"En_____s are as un_____ hood friends! *Always the Baker, FINALLY the Bride*, the final book in the Emma Rae series, provides immense satisfaction as a series-end. This is romantic comedy at its best! Novel Rocket and I give it our highest recommendation. It's a must read!"
—Ane Mulligan, Novel Rocket

"Only a few times have I experienced reading a book, falling asleep, and having the book's words follow me to dreamland. Sandra D. Bricker's *Always the Baker, FINALLY the Bride* did just that. Bricker's newest Emma Rae book reminds readers (those of us who have done all this) of all the joy and angst of wedding planning, and that life goes on in spite of our long list of 'to-dos.' But health and wealth aside, the big day comes, whisking us away to *happily ever after* Filled with recipes, trivia, and wedding cake drawings. Put this book on your 'to-do' list!"
—Eva Marie Everson, author of The Cedar Key Series

"Sandra D. Bricker has delivered the goods once again! *Always the Baker, FINALLY the Bride* offers readers a delightful story, sweet characters, and enough romance to make the heart flutter. In between chapters, readers will find surprise 'slices' of yummy goodness—recipes, wedding tips, and much more. What an enjoyable and satisfying read!"
—Janice Thompson, author of the Weddings by Bella Series

"This is a story with heart and humor, love and romance, a cake dilemma and a pig on a leash. Plus enough roadblocks on the pathway to wedded bliss to bring a runaway train to a screeching halt. But Emma Rae and Jackson have friends and

family, love, determination, and God to help them overcome any barrier that gets in their way."
—Lorena McCourtney, author of The Ivy Malone Mysteries and The Cate Kinkaid Files

"I always know I can count on Sandra D. Bricker to make me smile as I join her characters on their journeys to find love, and she didn't let me down in *Always the Baker, FINALLY the Bride*, the final book in the Emma Rae series. However, there is one problem: I'll miss Emma, Jackson, and all the other delightful people who grabbed my heart and still haven't let go."
—Debby Mayne, author of the upcoming Class Reunion Series

"Sandra D. Bricker writes charming, engaging stories with witty elements, large doses of romance, and a refreshing thread of non-preachy inspiration. *Always the Baker, FINALLY the Bride* brought the Emma Rae series to a delightful and wonderfully satisfying conclusion. I highly recommend the entire series for your keeper shelf."
—Sharlene MacLaren, author of The Little Hickman Creek and The Daughters of Jacob Kane Series

Other Abingdon Press Books by Sandra D. Bricker

Emma Rae Creations

Always the Baker, Never the Bride

Always the Wedding Planner, Never the Bride

Always the Designer, Never the Bride

The Big 5-OH!

Always the Baker, FINALLY the Bride

Sandra D. Bricker

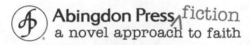

Abingdon Press fiction
a novel approach to faith

Nashville, Tennessee

Always the Baker, FINALLY the Bride

ISBN-13: 978-1-4267-3227-0

Published by Abingdon Press, P.O. Box 801, Nashville, TN 37202

www.abingdonpress.com

Published in association with WordServe Literary Group, Ltd., 10152 S. Knoll Circle, Highlands Ranch, CO 80130

Library of Congress Cataloging-in-Publication Data has been requested.

Printed in the United States of America

1 2 3 4 5 6 7 8 9 10 / 18 17 16 15 14 13

Barbara Scott
You saw the beauty in Emma before anyone else did
—the beauty in me as well—
and I love you more than this writer has words.

Rachelle Gardner
As my agent, you make it all come together
with such grace and charm.
I'm proud and humbled to call you my friend
as well.

Marian Miller and Jemelle Tola
I just don't think I could do it without you.
I love you so much.

And to D.
the voice in my head
(and the music in my ears since the iPod).
You're a true believer in this dream of mine.
Every writer chick needs a soft landing place like
the one you've given me.

Acknowledgments

Gratitude and appreciation to
Hanna Sandvig,
the *artiste* who took the cakes in my head
and put them on Emma's sketch pad.

See more of Hanna's artwork at
www.hanna-sandvig.com

Deepest thanks to my most delicious reader and friend,
Kris Bakken Mooney,
without whom there would be no final recipe
for Emma Rae's fabulous crème brûlée cake.
I forget how many stabs Kris took at this,
but she's a cake GENIUS!
Kris, Emma Rae and I salute you!

Love and appreciation to all of my readers, book clubs,
blogs, and reviewers who have supported and encouraged
me through this series.
And thanks to those who entered the contest to choose
Emma's final wedding cake, especially **Bonnie Cordova**,
the winner . . . and my new pal.

And finally to my Abingdon crew:
Ramona, Pamela, Julie, Teri (and Maegan).
Thank you so much for the ride of my life.
Bringing Emma and friends to the light of day
has been the best writing experience of my career.

Prologue

$\mathcal{A}$ champagne flute of vanilla bean gelato topped tableside with a shot of espresso."

"Seriously?"

"Chocolate chip bread pudding drizzled with warm caramel."

"Oh. My."

"Tiramisu lady fingers in coffee liqueur and cocoa."

Emma balled up the lapel of her jacket in her fist and whimpered. "Jackson. My heart."

Jackson leaned toward the waiter and clicked his tongue. "I'm thinking we should just move on to the sugar-free menu. She's diabetic."

"Oh. All right."

The gentleman pointed at the other side of the dessert cart as Jackson interrupted. "But I'll have that bread pudding," he whispered.

"Yes, sir. And for the lady, our sugar-free menu includes a warm berry tart with frozen vanilla yogurt."

"Oooh!"

"A red velvet cupcake with cream cheese icing sweetened with agave."

"You can stop right there," Jackson told him. "You had her at red velvet."

"Not so fast," she countered, and Jackson's heart began to thump. "Go on. What else?"

"Pumpkin spice cake with creamy buttermilk icing."

"Oh, that sounds lovely."

Perspiration puddled over his top lip, and Jackson wiped it away with his napkin. "Don't be ridiculous," he said. "Red velvet is your favorite."

"Yes, but I can make my own sugar-free red velvet. The pumpkin sounds—"

Jackson's attention darted to the waiter, and they shared a lingering exchange before the waiter offered, "The red velvet is our specialty. It comes highly recommended."

"Really?" she reconsidered. And by the time she nodded, Jackson's heart had begun to pound at double-time. "Okay. I'll try the cupcake."

"Very good."

"Coffee for me, and a pot of tea for my date, please," Jackson said, leaning back against the leather booth with a sigh.

"Are you all right?"

"Hmm? What do you mean?"

"I don't know," Emma replied. "You seem a little tense tonight."

"Oh. No. I don't know. I guess—"

Fortunately, the waiter reappeared so that he didn't have to concoct some lame excuse. He stopped breathing as the waiter set the beautiful red velvet cupcake down in front of Emma. A shiny pink cupcake tin held the confection, and a ring of intricate white chocolate made to look like a crocheted doily surrounded it. The carefully chosen diamond ring shimmered on top of it, catching the light from the chandelier overhead and reflecting the glint of recognition in Emma's brown eyes.

She looked up at him, and the expression in those spectacular eyes of hers crested into turbulent waves of gold-flecked understanding. Her perfect lips parted, but not a single syllable passed over them. She blinked several times before glancing back at the cupcake, and Jackson knew this was his moment. He slipped from the booth and hit one knee beside her.

"What . . .What are you . . . *Jackson?*"

He took her hand and grinned at her.

"Are you serious?"

"I've never been more serious in my life. You've changed me, Emma. You are the center of everything for me. I'm sorry it's taken me so long to get here, but I can't even think of living without you. Will you marry me?"

With that, she turned her head away from him and began to sniffle.

"Are you crying?" he asked on a laugh. "Emma, this is not a night for tears."

"I can't help it," she chuckled, and he watched her struggle to pull herself together. "You've really surprised me here."

"In a good way, I hope," he said, and he plucked the ring from the icing and gave it a quick lick.

"Frankly, I thought the best part of this night was going to be the cupcake."

"Emma. Will you give me an answer, please?" he asked, wiping the ring clean with the corner of a napkin. "Before my legs go numb?"

"Oh. Sorry."

He waited. "Is that a yes?"

A mischievous glint betrayed her amusement. "Can I let you know after I eat the cupcake?"

Jackson laughed. "I'd kind of like to hear it now, if you don't mind."

"If you insist," she told him, and she tilted her head slightly and smiled. If he'd been standing, he thought his knees might have gone weak under the weight of that sweet little smile.

"You're killing me here," he said with raspy emotion. "But I adore you."

"You do?"

"Oh, now you're just messing with me."

"You really do adore me?"

Jackson sighed, glancing at the floor.

Emma touched his jaw with one finger and nudged his face upward. "Yes, Jackson. I'll marry you."

1

*D*ude. When you said your family had a summer cottage near Savannah, I pictured something kind of different. More galley kitchen and bunk beds than *Great Gatsby* and mint juleps."

Emma smiled and yanked the camouflage duffle out of the back of Sherilyn's Explorer, heaving it into Fee's arms.

"*The Great Gatsby* was New York, wasn't it?" Sherilyn asked as she pulled her two floral overnight bags from the back. Leaning on the rear bumper, she wrapped both arms around her large pregnant belly and sighed as she gazed at the house. "It's been such a long time, Em. Are you glad to be back?"

Emma hummed her reply, slinging a burgundy tote over one shoulder and a brown leather bag over the other. She made her way across the sandy driveway and up the white-railed steps to the wraparound porch and pressed her grandmother's birthdate into the security pad. Once the beep of acceptance squawked its approval, Emma pushed open the massive double doors and turned around to grin at Sherilyn.

They sang it together: "Wipe *yaw fee-eet.*"

How many times had they heard those same three words over years of spring and summer holiday visits! They scampered into a quick, animated run-in-place atop the large straw welcome mat while Fee stood behind them, eyeing them curiously over the bridge of square black sunglasses.

Emma dropped her bags at the foot of the staircase and hurried toward the vistas calling to her from fifty yards beyond the wall of windows. She unlatched the French doors at the top, and again at the knobs, and shoved them fully open with dramatic flair, expectant and eager. The salty sea breeze caressed her face just as she'd imagined, and the distant purr of the rolling ocean waves brought the perfect music to accompany the lyric of chattering gulls.

Emma approached the porch railing and leaned against it, mesmerized by the foam-capped dance on the white sand shore. Aunt Sophie had always called it "Atlantic Therapy," a term that had popped immediately to mind when Sherilyn had suggested they go away somewhere relaxing where Emma could pull her thoughts together and make some solid wedding plans after months of avoidance.

Well. Not avoidance, really. More like . . . *inertia*. A numb sort of wedding paralysis that seemed to set in whenever key decisions needed to be made. Like the cake.

She wiggled the fingers of her left hand, allowing sunbeams to bounce off her beautiful engagement ring. She wondered for the hundredth time how Jackson had known that she'd always wanted a princess-cut diamond. She would have been pleased with a little square solitaire, of course, but the frame of smaller round diamonds that surrounded the stone and worked their way down to the platinum band caused the ring to catch that much more light. It was an exquisite ring. Perfect in every way.

"Sher, I never asked you before," she said as Sherilyn stepped up beside her. "Did you tell Jackson I wanted a princess diamond?"

"No, of course not. I was as surprised as you."

"Mm."

"Why?"

"No reason. I've just wondered, and I keep forgetting to ask him how he knew."

"Hey," she said after a moment's thought. "What do you say we unpack? Then we can head into town and get some groceries."

"No need," Emma said, breaking her gaze from the ring and fixing it on the sweeping blue horizon. "I faxed a list to Elmer and Louise. They took care of everything."

"Elmer and Louise!" Sherilyn exclaimed. "They still take care of this place? Are they still *alive*?"

"Twenty years connected to the Travis clan when they actually had a choice not to be," Emma summarized. "Boggles the mind, doesn't it?"

"Not really," she replied. "I've stayed connected without being required by blood." Emma glanced at Sherilyn, whose turquoise eyes were dancing with amusement as she mindlessly scratched her protruding stomach. "It's not such a bad deal, really."

"What's with this new move of yours?" Emma asked her, nodding at Sherilyn's belly.

"Oh, the scratching?"

"Uh, yeah!"

"I can't help it. My skin itches all the time now."

"You've got, what, a few more weeks? If you're not careful, you'll wear down the skin and the baby can step right out on her own."

"Stop," Sherilyn groaned, smacking Emma's arm playfully. "Wait! You said *on HER own*. Do you have a feeling? You think it's a girl?"

"If you wanted to know the sex, you should have had them tell you at the doctor's office, Sher."

"We want to be surprised," she sort of whined without conviction.

"You mean Andy wants to be surprised."

Twisting her red hair around one finger, Sherilyn shrugged one shoulder. "Yeah."

"Well, I can tell you this with total conviction. I absolutely know it's either a girl . . . *Or a boy!*"

Sherilyn swatted her arm again, and Emma rubbed her friend's stomach lovingly.

"Em," Fee called from inside. "Hey, Emma!"

Emma and Sherilyn went into the house, both of them looking around. When she spotted Fee standing at the top of the stairs leaning over the banister, Emma laughed.

"Can I have the blue room with the shells on the wall?"

She nodded, and Fee hopped away before she could utter the *s* in "Yes."

"Cool. This place has a lot of happy-looking rooms. But I think I can live with this one."

"What about you?" Emma asked Sherilyn. "Do you have any preferences?"

"Is the green room still green?"

"It is indeed."

Sherilyn grabbed her bags and waddled up the stairs. "I get the green room across the hall," she called out to Fee as she reached the landing, breathless.

Emma padded across the great room and through the open doors. Leaving her sandals behind on the porch, she rushed down the three wooden stairs and took off at a full run across the sand. She unzipped the heather-gray hoodie, discarded it at the halfway mark, and left her khaki shorts on the sand about three yards from the water's edge. She stopped where the sand darkened from a recent overflow of surf and adjusted the bottom of her red bathing suit. Knee-deep in the icy ocean, she tugged at the suit top before diving in and swimming out against the brisk green-blue current.

Just before surfacing again, she thought she heard her aunt Sophie's melodic laughter.

"Atlantic Therapy, Emma Rae. And the colder the better when you're looking for answers. They're all right out there in the Atlantic Ocean. God's hidden them there for us to find when we really, really need them."

✎

The elevator door creaked as it shut, and the car groaned slightly before setting out on its shaky ascent to his fourth-floor office. Something about the *klunk!* before the door opened again waxed familiar. Jackson had heard that noise before.

Emma's sweet face fluttered across his mind. And that pink sweater of his sister's that she'd changed into for their job interview after wiping out in the lobby and smearing fondant all over herself. She'd struck him as cute that day, with a speck of carrot cake still in her hair as they sat down to discuss the impending opening of The Tanglewood; even more so, a bit of a know-it-all when she stood there beside him as trapped passengers called out from the elevator car below a short while afterward.

"I'm assuming this is a hydraulic system, right? . . . Well, it probably is. Anyway, I'm thinking it's likely that the rails are just dry. A little oil can take care of that for you. But the door jamming like this is probably your drive belt. The service guy will take care of that when he gets the passengers out."

When the serviceman had confirmed her findings, Jackson recalled thinking that he'd better hire her, just so he could be around on the off chance that she might ever be proven wrong about anything. At the moment, as he pried the reluctant elevator door open, he felt pretty certain she hadn't been wrong about much of anything since.

"Call downstairs and tell them to place Out of Order signs on the west elevator on each floor, and call the repair service, will you, Susannah?" he asked his assistant as he passed her desk. "The doors are sticking. I think it could be the drive belt again."

"Will do," she returned as he entered his office and dropped into the chair. "Andy Drummond phoned. Says your cell goes straight to voice mail."

Jackson had turned it off after it rang about thirty times during his meeting with the front desk manager, and he'd forgotten to turn it back on.

"You can reach him on his cell for another thirty minutes."

"Thanks."

Jackson pulled his cell phone from his jacket pocket and dialed Andy. "Hey, buddy. It's Jackson. What's up?"

"Cats are away," Andy announced. "Mice must barbecue. You in?"

"What can I bring?"

"Whatever strikes you."

"What time?"

"Six thirty?"

"I'm there. You invite Sean since he's on his own too?"

"He's bringing soda and garbage bags."

"Garbage bags?"

"We're out. I thought since he was going to the store for drinks anyway—"

Jackson laughed. "Whatever. Later."

He ended the call and checked his watch. Twelve forty p.m. The growl from his stomach rumbled with regret that there wasn't time enough to grab some lunch before Bingham arrived for their one o'clock meeting.

Jackson produced a manila file of notes from his briefcase and opened it on the desktop. He'd been preparing all week to meet with Rod Bingham, and he probably didn't need to review the notes yet again. But he did anyway.

The possibility of franchising The Tanglewood into a start-up of six wedding destination hotels across the country flicked the back of his brain with excitement. Who could have ever imagined such a thing just a couple of years back when they'd opened their doors?

Desi.

More than likely, Desiree would have imagined it. The place had always been her dream more than his, but the death of his late wife had choked the life out of things for a while. Once his sisters, and eventually Emma, hopped onboard, however, he'd caught the fire, and The Tanglewood Inn had become a well-known and successful venture. Now someone wanted to clone the place, setting up Jackson for making a fairly obscene amount of money in the process. Maybe it would allow him to become a little more hands-off for a while and to pursue other interests and challenges. Maybe after the wedding, he and Emma could even travel a little and leave The Tanglewood in other capable hands for a bit now and then. Not forever. Just for a while. They'd swum around in that Paris-for-a-year dream often enough that it surfaced almost immediately every time he considered cutting back on hours and responsibilities.

"Jackson Drake! How are you, my friend?"

"Rod. Good to see you," he said, standing to shake Bingham's hand.

"I'm really enthused about our meeting, Jack." Tapping his briefcase with a grin, Rod added, "I think I've got something here that's going to put some real wind in your sails. Are you ready to talk?"

"I'm ready," he said, and they both sat down and faced each other from opposite sides of the large maple desk. "Tell me what you've got."

"Well, first of all," Rod blurted, "this thing is bigger than even I had guessed. Hold on to your hat, Jack. And tell me what you think about this idea. Not only would Allegiant Industries be interested in planting wedding destination hotels all across the United States, Canada, and Europe over the next five years—while making you a very rich beneficiary in the process, by the way—but they would also be interested in purchasing the original hotel from you."

"Purchasing . . . this place?"

"That's right, buddy. Allegiant wants to buy—"

"The Tanglewood?"

"Yes, indeedy."

"What do you mean?"

"What do you mean, what do I mean? They want to buy—"

Jackson gulped back the bubble of air stuck in his throat. "You want me to sell?"

"Yes. And not just for a song, Jack. For a *symphony!*"

He sat there quietly for a moment and rubbed his temple while the idea settled down on him.

"You want me to . . . *sell The Tanglewood?*"

⇛⇨

"Dude. What is wrong with you? Have you had a mental break?"

"No, I haven't had a mental break, Fiona. And you're not helping."

"Just decide. It's not like this isn't your forte, right? I mean, cakes are what you *do*. Picking a wedding cake design should be a piece of it for you."

The conversation was momentarily sidelined by the ghastly slurping sounds Sherilyn made from where she sat across from them, cradling a bowl on her basketball-shaped belly and scraping out the leftover chocolate muffin batter with a large rubber spatula.

"Sher, you're gonna make yourself sick," Emma scolded.

"No, I won't. It's just what was left in the bowl after you poured the rest out."

"Still. That can't be good for the baby."

"It's fine. It won't make me sick."

"Then it'll make *us* sick," Fee cracked. "Dude, you're gross."

"*Anyway*," Emma said with the shake of her head. "It's just not that simple, Fee," she retorted. "I'm a cake designer. How am I supposed to pick just one for . . . Oh, you just don't understand."

"No. You're right. I don't understand. You've got the greatest guy in the world convinced that you're a catch. So like, maybe, you should, you know, pitch or get off the mound."

"Don't say that! How could you say something like that?" Emma groaned and tossed herself into the thick cushions of the couch.

"Okay," Sherilyn said, licking the chocolate batter from her finger before setting the bowl on the table in front of her and struggling to stand up. "Okay, that's good. We're communicating. We have a dialogue going."

Emma shook her head, her sigh morphing into the *Pffft* sound of a deflating balloon.

"But . . . Fee . . ." Sherilyn continued with caution, "maybe a little less aggression in our communication would better suit what we're trying to accomplish here. How about this? Can I get anyone some more iced tea? The muffins should be out of the oven soon, shouldn't they? Do you want me to make coffee?"

"Just stop it, Sher. No need to play nursemaid here, okay? Just drop into a chair and prop up your feet before they spring a leak."

Sherilyn stood there, in the center of the room, her swollen pregnant frame wobbling from side to side as she glanced from Emma to Fee and back again.

"Relax, will you?" Emma said, more softly this time, punctuating her words with a smile. "Let's focus on the things we can accomplish, okay?"

Sherilyn sighed with relief and waddled over toward her. "Really?"

"Yes. I can't think about the cake. It's too much pressure. But how about we look at those flower pictures you mentioned on the drive down here?"

Sherilyn's blue eyes shimmered as she plopped down on the other side of the sofa, and a grin pushed her plump cheeks upward. "Great! Yes, let's talk flowers."

"I'm going for a walk on the beach." And with that, Fee hopped to her feet and headed out the door.

"Turn on the floodlights," Sherilyn instructed. "It gets really dark out there at night. The switch is on the—" With a single thump, the door closed, cutting her helpfulness in two. Deflated, she sent the rest of her words into the air over Emma's shoulder. "—wall by the door."

"You know Fee," Emma comforted. "She got married in a hallway at the hotel, for crying out loud. The details just aren't her thing."

"I know."

Sherilyn's pouty face made Emma chuckle. "Let's have a look at those flowers of yours, my wedding planner friend"

"Oh. Right."

Emma watched as Sherilyn struggled to balance the neon-pink laptop on her beach-ball belly. A few clicks later, she surrendered the fight and set the computer on the coffee table in front of them.

"Here. This will be easier."

Emma leaned forward and peered at the screen as Sherilyn arranged four rectangular photographs into symmetry.

"I thought because you chose such a lovely, simple silhouette for your dress, the flowers should—"

"Simple?" Emma interrupted. "Do you think it's too simple?"

"Not *too simple*, no. It's beautiful, Emma. It's just not one of those elaborate numbers where the flowers have to be bold and make a statement to stand out."

"Do you think Jackson will be disappointed? Because you know his family would so prefer some big extravaganza with three hundred guests and—"

"Emma Rae, of course not. Stop it." Sherilyn reached out and grabbed Emma's hand and shook it gently. "This is about what the two of you want. And I think you chose the ideal dress for an elegant, intimate ceremony. You're going to look so beautiful in your gown, Em. Timeless and perfect. Jackson is going to have to work to catch his breath when he sees you in it."

"Really?"

"Really."

Emma sighed and glanced down at the stunning platinum and diamond ring on her left hand. She heaved one more sigh. "You're a good friend."

"Yes, I am."

"And the flower choices are all really beautiful. What do *you* think, Sher?"

"Well, I love the calla lilies. Simple. Elegant."

"They remind me of a funeral," Emma stated. "Let's cut those from the possibilities."

"Done. What about this for your bouquet, then?" she asked as the calla lilies disappeared from the screen. She clicked on the next one and the image filled the screen. "Since you're going understated, maybe you want to go slightly bolder with your bouquet. This is a stunning combination of red roses, lily-of-the-valley—"

"No," Emma said, shaking her head. "It's really pretty, but I'm not feeling that one."

"Okay." Sherilyn clicked the X in the corner of the photo, and it disappeared. "I think you're going to love this next one, though. It really suits you, and since it's a spring wedding I think it's a great choice."

A beautiful arrangement of multicolored pastel tulips filled the screen, their long green stems wrapped in ivory satin ribbon.

Emma cooed at them. "Oh, Sher, that's really beautiful."

"I think so too."

"I love the way the light pink and lavender ones seem to blend into the white ones. Like cream."

"So . . . is this your wedding bouquet?"

Emma's blood pumped as she smiled. "I think so. Maybe."

Sherilyn minimized the photo and raised her hand in expectation of a victorious high five. But Emma didn't return the triumphant slap just yet.

"Wait. What's that one? Make that big, will you?"

Sherilyn opened the final image so it filled the screen, and Emma felt her blood pulse through every vein as her hand flew to her heart and she sighed.

"That's the one, Sher. Right there."

Just four stems of pale lavender-blue hydrangea, rhinestone-studded tulle ribbon wound tightly to hold them together.

"Flower paradise," she whispered. "That's the one."

"Really? You like the bling? I didn't think you'd like the bling. I mean, it's not that much bling, but still. I'm pleasantly surprised, Em. That's great. So this is the one."

"This is the one."

"This is the one!" Sherilyn repeated.

And when she raised her hand a second time, Emma slapped it in midair.

"Pull up your checklist and mark this off. I've chosen my flowers."

"I'm so proud," Sherilyn said as she *click-click-clicked* the laptop.

Emma sighed. "Me too."

"That's the dress, the venue, the invitations, and the flowers. We're cooking with gas now, Em! Am I pushing my luck to bring up the subject of music?"

Emma chuckled softly and fell back against the cushions. "Bring it on."

"Do you and Jackson have a song?"

"A song?"

"You know. A love song that belongs to just the two of you."

A nostalgic smile pushed upward at the corner of Emma's mouth. "Well, yeah. We have a song." Recovering, she added, "Do you and Andy have one?"

"Of course."

"You do? What is it?"

"Promise not to laugh?"

Emma thought it over. "No."

Sherilyn's eyes popped open wide. "No?"

"You know I can't promise that. Come on. Out with it. What's your song?"

She shrugged slightly and surrendered. "*Single Ladies.*"

Emma shook her head. "I don't think I know that one."

"Oh yes you do."

"I do?"

"Yeah. Beyoncé? *Single Ladies?*"

Emma pondered. As realization dawned, she smacked her hand over her mouth to catch the burst of laughter.

"Put a ring on it *Single Ladies?*" she exclaimed.

"Yes," Sherilyn admitted with some reluctance.

"Why on earth?"

"Emma, it's not like we chose it or anything. It was playing in the restaurant the night we told each other how we felt."

"Well," Emma said, and she pressed her lips together to hold back the grin. "I guess it worked. He put a ring on it, right?"

"Ha. Ha," Sherilyn commented dryly. "What's your song, smarty pants?"

"*The Way You Look Tonight.*"

"Oh, of course. It couldn't be something like *Disco Inferno*, now could it? If you were a better and more supportive friend, you would have lied."

"It was the opening night party for The Tanglewood; the first time we danced," she told her. "Jackson arranged this private little dinner for us after everyone had gone, and he asked Ben Colson to perform for just the two of us. It was magic. So—" She cut herself off when she noticed Sherilyn beaming at her, hand to heart. "Well, anyway. That's our song. Think you can do something with it?"

"Oh, I think so," she replied.

Traditional Wedding Flowers & Their Meanings

The Rose
Meaning: Deep and abiding love
Fragrant; in season all year

The Calla Lily
Meaning: Magnificence and great beauty
Mild fragrance; in season spring and summer

The Hydrangea
Meaning: Deep understanding and spiritual unity
No fragrance at all; in season early spring through late fall

The Peony
Meaning: Shy and virginal
Mild fragrance; in season late spring

The Tulip
Meaning: Passionate love
No fragrance; in season during the spring

The Lily-of-the-Valley
Meaning: Guaranteed happiness
Quite fragrant; in season spring and summer

The Orchid
Meaning: Unmatched beauty and appeal
No fragrance; in season all year

2

*J*ackson closed the back door and stepped inside the house just in time to catch the can of soda Andy lobbed at him.

"I think we've got about five minutes before the ribs need to be turned again."

Before Andy had a chance to reply, the dog barked as the front door gushed open and slammed shut again.

"Henry," Andy reprimanded. "It's Sean. Put a lid on it."

The very large sheepdog made his way toward the front door, his barks mellowing down to a soft yip as he escorted Sean down the hall.

"I stopped at Publix and picked up a few things from the deli," Sean announced, grocery bags in hand.

"Did you remember trash bags?" Andy asked.

Sean shot him a glance, revealing a peek of pearly white teeth as he began to unload several plastic bags, reciting his shopping list as he did. "I got everything that goes with ribs. Southern-style potato salad. Shredded cole slaw. Baked beans. A couple rolls of paper towels . . ."

"Good move," Jackson chimed in.

"The strawberry Twizzlers are for me."

Andy and Jackson exchanged glances before Andy piped up. "With ribs?"

"Nah. The drive home. Fee keeps a lock on my snacks when she's home. But it's my favorite candy, man."

"I get it. What about the trash bags?"

"Nah."

"No?"

Sean shook his head and dug deep into the bag. "Such low expectations, Doc." He tossed a roll of garbage bags into the air, and they landed in Andy's hand with a thud. "You don't know yet that I got your back?"

Jackson laughed and shook his head. "You gonna flip those ribs, or what?"

"Grab something to drink and join us," Andy told Sean on his way out the back door.

Making his way around Henry, Jackson followed and leaned against the deck railing. Andy Drummond, ortho man, monster-dog owner, and soon-to-be father, had found his sweet spot in life right there in front of the grill.

"How many times a week do you think you barbecue, man?" Jackson asked him.

"In weather like this? Not usually more than four."

"Four!"

Jackson couldn't imagine even just eating at home four nights a week, much less taking the lead in organizing the meal. The Tanglewood took up every spare moment of time for both him and Emma, leaving very little space for much else.

"Hey, Andy. Can I talk to you about something?"

"Sure," he replied without looking up from the rows of ribs rubbed with his secret recipe of brown sugar, chili powder, garlic, and whatever else he wouldn't give up. "What's going on?"

"I had a meeting today. Sort of intriguing, actually. But I just don't know how Emma will respond. How anyone at the hotel will respond, really."

Andy rolled the grill top closed and wiped his hands. "Yeah?"

"Just between us, right?"

"'Course."

"Well, there's an offer on the table about The Tanglewood."

"What kind of offer?"

Jackson inhaled sharply before he replied, "To buy the place."

Andy narrowed his eyes and shook his head. "What do you mean? Somebody wants to buy the hotel?"

"Yeah."

"Is it for sale?"

Jackson sighed. "I don't know."

"Are you really considering it?"

"Well, the offer is pretty great. And if the timing is right, Emma and I could have a really long, extended honeymoon before we start our life together."

"Sorry to say this, but I think The Tanglewood is a *big part* of your life together, isn't it?"

"I guess so."

"She's got the baking thing, and the tearoom."

"Yeah."

"And the staff is family to you both, literally *and* figuratively."

"Yep."

"Ah, man. Sherilyn."

"I know."

Andy folded his arms and gazed out over the back lawn. After a long and thoughtful moment, he chuckled. "Sorry, man. But you sell that hotel now and you're gonna be crucified."

"Don't I know it."

Emma tore off the top sheet of paper from her sketch pad and crumpled it with both hands before tossing it at the trash can at the side of the desk. It bounced off the rim and fell to the floor next to half a dozen others, and she let out a growl as she fell back into the chair.

"No luck?" Fee asked her, setting down a cup of tea on the desktop before making her way to the sofa and sinking into it.

"None," she replied, and she picked up the delicate china cup and gave it a sniff. "What is this?"

"Pumpkin spice."

"Really. I've never—"

"Premium black tea from Sri Lanka," Fee interrupted, looking up at the ceiling as she recounted the description from one of the canisters of loose tea she'd brought along. "Flavored with pumpkin and exotic spices."

Emma took a sip, and her eyes popped open wide. "It's wonderful. Is that what you're having?"

"No. Mine is gingerbread. It's got orange peel in it."

Emma joined Fee on the sofa and set her tea cup on the coffee table in front of them. "Let me try?" Fee handed her the cup, and she sniffed at the contents. "Mmm." She took a sip. "It really does taste like gingerbread."

"It's good, right? Very autumnal."

"Both of them are."

"Speaking of seasons," Sherilyn announced as she plunked down the stairs, rubbing her belly as she joined them, "we've got a spring wedding to plan. How did you do with the sketch of the cake?"

Fee shook her head and pointed one index finger over Emma's shoulder, toward the discarded paper wads on the floor by the desk. "Not so much," she said.

"Oh, Emma. You're actually having trouble with *the cake?* Really?"

She felt a flush of heat rise over her. "There's a lot of pressure about the cake," Emma defended.

"But that's what you do, sweetie. That should be the easiest part."

Emma stared Sherilyn down. "Are you joking? It's like Audrey choosing her own wedding gown, or—or you!—when you had to plan your own wedding. A wedding planner, planning her own wedding . . . but . . . remember how hard that was?"

"To be fair," Fee added dryly, "it would have been a lot easier for her if she'd been able to hold onto a dress rather than losing half a dozen of them."

"It was only two," Sherilyn objected. "And yes, I see your point. But you've got to narrow it down, Em."

"That's impossible to do," she told them. "When you have every cake in your repertoire to choose from, how do you finally say, '*THIS!* This is the one and only, be-all-and-end-all cake for Jackson and me,' huh?"

"Well, I don't know," Sherilyn said, trying three times before she finally rolled forward to grab Emma's cup from the coffee table. "How do you narrow it down for your brides?"

"That has caffeine," Fee pointed out as Sherilyn drank from Emma's pumpkin spice.

"Just a sip. Ooh, it's delicious." She handed the cup to Emma. "Just pretend you're one of your brides and sketch out a cake that tells your story with Jackson. Maybe a cake that represents The Tanglewood."

"Or it could have an Atlanta Falcons theme," Fee suggested, deadpan.

"Absolutely not!" Sherilyn exclaimed.

"Well, that *would* be right for Jackson and me," Emma teased.

"But it would not be right for the rest of the wedding."

"I don't know," Emma replied, holding back her amusement. "Nothing says romance like a candlelight ceremony in The Desiree Room, a hydrangea bouquet, and a wedding cake shaped like the Falcons' end zone."

"Stop. You'll make my water break."

"When exactly is the bambino due, anyway?" Fee asked. "You look like you're about thirty months pregnant."

"Feels like it too."

"She still has three weeks," Emma interjected. "Three long, long weeks."

"Not so long if you consider how many wedding plans we need to nail down before then, Emma. And just you wait!" Sherilyn warned her. "You'll be much more sympathetic about all of this once you and Jackson start *your* family."

"Actually," Emma said as she pushed back into the cushions behind her, "we're not entirely sure we want to have children."

The look on Sherilyn's face made Emma chuckle

"What? Of course you'll have babies, Emma Rae. You love babies."

"Yes, I do. And I'll be the best aunt to yours that ever lived. But Jackson and I are both really involved in our work, and what little time we have beyond that . . . we like to spend it wrapped up in each other."

"Emma." Sherilyn's voice clanked with disappointment, like a lone nickel dropped into a large metal jug. "Really?"

"We have so many things we want to do together. And apart, for that matter."

"Like what?"

"Well, we have this dream, sort of." Emma's heart began to race just thinking about it, and she grinned at her interested two-member audience. "We'd like to take a whole year and go live in Paris."

"Paris! What would you do in Paris for a whole year?"

"Everything!" she cried with enthusiasm. "We would go for walks through the Vergers de Champlain, explore the great art in the Louvre, take bike rides in the country, and stroll along the Seine. And I'd like to take those classes at Lenôtre while Jackson works on his book—"

"What book?" Sherilyn interrupted.

"The one he would write if we lived in Paris for a year."

"You'd really do that?" Her friend tried so hard to hide her incredulous astonishment, but Sherilyn had never been good at disguising her true feelings. "You'd move away?"

"Not forever. Just for a year."

"What about getting to know this little one?" she asked, rubbing her stomach and looking at Emma through misted eyes. "And the hotel. What about The Tanglewood?"

"We're not leaving next month," she reminded her with a soft smile. "It's just something we dream about for our future. My point was that children aren't really something either of us feels compelled to rush toward. It doesn't mean we don't like kids, or that we won't ever have any. Or that we won't love yours, Sher. It's just not something we see in our immediate future. After such a long time lost in trying to build our careers and then getting the hotel up and successful, we'd just like to spend some time getting lost in *each other* for a while."

Sherilyn looked to Fee, seemingly for a show of support. But Fee simply shrugged and turned her attention to her gingerbread tea.

"Paris," she breathed on a heavy sigh. "It's so . . . far away."

"I know," Emma said with a smile as she rubbed Sherilyn's hand. "But we'll get married first, so why don't you just focus on the wedding, okay?"

"The wedding," she replied, nodding. "So about that wedding cake, Em . . ."

I walked right into that.

⤮

"Did I wake you?"

The timbre of Jackson's voice, warm and rich, evoked a spontaneous smile, and Emma sighed and leaned into the cell phone cupped in her hand. "No."

"What are you doing?"

"Having a scavenger hunt."

"You're joking."

"Only in part. I'm on the hunt for a little creative inspiration."

"For?"

"The ideal wedding cake."

"That should be right up your alley, my friend."

Emma chuckled. "You'd think so, wouldn't you? But it's the detail of our wedding that seems to be causing me the most distress. Anything to contribute?"

"As long as you marry me, Emma Rae, I couldn't care less about the rest of it. I'd marry you on a running trail at Vickery Creek with no one around except the two of us."

"I both love and hate you for that, Jackson."

His laughter tugged at the heartstrings dangling inside of her.

"Relax," he urged. "You'll know it when it strikes you."

"Promise?"

"I do."

"Careful, buddy," she said with a snicker. "Save those two words for later, when you need them."

"Yes, ma'am."

Emma closed her eyes. "Are you at home?"

"No. Still in my office."

She pictured him there in the creaky leather chair, his suit coat folded neatly over one of the side chairs across from the desk, his shirt sleeves probably rolled up to mid-forearm, and his sleepy, milk-chocolate eyes narrowed.

"Go home, Jackson. Get some sleep."

"I can't sleep," he said. "Not until I talk to you about something."

"Are you breaking up with me, Jackson? Have you met someone else?"

He snorted in a chuckle and growled, "Not on your life. And when would I find the time?"

"Then lay it on me. What's on your mind?"

"You sure? It's not something you can discuss with the girls. It's just between us for the moment, *capiche*?"

"*Capiche* like a fox. What is it?"

"I took that meeting with Rod Bingham."

Emma's stomach did a little somersault. "Jackson, I'm so sorry. I've been so wrapped up in the wedding plans that I completely forgot about that. How did it go? Are they actually interested in franchising The Tanglewood?"

"Oh yeah, they're interested."

She listened as a low moan accompanied his breath as he exhaled. "And?"

"And there's an offer on the table to purchase the hotel as part of the deal."

She gulped. "Did you say . . . ?"

"Yep. Allegiant Industries would like to buy The Tanglewood too. And clone it across the country, into Canada and over to Europe within the next five years."

Emma knew she needed to reply, but the giant lump in her throat obstructed her voice.

"Emma?"

"Wow."

"I know."

"Sell The Tanglewood."

"I know."

She swallowed hard around the lump and sighed. "How do you feel about that, Jackson? Is that something you would consider?"

"Well . . ."

Oh, my. He's considering it.

". . . not at first. But I started thinking about the future."

"A future without The Tanglewood. That's hard for me to imagine."

"I know." He sighed again, "But we've talked about this, about how the hotel takes up every spare moment of our lives. And about how we'd love to have a little freedom to travel or pursue other interests."

"Or live in Paris for a year."

The coincidental timing of her earlier conversation with Sherilyn and Fee struck a hollow chord in the pit of her stomach, and Emma massaged her throbbing temple.

"Exactly."

"Oh. Jackson."

"It's not like we haven't talked about it before," he reminded her.

"Yes, but only in the most abstract terms. Now that it's a real possibility, it leaves me feeling—"

"Yeah, me too."

"—stunned."

Jackson sighed, and Emma could hear the rustle of his hair as he shook his head against the cell phone.

"When do you have to give them an answer?"

"Next week."

"Okay, then why don't we sleep on it?" she suggested. "Try to put it out of your mind for the moment. I'll be back tomorrow afternoon, and we'll take some time together. We'll figure this out, Jackson."

The line went silent, except for his gentle intake of breath.

"Go home and get some sleep," she said softly, and he exhaled. "And stop thinking about everyone else and how it might affect them. For the moment, lay down that big block of the weight of the whole world and just breathe. All right?"

"Mm-hmm."

"Jackson?"

"Hmm?"

"I love you."

"Somehow, that eases the pressure," he told her. "Say it again?"

"With pleasure," she replied, and her lips stretched into a grin. "I love you."

Jackson sighed. "See you tomorrow."

"Count on it."

Emma let him disconnect the call before she folded up her cell phone and laid it on the desk. She said a quick, silent prayer for Jackson to have an easy night's sleep, asking God to guide him to the right decision and thanking Him for such a wonderful man with whom to share her life.

And my pulse is pounding against my skull again, Lord. Please make it stop.

Staring down at the outline of a cake on her sketch pad, Emma recalled that first day when she met Jackson at the bakery where she used to work. She hadn't even known it was raining until she spotted the droplets on his jacket.

"You know, these brownies are awesome with hazelnut coffee. Can I interest you in—"

"No, thanks," he said, cutting her offer right in two. "Just black."

Emma tried to resist the urge to tempt him further, and she was successful for about twenty seconds. Then, with a charming smile, she extended a glass coffeepot toward him.

"Dark roast. Extra bold. Hazelnut's perfect with chocolate."

He didn't raise his chin, only his eyes, as he glared at her across the bakery case. "Just black. Thank you."

Emma shook her head and slipped the pot back to its place before grabbing the Colombian from one of the adjacent burners.

"Black it is."

He raked his dark hair with both hands, and his milk-chocolate brown eyes met hers without warning. There was a world of conversation between them in that one frozen moment in time, and she peeled her gaze away, trying not to stare at the slightly off-center cleft in his square chin.

"That'll be four dollars and eighteen cents."

He slipped a five toward her and muttered, "Keep the change."

She hesitated, wondering if she should bother to point out that she was the baker and not a waitress. And then she realized the tip was only about 80 cents.

Stand-up guy.

While GQ took his cup and plate and settled at a table near the window, Emma wiped down the counter and started a new pot of decaf.

A sort of happy grunt called her attention back to her customer, and she tripped over the crooked grin he aimed in her direction.

"What's in this?" he asked her, wiping a smear of chocolate from the corner of his mouth. "It's fantastic."

He'd ordered another six of them to take back to his office, and Emma hadn't realized until much later that the chance meeting in the bakery where she worked had actually marked the start of the rest of her life.

She opened the box of colored pencils and spilled them out on the desk. Less than an hour later, Emma's scavenger hunt ended in success, and she leaned back and admired the wedding cake on the page before her.

Flowers on top and between each layer . . . a simple ribbon adornment . . . and a thin, leafy scrollwork pattern on the sides . . . It was the perfect cake to represent the fairy tale that had begun that rainy day in The Backstreet Bakery.

Emma quickly scribbled a title beneath the cake and smiled. There wasn't another man on the planet she'd rather spend Once Upon a Time with.

Once Upon a time

3

"Do you have a minute for me, boss?"

Jackson glanced up from his computer screen to find his assistant, Susannah Littlefield, gripping the doorjamb, smiling at him.

"Of course. Come in."

She smoothed the salt-and-pepper bun atop her head and removed the wire glasses from her knob of a nose as she approached him.

"Have a seat," he invited, waving toward the chairs on the other side of the desk. "What's up?"

"I'm not sure how to begin," she admitted.

"Well, Susannah. Nothing good ever starts with *those* words."

She chuckled. "I suppose it's all in your perspective."

"After fifteen years together, I would think there's very little we can't talk about," he reminded her. "Just spill it out on the table, and we'll sort through it."

"All right," she said with a nod. "I would like to retire in the spring, Jackson."

He felt the words thump to a landing somewhere at the top of his gut.

"This *coming* spring?"

Susannah chuckled again. "I thought I might. After the wedding."

Jackson raked through his hair with both hands before leaning back against the leather chair. Susannah looked so expectant, but he couldn't think of anything to say in reply.

"There's time to hire someone else, and for me to train her in the basics of hotel business, and I think—"

"Retire, Susannah? Really?"

She nodded.

"I can't even remember what I did without you."

Susannah smiled at him, one of those maternal, knowing smiles she'd been smiling even before her dark hair entertained notions of silver strands.

"I won't leave you in the lurch," she promised. "I'll find someone just as accommodating . . ."

"Not possible."

". . . whose computer skills are top-notch . . ."

"Well, I'll need that, won't I?"

". . . with outstanding references."

Jackson fidgeted with the pen in front of him while he processed the thought of losing Susannah. When he'd left his corporate career in pursuit of his late wife's dream of transforming The Tanglewood Inn into a wedding destination hotel, this woman had blindly followed him into the great unknown. He'd once told her that he felt as if the two of them had entered a jungle armed with nothing but machetes and boots appropriate for wading through knee-deep mud. She'd done her fair share of swinging that machete since then, carving out a clear path toward a successful business. Without Susannah, and his sisters too, he never could have come through it with his sanity intact.

And, of course, there'd been Emma by his side.

Jackson sighed at the thought of her, and he checked the time on the clock that sat on the shelf by the door. She'd be home from Savannah in a few hours.

"You'll have to give me some time to digest this, Susannah."

"Of course," she said, rising to her feet.

"Can we talk about it again at the end of the week?"

"We can."

"But in the meantime, I'd just like to thank you," he told her in a hoarse, emotional tone. "You're a treasure."

She paused at the door and smiled at him. "Thank you, Jackson. I've enjoyed working for you more than I can tell you."

"Glad to hear it."

She started to turn away, but she stopped in her tracks. "Oh. Don't forget you have lunch downstairs with your sister in half an hour."

He grinned. "I did forget, Susannah. Thank you, yet again."

As he slipped into his jacket and straightened his tie, Jackson wondered if Susannah's impending departure wasn't just the first sign that the end of an era approached. Perhaps the sale of The Tanglewood was simply a logical conclusion?

"I'll be back in an hour," he told Susannah as he crossed through her office and headed down the hall.

Jackson pressed the call button for the elevator, and it rang almost immediately. His thoughts still behind him with Susannah and her retirement announcement, he took a step forward the moment the door slid open. But in the same instant, a small tornado blew out of the car and smacked hard into him.

"Whoa, whoa there," he said, taking the little girl by the shoulders. "Watch where you're going before you hurt yourself, or someone else, huh?"

A coarse mane of reddish-brown hair masked half of her face, and she glared up at him with one chestnut eye. "Sorry," she muttered halfheartedly, wriggling away from him.

"Wait a second. Where are you headed in such a hurry, huh?"

"Nowhere."

"Well, this floor isn't for hotel guests," he informed her. "This is our suite of offices. Where are you trying to go?"

"I told you, Nowhere."

"Well, Nowhere is not on this floor, so let's turn right around and get back on the elevator, all right?"

She thought it over, shrugged impatiently, and appeared to toss herself back into the elevator. Jackson followed her and pressed the Lobby button. "What about you? What floor is your room on?"

"Two," she said without looking up at him.

"Okay," he replied, and he pressed the button for her. "And when we arrive at the second floor, maybe you could dial it back, just a little, so no one gets run over?"

She chuckled. "Yeah, okay."

When they reached the second floor, the little girl slid through a minuscule opening and tromped down the hall before the doors even opened completely. Jackson shook his head as he pressed the button to close them again.

It wasn't until he reached Morelli's and Norma waved him toward her table that his thoughts drifted back to his conversation with Susannah.

"You look like you've had quite a morning," his sister observed.

"You have no idea."

"What is that all over your suit, Jackson?"

He glanced down at the smears of white powder and grimaced. One of them bore a strange resemblance to a small hand, and he groaned as he dusted it off.

"A small hurricane barreled into me on the elevator," he said. "I have no idea what she'd been into to make this mess."

"Is she a guest?"

"I assume so. She said her room is on the second floor, but she was trying to get off the elevator on four."

"Ahh," Norma nodded with a grin. "An explorer."

"A messy one."

"I would say so. Have a seat and let's get a little lunch into you. Now tell me, when is Emma Rae due back?"

"Later today," he replied, still brushing the front of his jacket as he sat down. "Seems like she's been gone for a month. Hey, did you know Susannah plans to retire?"

"Oh, she talked to you, hmm?"

Jackson looked up at Norma and glared. "You knew?"

"She may have mentioned it."

The youngest of his three sisters, Norma was the one who knew Jackson best. In turn, the glint in her hazel eyes, and the way she brushed back her sandy hair as she opened the menu before her, told him all he needed to know. Like everything else around his hotel, Norma had no doubt known about Susannah's plans even before she'd cemented them.

"Anything else I'm not privy to around here, Norma Jean?"

She giggled without answering his question. "I'm thinking . . . the beef stew in a sourdough bowl. What do you think?"

"I think you'd make a lousy spy. You can't bluff worth a dollar."

"I'm so proud of you, Em. Do you want me to order extra flowers for the cake, or will you make them out of sugar?"

Emma grimaced at Sherilyn and shrugged.

"Don't tell me."

"Well, I was sold on this cake last night. It just seemed to fit Jackson and me so perfectly. But in the light of day—"

Sherilyn's groan cut her words in two.

"What did I miss?" Fee asked as she blew through the front door. Sherilyn's expression drove her to pivot onto another topic. "I've got all of the bags in the car. Who's driving, Emma? Me or you?"

"You'd better drive," Sherilyn interjected. "Emma Rae is preoccupied. We might end up in Key West."

"Preoccupied with what? I thought things were great since she decided on the . . ." Fee paused, looking from Sherilyn to Emma and back again. "Ohhhh. That's not good."

"I just think there might be—" Emma began, and Fee pressed a hand to her shoulder, nudging her toward the front door. Sherilyn waddled past her and took the front porch steps with caution as Emma pressed the security code into the keypad next to the door. "—you know," she continued as she and Fee followed Sherilyn, "I just thought there might be another cake that is more representative of our whole relationship, you know?"

"You've got shotgun," Fee told her as they parted at the rear bumper of the Explorer. "Let Sherilyn sit in the back so she can put her feet up."

"Feet!" Sherilyn exclaimed. "They're nothing but big waterlogged stumps at the ends of my calves."

"Anything you need for the drive back?" Emma asked her.

"I don't know," Sherilyn began, rolling her eyes upward as she twisted her red hair into an elastic band. "Maybe some water. But then that might mean we'll have to stop in a few minutes. Maybe a snack instead. What do you think, Em? What snack is most representative of a pregnant woman whose best friend is plucking her last nerve?"

Emma began to laugh.

"Maybe a Snickers. Or wait! Some sesame sticks. Do we have any of those left? And do they really represent my full need for a snack?"

Reaching over the back of the seat, Emma slapped at the air in front of Sherilyn. "All right. I get it. I'll make a decision soon. I promise."

"Will you? Will you, really?" Sherilyn asked. "Because there's no hurry or anything. I can always finish up these pesky wedding details from the delivery room."

"The cake is my thing," Emma reminded her. "You just worry about the rest of it."

"Oh. Okay. I'll do that. It's not like it matters if everything fits together with some cohesive—"

"Sheesh, Sher!" Emma cried. "Hormonal much?"

"Oooookay!" Fee exclaimed. "That's enough of that, or I'll leave you two by the side of the road to duke it out."

Sherilyn growled loudly, and Emma laughed at her, pushing off her sandals and propping her feet on the dashboard as she closed her eyes.

"Ooh, you know what I have a taste for?" Sherilyn asked them, and Emma moaned. "Remember that fudge Pearl told us about?"

"Anton's secret recipe?" Emma teased.

"Yes. It sounded like heaven, didn't it?"

"Yes. But you heard Pearl. To get that recipe, you'll have to," Emma began, and Fee joined her as they completed it in stereo, "—pry it out of his cold, dead hands."

They all laughed, and Sherilyn began to whine, "But it sounded amazing, didn't it? Did she say it had marshmallows in it?"

"Marshmallow cream," Fee corrected.

"Ohhh," she whimpered. "I need chocolate. Do either of you have any chocolate?"

Emma shoved the sunglasses up the bridge of her nose and tuned her friend out, deciding instead to simply trust Fee to steer them home.

Four hours and five bathroom stops later, Sherilyn groaned again, this time with a slight whistle to it, and she followed it up with quick, noisy puffs of frantic breathing.

"Need another backrub?" Emma asked without turning around.

Her indecipherable reply came through more puffs.

"Sher?"

When Emma twisted to peer into the back seat, Sherilyn's wide turquoise eyes looked back at her from within a completely bunched-up face.

"Are you all right?"

Sherilyn shook her head with frenzied distress.

"No?"

She shook her head again, gripping her enormous belly with both hands.

"Oh, Sher. No."

Sherilyn nodded with the same frenzy.

"It's time? But there's still three weeks!"

Sherilyn's expression turned almost demonic, driving Emma's immediate apology: "Okay, sorry. So we're early."

Emma and Fee looked at each other for a resolution that neither of them had.

"How far are we from home?" Fee asked.

Emma checked out the scenery flying past them. "About twenty minutes. Sher? Can you wait twenty minutes?"

Sherilyn replied with a defeated shrug, followed by the shake of her head. "I don't know."

"Okay. Okay." Emma struggled to control her own breathing before urging Sherilyn to do the same. "Take slow, easy breaths, all right? Slow and easy." Turning to Fee, she whispered, "Step on it."

The motor revved as Fee complied.

She fumbled with her purse and pulled out her cell phone and dialed. "Andy. It's Emma."

"Hey, Emma," he replied, clueless.

"We're about twenty minutes from Roswell," she told him, "and I think Sherilyn is in labor."

After a brief silence, Sherilyn's husband, clueless no more, raised the pitch of his voice several octaves as he shouted at her. "I'll call the doctor. I'll meet you at the hospital. Is she all right? Can I talk to her?"

Emma glanced back at Sherilyn and made an executive decision. "I don't think that's a good idea at the moment, Andy. We'll see you at the emergency room as soon as we can. Call the doctor first. Remember that her bag is packed and tucked behind the driver's seat of your car. It has her iPod in it, and she'll need that. We programmed it with relaxation songs . . . and a little Seger. Meet us there, all right? Are you able to meet us there?"

"Okay. Okay. She's not driving, is she?"

"Of course not. Fee's behind the wheel."

"Let me talk to her."

"Fee?"

"Yes! Pass the phone to her, Emma."

She did, and Fee answered tentatively. "Hello?" Emma heard the hum of Andy's very loud voice from the other side of the front seat. "Yes, okay," Fee said after a moment. "Dude. Chill. I've got this."

"Uh . . . Emma?"

Emma looked back at Sherilyn, whose eyes were wider than she'd ever seen them before. The look of sheer panic as she glanced down at her belly caused Emma to follow suit.

"Your water broke?"

Sherilyn nodded, and her eyes puddled with tears.

"Her water broke," Emma told Fee as she flicked the buckle on her seat belt and tossed it aside. Heaving her entire body up and over the armrest, she awkwardly crawled through the small opening between the seats.

"What are you—youch!!—What're you doing? I'm driving here!" Fee cried as Emma used Fee's shoulder as a push-off point to catapult into the backseat beside Sherilyn.

"It's going to be all right," she promised, rubbing Sherilyn's rigid hand where it lay clamped to her belly. "Just relax. You're doing fine, and we'll be there very soon. Does it hurt?"

"Only at the beginning of the pains. I just thought I'd eaten too much bologna at breakfast."

"You had bologna for breakfast?"

"I had a taste for it."

"Where did you get bologna?"

Sherilyn's wide eyes flashed suddenly, and she began pushing out short puffs of air through clenched teeth.

"Contraction?" Emma asked.

Sherilyn nodded again and, before she knew it, Emma had joined her in the strange rhythmic ritual.

"Chhoo-chhoo-chhoo-chhoo."

She checked the clock on the dashboard as Sherilyn muttered Emma's name and squeezed her hand so tightly that Emma's entire body coiled into it. She pressed both feet against the back of Fee's seat.

"Hey!" Fee exclaimed.

"Sorry."

Tendrils of moist red hair framed Sherilyn's pale white face, and Emma smoothed them back with her free hand as she whispered words of comfort to her friend.

"It's all right, Sher . . . We're almost there . . . You're doing great."

Once the contraction appeared to pass, Emma scanned the surroundings beyond the car window. "We're just a few minutes out," she told Sherilyn softly. "Just hang in there, okay?"

"Okay," she agreed. "Is Andy meeting us there?"

"He shouldn't be too long after us."

"Oh, good. I'll bet he's . . ." Sherilyn gasped. "*Fraaaaan-tic.*"

"Another one?" Emma asked, and she checked the clock again.

"Emmm-mma," Sherilyn squealed.

"I know. I know. Just hang on, sweetie. Hang on."

Emma perked up when she saw the square sign with a large *H* in the middle. At last, North Fulton Hospital, right around the corner.

"When Fee stops out front, you stay right here, okay?" she instructed Sherilyn. "I'll get a wheelchair and push it right up to the car door. You just keep on breathing, okay?"

Sherilyn shot her a frenzied nod. "Chhoo-chhoo-chhoo-chhoo."

"Good girl."

The tires squealed as they flew past the blue-and-white entrance sign toward the emergency room. The Explorer hadn't come to a full stop when Emma threw open the door and jumped from the backseat into a full run.

"Wheelchair," she shouted at the woman behind the desk. "Pregnant woman in labor. I need a wheelchair!"

Before the nurse had a chance to reply, Emma spotted an empty wheelchair parked near the entrance. She jogged toward it, flicked off the brakes and pulled it behind her as she ran out the door.

"Here," she said, breathless. "Can you get out?"

Sherilyn nodded, and she flung her legs out of the back seat. But instead of rushing into the chair, she stopped and stared at it.

"What are you waiting for?" Emma asked her. "Let's go."

"Emma, what kind of wheelchair is that? I think that's made for a child "

"So? What's the difference?"

"That tiny seat," Sherilyn declared, wielding a pointed finger at the chair. Turning her hand, she added, "And this enormous butt. Never the twain shall meet!"

Emma's blood pressure shot up, and her ears began to ring. "Put that massive butt into this chair right now, Sherilyn Drummond, or I will fling you over my shoulder and *carry you* inside. Is that the way you want to do it? Because I will!"

"Fine."

Sherilyn pouted at her as she stepped out of the car and wedged into the wheelchair. Emma groaned as she pushed the chair through the arch and into the hospital.

"Her water broke a while ago, and her contractions are about four minutes apart," Emma instructed as a male nurse moved into position behind the wheelchair. "Her husband has paged Dr. Caldwell, and they both should be here very soon."

Emma snagged Sherilyn's purse from her arms. "I'm going to give them your insurance information while they get you settled. Is there anything you need?"

Sherilyn nodded.

"Okay." Emma squeezed the nurse's arm, and the wheelchair came to a stop. "What is it?"

"If I can't get my hands on some of that fudge Pearl was telling us about—"

"And you can't."

"Right. But remember that girl from Rhode Island? She got married in the courtyard, and her husband works at the zoo?"

Emma's eyes narrowed. Curious, she cocked her head slightly. "Loretta?"

"Right! Loretta."

"You . . . want me to . . . call Loretta? Why?"

"Oh, no. But remember that wedding cake you made for them? It was cheesecake, but it was all chocolate?"

"Y-yeah. What about it?"

"I need some of that."

Emma groaned. "Go ahead," she told the male nurse, and she tapped his arm a couple of times.

"Something chocolate, then," Sherilyn called over her shoulder. "I don't care what. But I really want something—"

The doors closed behind them, muffling the rest of Sherilyn's plea.

"*—chocolate!!*"

୬୫ଡ଼୬ଡ଼

Emma's *Oh-You-Better-LOVE-Chocolate* Cheesecake

Preheat oven to 350 degrees.

9-ounce package of chocolate wafers
1 tablespoon sugar
6 tablespoons melted butter

Grease a 9-inch springform pan.
Blend the chocolate wafers until they are finely ground.
Mix wafer crumbs with sugar and add the melted butter.
Press the crumbs onto the bottom of the pan.
Bake for about 5 minutes until the crumbs are set,
and put aside to cool.

10 ounces semi-sweet chocolate, broken into pieces
4 8-ounce packages cream cheese at room temperature
1 ½ cups granulated sugar
¼ cup unsweetened cocoa powder
4 eggs

Melt the chocolate until smooth, and cool slightly.
Blend cream cheese, sugar, and cocoa powder with mixer.
Add eggs and continue to mix.
Mix in the warm chocolate.
Pour filling over the crumb crust and smooth the top.
Bake for approximately 1 hour, until the center appears set.
Remove from oven and cool on a wire rack for about
10 minutes.

Run a cool knife around the sides, cover,
and refrigerate overnight.

¾ cup whipping cream
6 ounces semi-sweet chocolate, broken into pieces
1 tablespoon sugar

Stir ingredients over low heat until smooth, and cool slightly.
Pour over the center of the cheesecake, out to about ½ inch
from edges.
Chill for 2 hours, then let stand at room temperature for
1 hour before serving.

4

"It's a girl."

"That's great," Jackson muttered into the phone. "Really, that's great. What time is it?"

"I don't even know," Emma told him. "It looks like the sun is yet to come up though."

Jackson squinted at the alarm clock on the cherry nightstand. "Almost four thirty," he told her. "Will you go home and get some sleep?"

"Can't," she said. "Although I'd love nothing more than a couple of aspirin and eight hours of uninterrupted sleep, I promised Sherilyn I'd stay a while. And I've got some interns coming in at nine to help us finish up the cookie favors for the Bristol bridal shower."

"Fee can't handle that?"

"Probably, but you know . . ."

Jackson did know. Perfectionist that she was, Emma never seemed to leave anything she'd started to someone else for completion.

"I have a client in the afternoon and I need to go through the paperwork for when Kat arrives on Tuesday to take over for Sherilyn while she's on maternity leave. Then—" Emma cut herself off and smiled. "Sorry. I'm kind of chasing myself, and the sun hasn't even come up yet. I'm going to run home for a shower and a change of clothes," she told him. "Want to meet at the hotel for breakfast around eight?"

"Sounds good," he replied. "I'll see you then."

It seemed like he had just set down the phone and rolled over when the 6:45 alarm went off. After a hot shower and a shave, Jackson wrapped a thick terry towel around his waist and stepped into his closet. Gray dress slacks . . . the charcoal-striped Van Heusen shirt his sister Madeline had given him for his birthday . . . black leather suspenders . . . underwear, T-shirt, socks, and shoes. After laying it all out on the corner of the bed, he returned to the bathroom. He'd just spread a dollop of Colgate on his toothbrush when the phone rang, and he hurried into the bedroom to pick it up.

"Sorry to bother you, boss."

"Susannah, don't be silly. What's up?"

"I think you'd better flip on the local news. Channel Eleven."

He found the remote and aimed it at the flat screen on the wall as he asked, "Why? What's going on?"

"I'm pretty sure your day has just been ruined."

Jackson grimaced when he saw his own face occupying a small square behind the reporter.

". . . and as we reported on our early morning broadcast, it seems that Jackson Drake, the owner and creator of Roswell's Tanglewood Inn, is about to sell the unique wedding destination hotel to Allegiant Industries, the conglomeration that took so many Buckhead and Alpharetta small businesses out of commission just last year. More to follow on our noon broadcast right here on *11-Alive*. Now back to the *Today* show with Matt Lauer."

Jackson flipped off the television and sat down on the edge of the bed.

"The phone should start ringing in a few minutes," Susannah told him. "What is our official response?"

"No comment."

"And your unofficial word? Are you really selling the hotel, Jackson?"

"Can we talk about this when I get there?" he asked.

"Certainly."

"And will you call downstairs and make breakfast reservations for Emma and me before you leave for the office?"

"Of course. For what time?"

"About eight."

"I'll see you afterward then."

Not if anyone else sees me first, I'm afraid,

He'd so hoped to have the opportunity to discuss the offer in detail with Emma before the word spread that he might be selling The Tanglewood. The faces of so many of his employees flashed across his mind's eye, and their varied-but-similar reactions evoked a shake of his head to clear them away.

He unfolded his cell phone and looked up Rod Bingham's phone number.

"Hey, buddy," Bingham greeted him. "Do you have an answer for me?"

"Does it matter?"

"What do you mean? Of course it matters."

"Well, since the local news is reporting that I'm already selling out to Allegiant, I don't know that it does."

"Oh." Bingham cleared his throat. "Did that leak out?"

❧

"Did you catch the news this morning?"

Emma looked up from her tea and smiled at Jackson. Her heart fluttered a bit at the sight of him in those leather suspenders she liked so much. He had a long, lean angle to him: broad shoulders and chest, tapering to a narrower waist.

"Yes," she told him. "And so did Sherilyn."

Jackson groaned as he slipped into the chair across from her.

"It's far too early in the day for you to look this tired, Jackson. Maybe you should turn around, go home, and start again."

"If only."

She reached across the table and took his hand, caressing it with her thumb. "How about we go one better? You go up to your office and close the door behind you. I'll have some breakfast sent up for us and meet you there in ten."

He looked unsure in that fleeting moment before Pearl emerged from the kitchen and made a beeline for their table. Suddenly he nodded and popped up from the chair.

"You're a genius," he muttered, squeezing her hand.

"Jackson, wait!" Pearl called after him, but he was well on his way across the lobby.

"Pearl," Emma sidetracked her. "Can I have a breakfast tray sent upstairs to Jackson's office? We're having a working meeting."

Pearl's focus remained on Jackson's trail as she replied, "Sure. For how many?"

"Just the two of us."

"The usual?"

"Please."

Emma took a final sip from her teacup and wiped the corner of her mouth with the linen napkin. She stood up and grabbed her bag from the back of her chair.

"So is it true?"

Pearl had always reminded Emma a bit of an elf with her silver pixie haircut, but this morning she appeared stoic and quite serious. Her starched white uniform hadn't yet been splattered with anything from the kitchen, and her striking indigo eyes flashed with questions Emma knew she couldn't answer.

"Pearl," Emma said, patting the woman's arm. "Nothing has been decided yet. It's no more than an offer on the table at this point. Jackson hadn't even had time to seriously consider it before someone leaked half-truths to the press. Believe me, if there's anything to tell, Jackson won't waste any time in telling it."

After a long and silent moment, the woman sighed. "Orange?" she asked.

"Pardon?"

"Juice. Orange or grapefruit?"

"Oh. Yes, orange."

More of the same awaited her on the trek from Morelli's, through the lobby, and to the elevator. The restaurant hostess, two guests, and the front desk manager all inquired about the report on the morning news. She felt almost relieved to find Susannah's desk unoccupied, and she slipped into Jackson's office and closed the door behind her.

Leaning against the door, she sighed. "Well, you've opened up quite a can of worms around this place, haven't you?"

Jackson chuckled. "Long walk through the lobby?"

"Very. Breakfast should arrive in a few minutes."

"Any danger it will be poisoned?"

"Only a little," she teased. "Why don't we sit down and talk it over? What have they offered, Jackson?"

He pulled a leather notebook from his briefcase and opened it on the desktop. Reading to her from the notes he'd made, Jackson provided an overview of the buyout offer. Emma tried—*and failed!*—to disguise her astonishment at the generous numbers.

"Jackson!" she breathed.

"I know. Turns your head, doesn't it?"

Emma nodded. "Dreaming about living in Paris for a year is one thing. Having it financed with a fortune to spare is quite another. Where's your head on this, now that you've had time to think it over?"

"I'm torn. On one hand, there's the—"

A knock at the office door cut his thoughts in two, and they fell silent as Rafael, one of the wait staff, wheeled in the breakfast cart.

"Morning, Rafael," Emma greeted him. "How are you?"

"Good morning." His cool tone announced that he had either seen or heard about the morning news broadcast.

Emma's gaze remained fixed on Jackson's, and his on hers. Not another word was spoken until Rafael headed for the door.

"Thank you, Rafe," Jackson offered.

Nothing in return.

Once the door closed, the corner of Jackson's mouth twitched.

"All rightie then," Emma said with a sigh. She removed the aluminum dome from Jackson's plate and slid it toward him. "Shall we?"

Jackson examined the plate thoughtfully and smirked. "You first."

❧

"Thanks for coming in," Emma announced as she handed out aprons to the three young ladies lined up on the other side of the rectangular stainless steel worktable. "Today's project is preparing the guest favors for twenty-five women attending a bridal shower in the courtyard tomorrow afternoon."

Three sizes of sugar cookie rounds lined both counters and two rolling workspaces. Plastic boxes and precut ruffled pink ribbons sat in stacks on a four-level stainless steel shelf.

"If you'll look over at Fee," she instructed them, "she's going to demonstrate how to assemble each cookie cake before placing it inside a plastic box and tying it shut with one of the ribbons."

Three fresh, eager faces turned toward Fee.

"Each cake consists of three tiers," Fee told them. "The bottom two are made up of three layered cookies, like so. And the top layer is just two of the smallest ones. Now, one of you will be assigned to each of the three sizes so that you can ice together individual tiers with lavender royal icing, like this."

Spreading frosting between each of the cookies, she demonstrated.

"And remember, no finger-licking!"

The girls shared chuckles before turning their attention back to Fee.

"After all of the tiers are assembled, we'll focus on constructing a perfect three-tier cake out of cookies, like this one. The top layer will be frosted, and a pastel-green sugar flower will be angled on top, like this. And two pink pearls will adorn the cake like this. Any questions?"

When no one piped up, Emma rubbed her hands together and smiled.

"Excellent!" she said. "Why don't you get started while I speak to Fee privately for a moment."

Fee removed her apron as she followed Emma to her office.

"Should I close it?" she asked, nodding at the door.

"Please," Emma replied. "Sit down for a second."

Before Emma could even find her chair, Fee sat down and peered over the top of her square black glasses, lightly scratching her tattooed arm. "It's true then. Jackson's selling the hotel?"

Emma sighed. "You saw the news."

"Nah. I don't get up that early, you know that. Ramon down in the laundry told me. Do I need to start job-hunting?"

"No." Emma closed her eyes and massaged her temples for a moment. "This company started out talking to Jackson about franchising the whole wedding destination hotel idea. Then the guy makes this offer to buy the hotel, and it came out of left field. Jackson didn't even have a chance to take a breath before it was all over the news that he'd agreed to sell."

"And?"

"And that's all," Emma assured her. "No decision has been made. But the minute he decides, either way, I promise that you and Sher will be the first to know."

Fee scowled for a moment as she thought it over. "You have a preference?"

"About selling?"

"Yeah."

Emma sighed. "Of course. But it's not my decision. This is all Jackson, and I'll support him in whatever he decides."

"Not exert even the teeniest bit of influence?" Fee prodded. "You know. So we can all keep our jobs."

"I'm not in this, Fiona."

Fee hopped up from her chair with a nod. "Good, then."

"That's all?" Emma asked with a chuckle.

"Well, yeah. You'll let me know when there's anything else to know, right?"

"Yes. Right."

"The petit fours are complete and in the fridge," she said, shifting gears so quickly that Emma's head spun a little. "When the cookie favors are complete, I'll start the miniature cheesecakes. After that, Sean and I are meeting our realtor to check out a house in Sandy Springs, then I'm headed over to the hospital to see Sherilyn and to take a gander at the little guy."

"Girl."

"Right. Girl. Want to come along?"

"I wish I could, but I'm finalizing the shower menu, and I have a ton of stuff to do before Audrey and Kat arrive on Tuesday."

"Right. Your dress. Kat's coming too? That's new."

"Oh, you didn't know? Kat's filling in for Sherilyn for a few weeks while she's home with baby Isabel."

"You know, she's left me a couple of messages, but I haven't had time to call her back. Is Russell coming with her?"

"No. He's filming a movie in Brazil, and she's coming off some big jewelry show in New York."

Another nod. "It will be good to see Kat again."

"Yes, it—" Fee was on her way before Emma could complete the thought. "—will."

Emma guessed that was the simplest discussion she or Jackson would have with anyone in the hotel on the subject of the possible sale of The Tanglewood. The relief hadn't had a chance to settle in when—

"Emmy, where's that fiancé of yours?"

Her heart tapped out a beat against her temples at the unexpected arrival of her father.

"I want to talk things over with him," Gavin announced as he filled the doorway to her office. "Has he got an attorney to walk him through the sale?"

"Hi, Daddy," she said, kissing his cheek.

"You can't be too careful when those corporate raiders come swooping in, Emmy."

"Jackson used to be one of those corporate guys, Daddy."

"Yeah. That's right. Still. Can't be too careful. Jackson in his office?"

She considered an outright lie. Instead, though, she just nodded. "I think so."

⤳

Audrey Regan had become a bit of a phenomenon since taking her mad design skills to the renowned house of Riley Eastwood last year. She'd left New York and settled in the Atlanta area to be closer to her friend Carly, but she hadn't been in town much since Thanksgiving, when Carly's military husband returned from the Middle East. In February, she debuted on a London runway with Riley's grand finale piece, a spectacular couture gown to announce House of Eastwood's new plus-size label.

Emma knew how fortunate she'd been when Audrey agreed to design her wedding dress. She hadn't exactly been great with the planning details—flowers, music, and, of all things, the elusive wedding cake!—but Emma had a clear picture of how she wanted to look in her gown. And Audrey Regan was just enough of a genius to take the picture out of her head and sketch it into reality.

Kat had phoned from the airport to say they were on the way to the hotel, and Emma made every attempt not to hover over the entrance like a nervous bride. Instead, she'd been casually pacing between the vicinity of the door and the front desk for the last fifteen minutes.

A ruckus at the desk dragged her attention to Mrs. Montague, the mother of next Saturday night's bride with the seven-tier lemon-filled cake. The woman inched her way toward the manager as she pinched the ear of a young girl and pulled her along.

"Let go!" the child cried, wincing and flailing her arms at the woman in slaps that never quite hit their target. "Let go of me!"

"I caught this ragamuffin pawing through the leftovers on our room service cart," Mrs. Montague explained as Emma joined them at the desk.

"Let go of my *eeeeeear*," the girl squealed as she wriggled and twisted in a jagged circle until she managed to escape the woman's grip. "Dang!" she groaned, rubbing her ear.

Glaring at the child, Mrs. Montague spoke in quiet, unmistakable syllables. "I hope someone will call her parents before she gets into some real trouble."

"Look, I'm sorry," the girl said. "It smelled good and I couldn't help myself."

"Well, someone should have taught you to try harder."

"I'm . . . *sorrrry*." It almost seemed like she'd choked on the word. "I won't do it again."

"See that you don't." The woman shook her head at Emma before glancing at the front desk manager. "You'll call her parents, won't you?"

"Yes, ma'am."

Mrs. Montague adjusted her large designer handbag and headed off toward the front door, her high heels clicking on the tile floor, the child she left behind doing a cartoonish impression of her as she went.

"Hey," Emma said sharply, and the girl stopped in her tracks. "What were you doing going through the room service cart?"

"You answered your own question," she snapped, pushing a mass of tight, reddish-brown curls away from her face. Emma noticed a smear of what looked like barbecue sauce or ketchup on the side of her chin.

"Don't be smart," she said as she wiped it away. "What's your name?"

"You first," the girl snarled, backing up.

"Emma Rae Travis."

"You work in this dump?"

Emma glanced at the manager before she replied, "I'm the baker. Now it's your turn. What's your name?"

"Hildie."

"Hildie. That's pretty."

"It's stupid. Sounds like an old southern fart."

Emma couldn't help herself, and she popped with laughter. "Hildie what?"

"Just Hildie."

"And how old are you, Just Hildie?"

"How old are *you*?"

Emma narrowed her eyes. "I'm guessing you're, what, around ten?"

"Eleven!" she corrected.

"All right. Now we're getting somewhere. Tell me, eleven year-old Just Hildie, what room are you in, and where are your parents?"

"Well . . . I . . ."

"Emma!"

She pivoted toward the call and saw Audrey make her way into the lobby behind Kat, who waved her arm and grinned from one ear to the other. Tomás, one of the day shift bellmen, pushed a loaded brass cart behind them.

"Hey!" the manager called, and when Emma turned back around, Hildie had disappeared around the corner and up the stairs.

"Find out who her parents are," Emma told him before hurrying across the lobby to greet her friends.

The closer she got to her, the more profoundly Emma felt the impact of Audrey's beauty. With her platinum blond hair, voluptuous curves, and catlike eyes, she looked like an updated version of a 1940s pinup girl. And Kat, Audrey's former assistant, looked like a fresh-faced model in an ad for peach shampoo or some great new minty toothpaste.

"Look at the two of you!" Emma exclaimed as they exchanged embraces. "Together again, and walking through the doors of The Tanglewood Inn."

"It's so good to be back," Kat said with a wide grin. "And wait until you see your dress!"

Audrey beamed, her full red lips stretched out into a perfect smile. "Let us get checked in and you can come up to the room for a fitting."

"That works!" Emma replied. "Half an hour?"

"Perfect."

Kat followed Audrey toward the desk, then stopped abruptly and turned around. "Emma, is Fee in the kitchen?"

"She is. I'll bring her with me."

"Great!" Kat wrinkled her nose and shot Emma a crooked grin. "It's so good to see you again."

"You too."

৯৫২৯

"Your wedding invitations are here," Sherilyn told Jackson as she poked her head through the door. "Would you like to peek, or shall we wait for Emma Rae?"

She looked harried as she rushed through the door with a small cardboard box under one arm, her infant child cradled across her in a strange sideways sack. She wore a floor-length paisley dress, her hair was knotted into something slightly resembling a ponytail, and a large quilted diaper bag was slung over her shoulder.

"Emma is having her dress fitting at the moment," he replied with a grin. "She may not come up for air until who-knows-when. Let's have a look."

"Audrey and Kat are here? Why didn't she call me?" she exclaimed as she thrust the box toward him. "Here, can you just pull one of those out so I can show it to her? What room is Audrey in? Do you know? Oh, never mind, I'll call Kat's cell."

Jackson chuckled as he pulled out one of the invitations from the top of the box and handed it to her.

"I hope you like them," she called over her shoulder as she scurried out the door.

Ivory linen set against a black card border held the raised black letters inviting their chosen few guests to join them in celebrating their nuptials. A silk ribbon wrapped cleanly around the invitation, tied in a bow.

"Pale orchid" was the label Emma had given the light purple ribbon when she'd presented the option to him. "Kind of elegant, very classic. This one's my favorite."

She'd gone on about something having to do with hydrangeas and centerpieces, but he'd zoned out a little on the rest of it. Frankly, she'd sounded more like Sherilyn than his Emma.

"Then pale orchid it is!" he declared when she'd finished.

It turned out to be a fine choice he realized as he looked at it, and his stomach squeezed a little as he traced the glossy raised letters of their names on the card.

Finally. Emma will be my bride.

Jackson felt as if he'd been waiting a lifetime to see those two names sharing the same invitation card. He asked himself why he'd waited so long.

Desiree flickered across his mind with a sweet, gentle smile, and his stomach squeezed again. She'd looked so beautiful on their wedding day, like a princess in a ball gown, a strand of her grandmother's pearls around her neck, and a long veil that brushed the floor. He struggled to remember what their invitations had looked like, but he couldn't quite nail down the image. It felt a little disloyal for a moment before he realized Desiree wouldn't care in the least whether he remembered the invitations or the flowers or the cake, as long as he remembered her. And Jackson did.

He remembered every curve of her face, every freckle on her arms, every single one of her always-readable expressions; and as he mentally browsed over each memory, he landed on what Emma had promised him early on in their romance.

"There's room enough for all three of us in this relationship, Jackson. There's you and me, and there's your memory of your late wife. You don't have to choose."

He'd already known he loved her by then. He just hadn't known quite how much.

You'd actually like her, Desi. If you'd have met somewhere, you might have been friends.

Warmth surged through Jackson, and he closed his tired eyes for a minute and leaned back until his desk chair creaked. He felt pretty certain that she'd have encouraged him to move on without her. But he couldn't help wondering about something else . . . hoping that Desiree would understand . . .

Tips for Choosing the Best
Wedding Invitations

It used to be that all wedding invitations were formal:
white or ivory paper with raised black lettering.
Guests wore formal attire, such as evening gowns
and tuxedos.
Today, however, the wedding invitation is a reflection
of the bride and groom's personal style
as well as the theme, tone, and location of their wedding.

- The invitation should match the tone or theme
chosen for the wedding.

- Today's wedding invitations can include such personal
choices as dried flowers, recycled papers, and gilt edges.

- Traditional and formal weddings usually require a
more formal invitation with engraved lettering,
a technique that raises the letters slightly.

- For a more casual invitation, a professional portrait
of the bride and groom can be a nice touch to make
a personal statement, and it is a particularly nice touch
for those invitations going to out-of-town recipients who
will likely not be able to attend the wedding.

- The wording of the invitation may also vary; however, the name of the hosts should always be included in addition to the date, time, and location.

- When cost is a priority, some lovely invitations can be created with a little imagination and a good-quality printer. There are many templates available, and a fine stationery store will offer everything from cardstock to linen papers and vellum overlays.

5

Pleated sweetheart bodice.
Hand-embroidered and beaded cap sleeves.
Side-draped cascades of chiffon.
A two-inch belt of rhinestones circling a natural waist.
Twenty rhinestone buttons down the back.
A-line silhouette with draped chapel-length train.

Those were the notes Audrey had scribbled while they conferenced about Emma's gown. A week later, she'd included them in the e-mail to Emma with a jpg of the sketch attached. She had meticulously included every idea Emma had somehow managed to express, times ten. And now—seeing the end result before her—Emma could hardly breathe.

"Oh my!"

"Yes?" Audrey asked eagerly.

"Oh . . . Audrey . . ."

"I think that's a yes," Kat added. "Isn't it?"

"Well, come on. Don't keep us in suspense," Fee declared.

"It's beyond—" That was all she could manage.

Emma sank to the edge of the king-sized bed, both hands over her heart, trying to breathe as she gazed at the dress form angled toward her. Every detail of the gown came together to stop her heart, every rhinestone on the belt perfectly placed, every pearl and bead on the delicate cap sleeves shimmering. Even the way the hem sat arranged on the floor brought a mist of emotion to her eyes and a lump to her throat that kept her from speaking.

"It's a gorgeous dress," Kat said with a sigh as she dropped to the bed beside Emma.

"Exquisite," Emma managed.

The four of them lined up along the foot of the bed, gazing at the gown as if it had descended from a cloud, affecting the mood of the room full of women the way only a wedding dress could.

A sudden bang-bang-bang against the door drew Kat to her feet, and she hurried to answer Sherilyn's frantic calls from the corridor.

"Let me in! Don't you dare leave me out of this!"

Emma couldn't manage to look away from the gown as Sherilyn blew into the room. But when Sherilyn gasped and the others fell eerily silent, she looked up to find her friend standing in the middle of the room, her baby strapped across her chest, bulging diaper bag flung over her shoulder, and her glassy eyes trained on the dress before them.

"Is that it?" she slowly asked. Fee's dry glance at her elicited a further reply: "Oh. Well, of course it is. It's . . . it's . . . exquisite!"

"Isn't it?" Emma said.

Sherilyn sat down next to Emma on the bed, cradling the tiny pink bundle in her arms.

"Hi, Isabel," Emma cooed at the baby. "Did you see my wedding dress? Isn't it beautiful?" Looking up at Sherilyn, she asked, "Can I hold her?"

Sherilyn nodded absentmindedly, pulling a bottle of antiseptic gel from the bag and handing it to Emma without glancing away from the gown.

Emma squirted out a dollop of gel and rubbed her hands together as Sherilyn exclaimed, "Oooh!" She plucked something else from the front flap of the diaper bag and waved it at Emma.

"The invitations arrived!"

"They did, and I think they're really lovely, Em."

Emma wiped her hands again before she gingerly accepted the invitation. Tracing the glossy, raised letters of Jackson's name with her index finger, she grinned. "They're perfect."

"Let's see," Fee said, and she pulled the card from Emma's hand. "Nice."

"And how's the wedding cake project coming along?" Sherilyn asked her.

Emma shrugged. "I got another one down on paper last night. But . . . I don't know. Maybe. Maybe it could be the one."

"That's what she said about the last one," Fee commented, but Emma's attention was fixed on the gown again.

Reaching across Sherilyn, she grabbed Audrey's hand and gave it a playful shake. "And you! You're a genius," she said, and Audrey smiled in reply. "No, I mean it. You're an absolute genius. I may be a little lost in getting to my wedding cake, but this dress is a touchdown. It's what I pictured in my head, and so much more. The rhinestone buttons . . . the detailing on the sleeves . . . It's genius, Audrey. How can I ever thank you?"

"You can marry that fabulous man of yours and live a happy life. But before you do that, why don't we do a fitting?"

"Oh!" Emma squealed, and Sherilyn shushed her, pointing down at Isabel.

"I forgot I get to try it on," Emma whispered, tugging off her blouse before she even hit her feet. "I can't wait to try it on!"

જીશ

From the time that he'd opened the place, Jackson had taken to enjoying his mid-morning coffee at this one particular table in the restaurant whenever he could manage it. He'd actually preferred it there before the hotel had officially opened because the tables around him sat unoccupied back then, but he wouldn't trade the steady stream of patrons for all of the peaceful coffee experiences on earth. The Tanglewood had evolved from a questionable venture in those early days into the solid success that it was now, all thanks to those customers who churned through the doors day after day.

Behind him, a family of five chatted softly over their breakfasts, and a young businessman sipped coffee in the corner. Chiffon-filtered streams of sunlight pointed to the floor beside the man as he exchanged pleasantries with his waitress.

Jackson poured the last drops from the pot into his cup as rubber-soled shoes padded their way toward him, and he looked up as they came to a muffled halt next to his table. The warm and familiar smile of Emma's Aunt Sophie greeted him, and he found himself remembering that first morning when he'd looked up at her from that very spot in the restaurant to find that she wore a mint-green evening gown, long white gloves and—of all things!—a tiara.

"What is your name?" she'd asked him, and less than three minutes later, Jackson had fallen a little bit in love as she quoted Scripture to him from the Book of Isaiah, promising him that whatever situation had him so engrossed in his own thoughts was sure to look up very soon.

"Good morning, Jackson," she said to him now, as she smoothed back her halo of beautiful silver hair with both hands. "Am I interrupting you?"

"I think that's what you asked me the very first time you walked through those doors, Sophie. You asked if you were interrupting me."

"Did I?"

"And you were dressed in green, like you were going to a ball at the palace."

Sophie smiled. "I must have looked happy. Was I happy, Jackson?"

"You always seem happy to me," he remarked. "It's one of the things I love most about you."

He took a final draw from his cup and set it down on the table.

"How about you?" she asked, and Jackson leaned back against the chair. "Are you happy? Because you look unusually burdened this morning, dear."

"I'm just in the process of making a business decision," he explained with a smile.

"Then I won't keep you from it," she replied, turning on her heel and heading toward the door.

"Wait, Sophie. Are you here alone?"

"I came with Avery. And she's . . . she's . . ."

Jackson watched her closely for a moment, noticing the spark of confusion that flashed in her bluish eyes as they darted about the restaurant.

"Oh, dear. I'm afraid I've . . . I don't know . . ."

"I was just headed into the kitchen to say hello to Emma," he said, standing up and offering his arm. "Would you like to come along?"

"Well . . ."

"I know she'd love to see you. Come for a walk with me."

Sophie grabbed hold of his arm tightly, and he covered her trembling hand with his as they strolled out of the restaurant.

"Kathy, if Emma's mother comes in looking for this beautiful young lady," he told the hostess at the door, "would you direct her to the kitchen? I'm just borrowing Miss Sophie for a few minutes."

"Certainly, Mr. Drake."

Sophie sighed, leaning into Jackson as they headed for Emma's kitchen. She'd become so much stronger and more confident over the last year, and her periods of lucidity were much more frequent now that the family had built such a familiar and established environment for her. But every now and then, he saw that fearful glimmer of someone momentarily lost, and it broke Jackson's heart every time.

"Aunt Soph!" Emma cried as they pushed through the swinging door into the kitchen. "Your ears must have been twitching. I was just thinking about you!"

"Were you, dear?"

Emma shot Jackson a grateful glance as she wrapped her arms around her aunt's shoulders. "I need to tell you all about the wedding plans. Are you up for a little chat?"

"Of course I am, Emma Rae. Of course I am."

Avery scurried through the kitchen door and halted next to Jackson as Emma and Sophie wandered away toward the office. Her hand to her heart, Avery sighed, and Jackson squeezed her shoulder.

"Thank the Lord," she whispered. "Some days, Jackson, keeping an eye on my sister is like herding kittens. I don't know how those people at the center keep up with her!"

"They're trained professionals," he teased, and Avery chuckled.

"How are the wedding plans coming along?" she asked, threading her arm through his as they left the kitchen.

"You're asking the wrong guy. As I understand it, I'm just supposed to show up in a tuxedo at the appointed time."

"That sounds like Sherilyn."

Jackson laughed. "A direct quote. And now that she's had the baby and she has Kat here filling in, it's double duty with the organizational directives. There's nothing going to slip through the cracks, believe me."

"Oh, I've known Sherilyn for many years," Avery said with a nod. "I believe you."

As they reached the restaurant, Avery tapped Jackson's arm before releasing it. "I have an early luncheon here at Morelli's."

"With Gavin?"

"Oh, don't be silly, dear boy. The day your future father-in-law schedules an early anything is the day Biloxi freezes over."

A pop of laughter burst out of Jackson, and he shook his head.

"No, I'm meeting your sister for an early lunch."

A twinge of curiosity pinched him. "Which one?"

"Georgiann," she replied with a smile. "Would you like to join us?"

"I wish I could, but I'm due back upstairs for a conference call."

"A pity," she remarked before pecking his cheek. "You have a lovely phone call, then. We'll just chirp about you behind your back."

"Little *bruthah*, I haven't seen you in a month of Sundays."

"Hi, George." He greeted her with an embrace as they passed.

"Wait, you can't join us?" she asked him. "We're having—"

"Sorry, I can't. Conference call. You two enjoy yourselves."

Georgiann tossed her hands with dramatic flair, and Jackson grinned at her as he crossed the lobby.

"I swanee," she grumbled as he went. "That boy!"

Georgia 400 was uncharacteristically free of traffic, and Emma had an easy fifteen-minute drive from the hotel back to her apartment. She rounded the building and pulled into the parking space painted with a faded orange #6. Propping open the door of her idling candy-apple-red Mini Cooper, she tilted her head back against the seat and closed her eyes, humming back-up *do-wops* for Aretha Franklin.

Traffic droned in the distance while the murmur of the Egglestons' conversation wafted through their open door, reminding Emma of another night like this one a long time ago. She'd come home to find Aunt Sophie seated on the back step in her bathrobe, and Jackson had shocked her when he unexpectedly leaned in over the top of Emma's open car door.

His kindness to her wandering aunt had touched Emma's heart that night. And after they got Sophie settled in the guest room, Emma and Jackson had shared their very first kiss. It felt like only a moment ago as she recalled how she'd had a sudden urge for tea . . .

She had risen from the couch, and padded off toward the kitchen in bare feet, and filled the stainless steel kettle with water. When she turned back again to ignite the stove, she thumped into Jackson.

"Oh! Sorry. I didn't know you were—"

He didn't let her finish. He just wrapped his arms around her waist and pulled her into him, angling his face and pressing his lips against hers. She was so surprised that she drew in a long, deep breath through her nose and then just held it there as the warmth of his kiss began to settle on her. Aware of a ticklish tingle to her lips, she pursed them a little more, pressing in.

Suddenly the kettle that had been in her hand clanged to the floor . . .

As she let the memory wash over her, Emma's lips began to tingle. That kiss had been the start of something, a catalyst that changed everything. How could she ever have known how accepting a new job and getting to know her new boss could have led to . . . *this?*

She rested her left hand atop the steering wheel and wiggled her fingers. The shimmer of light-play bounced off her engagement ring and against the glass windshield, and she squinted at the ring for a moment before reaching for her cell phone.

"Emma."

"Are you tied up?"

"Why? What did you have in mind?"

She giggled. "I just didn't want to interrupt anything important."

"No," he sighed into the phone. "I'm just cleaning off my desk, getting ready to head out. Did you forget something?"

"No. I remembered something."

"What's that?"

"I just parked out back at my place," she told him, fluttering her ring against the light again. "And I remembered that night I came home to find you and Aunt Sophie here. Do you remember?"

"Mm-hmm."

"Do you remember what else happened that night?"

"Yes, I do."

"What," she challenged him with a grin. "What else happened?"

"You kissed me for the first time."

"I think *you* kissed *me*."

"Oh," he teased, "you kissed me right back, my friend!"

She paused before letting out a chuckle. "Okay. I did. You're right."

"So you're home for the night?"

"I just pulled in. Did you want to do something?"

Jackson sighed. "I really need to see you."

"Want to come over?"

"Be there in half an hour."

At first glance, it didn't look to Emma like she had much in the refrigerator to work with, but by the time Jackson arrived she'd put together a pretty fair spread. Slices of ham rolled around softened cream cheese and cucumber slices; warm brie and stone crackers; a bowl of red seedless grapes; chilled sparkling water with lime wedges.

"Not bad," she said aloud on her way to open the front door. But the moment she saw Jackson's weary face, her own amusement fizzled. "Jackson? What's wrong? You look . . . awful."

"Shhh," he said, drawing her into his embrace.

Minutes ticked by as Jackson held her there, the front door standing wide open as his strong arms wrapped around and buoyed her, their bodies rocking slowly from side to side. Emma's heart began to race, first with that familiar rush of adrenaline she'd come to know so well, the one initiated by physical contact with Jackson. Then came another type of heart thumping, the kind ultimately followed by anxiety. Something wasn't right.

"Jackson?"

"Shhh," he repeated, nuzzling his face into her hair and kissing her lightly behind the ear.

"Come inside," she insisted, closing the door and helping him out of his suit jacket. "Come on. Sit down and have a snack. Let's talk."

Jackson collapsed on the sofa and sank into the plump cushions behind him. He tilted his head back and sighed, closing his eyes. The dim light from the mission-style torchiere in the corner cast a yellowish glaze over his tired, worn countenance, and Emma sat down next to him without making a sound. After a few moments, she gingerly raised her hand and ran her fingers lovingly through his dark hair.

"It's all right," she whispered. "Everything's going to be all right."

Jackson lifted his head and eased his eyes open. "Somehow, I believe it when you tell me that."

"Because I never lie. I'm a very honest girl."

"That you are," he said with a weary smile punctuated by a sudden spark in his eye. "You are also a very beautiful girl."

"Now, don't you start lying, Jackson Drake!"

"I don't lie, either. You know that. You have no idea how stunning you are, do you?"

Emma's lips parted, on the verge of a witty retort, but Jackson pressed one finger across them to hold it back.

"Don't say another thing unless it's to tell me how much you love me," he said, gravel in his voice.

Emma kissed his finger before pushing it away. "To the moon and back again," she whispered. "And if you love me that much in return, you'll start talking and tell me what's got you so tangled up."

He sighed again, this time with an undertone of a soft growl as he dropped his head back on the cushion. "Ah, where to start."

"Just tell me." Then, as an afterthought, "Jackson. Let me help."

He lifted his head and gazed at her for a moment before narrowing his eyes. The weight of his stare felt like hot wax pressed against her cheeks and throat.

"Your father came to see me the other day, you know."

"Oh, no." Emma's heart palpitated and fluttered. "What's he done?"

Jackson snorted in amusement, shaking his head. "No. Nothing."

"No?" she asked. "Because I've come to understand that, when it comes to my parents, Jackson, I really have no control over them whatsoever."

Jackson squeezed her hand. "Emma, he gave me some good advice, actually."

She swallowed around the lump in her throat. "Do tell."

"He taught me a little something about poker."

She took a moment to think that over, but she came up blank. "Sorry. I don't understand."

"He told me you need to know when to hold 'em and know when to fold 'em."

Emma cocked her head slightly. "Know when to walk away, and know when to run? Like the Kenny Rogers song?"

Jackson belted out a laugh and lifted her hand, kissing her knuckles. "Just like that."

"So . . . you're going to play cards with my father?"

"No," he stated. "I think it's time to fold 'em."

Emma's heart began to race again, and her face flushed with sudden heat. The pressure in her ears caused her words to sound hollow as she spoke them.

"You're selling The Tanglewood?"

Jackson heaved another sigh. "I'm selling."

A little topsy-turvy

6

*Y*ou have got to be kidding me!" Sherilyn exclaimed. "Didn't you tell him how you feel? That you don't want him to sell the hotel?"

Emma felt the grind of a headache coming on. She leaned forward, propping her elbows over the cake sketch on the desk as she massaged her throbbing temples. For some reason, the topsy-turvy wedding cake idea seemed very appropriate for her marriage to Jackson.

"You can't give up The Tanglewood, Em."

Sherilyn's turquoise eyes brimmed with tears, and the moment she blinked they spilled over and ran in streams down her face. A few droplets plummeted from her chin and landed on the large pink strawberry embroidered on baby Isabel's cotton sack.

"I don't want to sound terrible here," she continued, caressing Izzy's peach-fuzzed head, "but this place doesn't just belong to Jackson anymore, Emma Rae. It belongs to all of us now."

"In our hearts, yes. But the deed just has one name on it, Sher. And he's the one who gets to make the choice."

"And he's made it," she said, "just like that?"

Emma's blood simmered a little at that. "Of. Course. Not."

"Sorry. I get it."

"Jackson has been tortured over this decision, Sher."

"Then . . . why?"

Emma lifted her eyes and gazed at her friend's mournful expression. The grief seemed almost palpable. It really was a bit like a death, she supposed.

"Can't you change his mind?"

Emma replied in a raspy whisper. "It's not my place to do that."

"If not yours, then whose?"

Emma wrung her hands and sighed. "No one's. It's Jackson's hotel, Sherilyn. Do I wish he'd gone another way? Of course. But it's his decision."

"You can't just tell him how you feel, Em? You can't just weigh in on this? He'll listen to you."

Muted conversation drew their attention to Jackson and Fee in the kitchen beyond the other side of the closed office door.

Sherilyn turned back toward Emma and raised one arched eyebrow. "Now's your chance. Tell him how you feel."

Jackson nodded at Emma through the glass and headed toward them.

"Tell him," Sherilyn blurted just before he turned the knob and opened the door.

"Hey, Sherilyn. How's little Isabel today?"

She stood up and stared at him for a long and serious moment. Jackson glanced at Emma before half-smiling at Sherilyn. "What did I interrupt?"

"How could you, Jackson?" she asked him. "I mean, I know it's your hotel and you get to make the choice about what to do with it, but there's a whole community of people here who feel like family. You're going to just pull the rug out from underneath every one of us."

"Sherilyn, selling The Tanglewood does not mean you'll all lose your jobs," he told her. "The concept of the hotel will remain intact, and they'll need you all to stay on staff."

"Oh, goodie," she cracked. "From a family environment to . . . to . . . a *corporation*."

"It's not—"

"Look!" she exclaimed as she gathered her things. "You're going to do whatever you're going to do, but at least talk to your future wife about how she feels instead of just making a decision and issuing a sentence without even asking her because, you know what, Jackson? You're the only one who thinks this is a good idea. And I'm just so . . . so . . . disappointed in you."

And with that, Emma's forthright friend stomped out of the office and through the kitchen without a word to Fee as she passed her. At the door, she paused for a good, long moment before turning back and grabbing one of several dozen miniature chocolate muffins on Fee's worktable and throwing the thing into her mouth.

"They're really GOOD!" she snarled before reeling back toward the door and blowing through it.

Emma pulled a bottle of aspirin from her desk drawer and took two of them.

"Nice, Emma," Jackson snapped.

"What? You said I could tell her, Jackson. You had to know she would take it like this. I mean, you *have met Sherilyn* before, right?"

"You told her you don't want me to sell?"

"Well . . . no . . . not exactly."

"Great. You don't want me to, they don't want me to, and me . . . I'm just the big tyrant yanking their lives out from under them and tossing them to the corporate wolves to be eaten alive. Way to stand beside me in this, Emma. Way to present a united front."

"Jackson, that's not—"

"And for the record, I did ask you what you thought, didn't I? You just chose to say it was my hotel, my decision."

"Well, it is!"

"You should have spoken up, Emma. Told me your opinion. But you sure did manage to tell Sherilyn, didn't you?"

"I think you're—"

"A tyrant. I know."

Emma hadn't even known her office door was capable of such a good, hard *Slam!* But Jackson showed her that it was. And even though the swinging door at the other end of the kitchen couldn't manage another one, the way it flew back and forth behind Jackson made the point in its own gaping way.

⟡

The elevator doors couldn't open fast enough for Jackson once the car came to a stop on the fourth floor. Pushing his way through them, he stomped down the hall and rounded the corner into his office. He might have tromped right on past reception if not for the *What's Wrong With This Picture?* flash of neon that stopped him.

"Hello."

The fortyish brunette wearing a bright orange jacket and seated behind Susannah's desk didn't strike him as even remotely familiar.

"You must be Mr. Drake?"

He squinted at her for a moment before replying. "Yes."

She hopped up and sidestepped the desk with her hand extended. "I'm Bree Olding. Like the cheese?"

The cheese?

"You know. Brie. The cheese."

"Oh. Right," he said, shaking her hand vacantly. "And Bree, you're . . . here . . . because . . ."

"I'm helping Miss Littlefield."

Still. Why are you here?

"Oh, Jackson," Susannah said as she emerged from his office. "You've met Bree."

"I have. And I was just asking—"

"I'll explain all that to you. Why don't we step into your office then?" Susannah started back inside as she added, "Hold down the fort, will you, Bree?"

"Right you are!" the woman declared.

Jackson pushed the door shut behind him and slipped into the leather chair. Propping his elbows on the desktop, he stared Susannah down for a moment before prompting, "Well?"

"My sister, Mona?"

"Yes," he said with a nod. "The one in Jacksonville."

"Yes. Well, she has taken a fall," she told him, standing on the other side of the desk. He motioned for her to take a seat, but she shook her head and continued, "Her hip is broken in two places, and they performed surgery yesterday."

"I'm sorry to hear that."

"She's going straight to the rehab center for a bit, and then she's going to need some help at home. So I'm going to fly out over the weekend. I shouldn't be gone more than a couple of weeks."

"Weeks."

"I called Cheryl Delbert at the employment agency, and she sent Bree over. I'll spend a couple of days with her to make sure she knows the lay of the land, and I'm sure she'll be a fine replacement for me until I come back."

"You're irreplaceable, Susannah. You know that."

Her sudden grin cast a shy shadow. "If she works out, perhaps we can discuss full-time employment as my retirement date approaches."

Jackson groaned. "Don't remind me. Let's just get your desk covered while you take care of your sister. We'll think about all the rest at a later date."

"All right, Mr. Scarlett O'Hara," she teased. "You think about all that tomorrow."

"She comes with good references?"

"Cheryl seems very confident in her abilities."

He sighed and thumped the desk with one fist. "All right. I guess I'll leave training to you."

"Thank you, Jackson. I'm sorry to do this with so little notice. But it really couldn't—"

"It can't be helped," he finished for her. "Don't worry. We'll manage."

Jackson drummed his fingers on the desk as Susannah turned to leave the office. "Uh, wait just one second, will you?"

She turned and looked at him expectantly.

"I've decided to go ahead with the sale of the hotel, Susannah. Do you have any feelings about that one way or the other?"

"Well, of course, I'm retiring," she said, and he waved at her and grimaced. "Sorry to mention it again, but I am, Jackson. So it won't really affect me in any significant way. I imagine the rest of the staff will be distressed."

"You have no idea."

"But I think this is ultimately your decision."

"So I've been told."

"I know you well enough to know that you're weighing your options and the toll on others, and you'll make the best choice for everyone. Especially for you and Emma Rae as you start your new life together."

"Well. That was my plan."

"I wish you a very happy life, Jackson. You know that."

He sighed. "I do know that."

"Closed or open?" she asked as she reached the door.

"Closed, please."

After Susannah had gone, Jackson strolled over to the window and surveyed the Roswell streets splayed out before him. Traffic moved along at a nice clip, and the offices over near the old Roswell Mill bustled with activity.

Jackson loved the community that The Tanglewood called home. From the historic homes to the nature trails to the lovely old town square, Roswell evoked Old South charm. It ranked as the third largest city in Fulton County, the eighth largest in the state of Georgia, while still presenting itself as having the allure of a small southern town. If Emma ever spoke to him again and actually followed through with their marriage, perhaps they could think about settling here once both of them sold their current places.

Chastising himself for walking out on her the way he did, Jackson returned to his desk and picked up his cell phone.

I'm an idiot, he typed into the text box.

And? came the reply.

Still want to marry me?

Thinking. Will let you know. Would be hard to give up the ring.

Jackson laughed out loud.

Keep it. It's the least I can do.

True. What about the Falcons tix?

Not giving those up.

Then I suppose I'll have to marry you. I'm not giving them up either.

He leaned back in the chair and released a heavy sigh.

I love you, he texted her.

Adore you more. Fondant 911. See u later.

The intercom on his desk phone buzzed.

"Mr. Drake, your conference call is on line one," the cheese woman announced.

But when he picked up the phone, the line hummed.

"Sor-ry. I'll get them back again," she exclaimed from the other side of the closed door. An unexpected expletive followed, and Jackson snickered as Susannah hushed her.

"No, no! That kind of language isn't appropriate at The Tanglewood."

Another breach followed an instant later.

"Bree! Really!"

"Sor-ry. But this phone system is—"

The muffled completion to the sentence led Jackson to envision Susannah covering the cheese woman's mouth with her hand. He almost gave in to the temptation to go and have a look, but Susannah creaked open his office door and poked her head inside.

"Give it another try. We've got them back on line two."

Jackson nodded and picked up the phone. "Dale, it's Jackson Drake. How are you?"

"Better than you. What's going on down there in your offices, Drake?"

"Ah, you haven't got the time."

Dale Eeks cackled with laughter. "Well, if you're ready, we've got everyone on the line. Let's talk about your Roswell team."

❧

"Seriously. How does she do it? I'm starting to think Sherilyn Drummond is a robot!"

Emma chuckled. "I hear that a lot. She just really loves what she does, and she's well suited to it. Just hang in there, Kat. It's a process, and she's only out for a few weeks."

Kat shook her head as she climbed atop the stool at the far side of the stainless steel worktable where Emma and Fee dipped round, coffee-flavored cookies into chocolate.

"I don't think I knew what I was in for when I agreed to handle things for her while she's on maternity leave. I guess I thought it was just a matter of making sure things stayed organized. But, man!" Her words trailed off as she caught a glimpse of the cookie in Fee's hand. "Man, those look good. What are they?"

"Mocha latte cookies," Fee replied. "One of Emma's creations."

Kat watched, riveted, as Fee dipped the small round into the pan of warm chocolate to cover half of the cookie, then placed it next to the other cookies on the wax paper.

"Do you want one?" Fee asked dryly.

"Can I?" Kat cried, and she plucked a cookie from the table before either of them could reply.

At the first bite, she moaned, and Emma laughed at the reaction. "Those cookies get that response a lot."

"They're wicked!" Kat exclaimed. "So good!"

Emma smiled at her as she continued her work. Taking great care with the spatula, she loosened the next batch of cooled cookies from the sheet, lining them up for dipping.

"Oh! Where are you with the invitations?" Kat asked as she pilfered another cookie.

"Thirty-four of them, addressed and stamped, all ready to go."

"Thirty-four," Fee commented. "I thought you were only having a group of less than twenty."

"So did we."

Fee nodded knowingly, and Kat chuckled.

"Our guest list is what happened when we were busy making other plans."

"Jackson's sister?"

"Yeah. The only thing more frightening than Georgiann Markinson is putting her in a room with Avery Travis. But we've put our collective foot down, and thirty-four invitations is the line in the sand."

Kat looked up from her iPhone and asked, "Sherilyn wants to know if you mailed them."

"Text her back and tell her I said they're lost. We need to reorder."

Kat's eyes danced with the fire of surprise. "I'm not telling her that."

"Atta girl," Fee teased. "Save yourself."

"Hey, do either of you want to come to Carly's for dinner tonight? She told me to ask you and I completely zoned."

"Can't," Fee replied as she set the last of the chocolate-dipped cookies on the wax paper. "We've got two more houses to tour, and then Sean's brother is coming over."

"Jackson and I have some making up to do," Emma said with a grin. "We need to do that in private. Will Audrey be there?"

"No. She flew out to Las Vegas to meet up with J.R. for a couple of days."

Emma smiled. "How is J.R.?"

"He's on top of his game. Audrey says he's been consulting on a Matthew McConaughey movie out there, lining them up with vintage motorcycles."

"Oooh! Good for him! And how is your movie star paramour?"

"Russell's fine," Kat replied, blushing. "He's in Brazil for another month."

"A month." Emma shook her head. "I can't imagine being separated from Jackson like you two are."

"Well, Jackson isn't quite as exhausting as Russell," she quipped.

"True enough."

The three of them shared a laugh, and Kat added, "Truthfully, this has been a long stretch, so a little harder than normal. But sometimes a few weeks apart is just enough time for me to recharge."

"He is a handful, as I recall," Emma said with a grin.

"Indeed."

"It would have been nice if he could make it for the wedding, though."

"It's not completely out of the question, but it doesn't look good. He does send his love."

"Back at him. He's a terror . . . but a lovable one."

Kat nodded. "And speaking of lovable, I've got a consultation with next weekend's bride."

"Send my love to Carly and Devon." Emma called as Kat left.

"Will do."

The kitchen door still swung after her as Fee dried her hands and asked, "So what next? Scones or lemon squares?"

"Squares," Emma declared, and Fee nodded.

"I'll prep the counter."

Emma Rae's Lemon Squares

Preheat oven to 300 degrees.

2 cups all-purpose flour
½ cup powdered sugar
2 sticks butter
2 cups granulated sugar
1 teaspoon baking powder
¼ teaspoon salt
4 eggs, beaten
1 tablespoon grated lemon rind
¼ cup juice from a lemon

Sift the flour and powdered sugar together.
Cut in the butter until blended.
Press the mixture over the bottom of a 9x13x2-inch pan.

Bake for 20-25 minutes until lightly browned.
Combine granulated sugar, baking powder, salt, eggs,
lemon rind, and juice.
Spread over the baked crust.

Turn the oven up to 350 degrees.

Bake for 30 minutes.
After removing from oven, sprinkle with additional
powdered sugar.
When fully cool, cut into squares.

7

"I'm so grateful that you could meet with me this late in the day."

"Not a problem," Emma replied, passing a glass bowl of sugar cubes to the eager blond beauty across the table from her. "My fiancé is caught working too. You're helping me kill some time before we meet for a late dinner."

"Oh, good."

Holly Norris had great bone structure. Her face looked to Emma like a sculpture in a museum, and the deep set of her blue eyes added intensity.

"So Kat tells me that you've officially nailed down all of the details except the cake," Emma said, leaning back against the cool wrought iron chair and crossing her legs.

"Finally. Planning a wedding is far more complicated than I expected."

"You don't have to tell me," she said on a chuckle. "I'm in the midst of planning my own."

Holly's eyes twinkled as she nodded toward Emma's hand. "I noticed your ring. It's breathtaking. When is your big day?"

"Just three weeks from tomorrow."

"Are you having it here at the hotel?"

"Yes. This place is sentimental for us. It kind of brought us together."

Holly wrinkled her nose and grinned. "Oh, that's so romantic. Which ballroom will you use? I'm in The English Rose."

"That's the largest room," Emma observed, and she picked up her pen and made a note. "So you'll have how many guests then?"

"A hundred and fifty-two are confirmed," she replied.

"Ours will be much smaller. Twenty or thirty guests," Emma told her as she completed her notes. As she set down the pen, she glanced around. "Our ceremony will be right out here in the courtyard, and our reception in The Desiree."

"I did sneak a peek at that room. It's gorgeous."

Emma's heart fluttered slightly. She'd excitedly chosen the room Jackson had named after his late wife because it felt right to incorporate her memory into their wedding. If not for Desiree's dream of turning the hotel where she worked into a full-fledged wedding destination, Jackson would certainly never have followed through and bought the place. And then he'd never have needed a baker, and they might never have met.

Although . . .

The hotel wasn't where they had met for the very first time. It was the bakery where she used to work.

Perhaps we'd have found our way to each other anyway, with or without The Tanglewood.

That lovely thought pressed Emma's mouth into a soft smile that Holly noticed right away.

"You're thinking about your future husband, aren't you?" she prodded with a sigh.

"Actually, I was," Emma admitted. "Sorry about that."

"I think it's so romantic that my cake baker is this much in love. It's a sort of good vibe."

"Well, speaking of your cake baker," Emma declared, pen in hand once again, "let's talk wedding cakes. Do you have any thoughts about what you want?"

"Something different," Holly replied, and Emma grinned. Nearly every bride uttered those same two words when asked about her wedding vision. "Something in keeping with the theme of the wedding."

"Which is Victorian?"

"Yes. Kat told you?"

"She did. We talked about your colors and flowers, and she showed me the photograph of your cake topper. It really inspired me. I was thinking about something like this." Emma opened her sketch pad and nudged it toward Holly "This one is four tiers, very ornate, with detailed floral elements and pearl beads around the edge of each tier."

"Oh, it's beautiful."

"And this second idea," she said, flipping over the page, "is less ornate, with slightly more whimsy to it. Each tier would be edged with very small roses, and then spiral ribbons would cascade down from the top tier."

"Are those real ribbons?"

"No, everything on our cakes is edible. The flowers, the ribbons, the pearls, all of it."

"Oh, my goodness." Holly picked up the sketch pad and took a closer look.

"Kat showed you the photographs online of some of our cakes, yes?"

Emma's meeting with Holly lasted another forty minutes, during which they covered flavor options, adding sparkle dust to the pearl edging, and making various tweaks to Holly's final choice, the first cake with the pearl beads.

"I'll have you and your fiancé back next week for a tasting, and we'll decide on whether to go with one flavor for the whole cake, or perhaps a different flavor for each tier. Kat will sync that up with our caterers so that you can do a tasting for the reception meal as well while you're here."

"That sounds perfect, Emma. Thank you so much. I'll see you then."

Emma walked Holly as far as the glass doors leading back into the lobby, and she returned to the courtyard to gather her things. Out of the corner of her eye, she noticed a bulky dark shadow rush across the brick, and her gaze darted after it.

The white lights strung through the trees had only just come on a few minutes earlier, and the flickering gas lamps in each corner of the courtyard didn't provide enough light to clearly make out what it was. She moved toward the brick planter along the far wall as something rustled the flowering shrubs, and she hurried toward it and pushed back the branches. One chestnut eye peered out at her.

"Come here," she said. "Hildie. Come out of there right now."

The little girl who'd been discovered going through discarded food on a room service cart a few days before emerged from the bushes, stomped her feet hard against the brick, and looked up at her defiantly. "What?"

"Don't you *what* me, young lady. Why are you always turning up in places where you shouldn't be?"

"Who makes the rules about where a person should and shouldn't be?" she asked. "You? Who are you, anyway?"

"I told you who I am. Now I want you to tell me who you are. The truth!"

"I did tell you the truth. I'm Hildie and I'm eleven."

"Hildie what?"

"Now you're *whatting* me."

Emma shifted as she glared at the girl. "You have quite a mouth on you, don't you?"

"Everybody's got a mouth," she snapped.

"Yes. But you'll learn soon enough that it's all about how you use it. Now tell me what room your parents are in."

"Why? So you can call them and rat me out for getting into your precious bushes?"

Emma sighed, but before she could reply, the little girl's stomach began to rumble noisily, and she grabbed at it in an effort to silence it.

"It sounds to me like you're hungry."

"So."

"So . . . maybe I can do something about that if you'll try being a little less disagreeable."

"In return for what? Information?"

"Absolutely."

"Then, no thanks," she snapped, and Hildie shoved her massive mane of reddish-brown curls away from her face and turned to leave. When Emma grabbed her arm, the girl shouted. "Let loose!"

"I'll tell you what. You come with me to the restaurant. I'm meeting my fiancé for dinner, but he won't be there for half an hour or so. We'll get you something to eat, and you and I will have a conversation."

"Or what?"

"Or I'm going to march you up to the front desk, where I'll ask the manager to send a message to every room in this hotel until your parents are notified to come down and talk to me."

Hildie thought it over for a long moment before asking, "I can have anything I want?"

"Anything on the menu." Thinking better of it, she added, "Within reason, of course."

"Let's go, then."

Emma snagged Hildie's arm before she went any farther. Leaning down to look the child in the eye, she said, "And if you take off again when I'm not looking, I'll still have a message sent to every room in this hotel. There won't be anywhere for you to hide. Do you understand me?"

"Yes. Whatever."

Emma let Hildie lead the way, and she followed close behind. The hostess met the child at the entrance with a curious glance.

"She's with me, Lucy. There should be a table waiting for Jackson and me?"

"Sure, Emma. Right this way."

They sat down right next to the window at a table with four place settings. Lucy handed them both menus, leaving one behind for Jackson. Hildie immediately peeled hers open and began to pore over it, giving Emma a chance to really look her over.

"What?" the girl asked without glancing up from the menu. "Are you checking me for fleas or something?"

Emma chuckled. "Why? Do you have any?"

"Ha. Ha. You're *high-larious*."

"And you so aren't."

Their eyes locked for a moment before Hildie shrugged one shoulder and returned her attention to the menu.

"Can I get you something to drink while you decide?" the waitress asked them.

"Iced tea, unsweet," Emma replied. "No lemon."

Before she could prompt Hildie, the girl jumped right in. "You got any chocolate milk?"

"I think we do." The waitress grinned at Emma.

"Then I want a big one, and a glass of ice," she told her. "Do you get that? An extra large chocolate milk, and a separate glass of ice on the side."

"Right away," she answered. "I'll be right back to take your orders."

Hildie shoved back her slightly matted mop of hair and sighed. "Everything on this menu is *frou-frou*. Don't you have any plain old fried chicken?"

"There are chicken tenders on the children's menu. Those are like—"

"Hey, you didn't say anything about sticking to the children's menu. You said I could have anything I want."

"I'm not saying you have to stick to the children's menu, Hildie. And lower your voice."

"Sorry," she blurted. "But I want a regular-size supper. That all right?"

"Yes. All I was going to say was that perhaps, if the chicken tenders appealed to you, we could request a larger portion."

"Oh. Right. Okay. Can we do that with the spaghetti and meatballs?"

"Certainly."

"Okay. That's what I want. The spaghetti and meatballs. Super-size it."

Emma stifled the chuckle that tried to pop from her throat. This girl was an odd combination of annoying, incorrigible, and adorable.

"What are you getting?"

"Just a salad for now," she replied. "I'd like to wait on Jackson."

"Is that your boyfriend? Jackson?"

"Yes," she said with a nod.

"There was a girl in my fourth-grade class with that name. But it was her last name."

"What grade are you in now, Hildie?"

"Fifth."

"And where do you live? I assume you and your family are in town for—"

"Nice try," she snapped.

"We made a deal. I feed you, you give me some information," Emma volleyed back at her.

"Eats first. Information after."

The waitress set their drinks down on the table. "What can I get you?"

"I'd just like to start with a house salad," Emma answered. "Balsamic vinaigrette on the side. Jackson will be joining me for dinner in a while."

"And you?" she asked Hildie, who was involved with the very delicate operation of pouring a portion of her chocolate milk over ice. "What can I get for you?"

"She'd like the spaghetti from the children's menu," Emma said.

"But I want it super-sized," Hildie added without looking up from her project. "And don't skimp on the meatballs."

Emma sighed. "Can you increase it to an adult portion?"

"Certainly. I'll speak to Pearl."

"Thanks so much."

"Hey, wait a sec!" Hildie exclaimed. "Can I get another straw? I like to have two."

The waitress produced a second straw from the pocket of her starched apron and set it down on the table.

"Why two?" Emma asked once the waitress departed.

"I dunno. I like the way it feels." Emma grinned as the girl poked the second straw into her glass and took a sip. "Wanna try?"

"No, thank you. But you enjoy that."

Once Hildie had noisily slurped up the last of the milk in the glass, she poured in the rest and stirred it around with the straws.

"Listen, Hildie," Emma began, but the girl didn't even glance up at her. "I need to know what's going on with you."

Still no reply. "Come on. I think I've shown good faith here. Now you need to do the same."

She shrugged one shoulder and stared into the depths of her glass of chocolate milk and ice. "Nothin'."

Emma folded her arms and leaned back against the upholstered chair. "Hildie, look at me." When she didn't, Emma repeated the request. "Look at me."

Hildie raised her eyes slowly. "All right already."

"Your parents aren't staying in this hotel, are they?"

Darting her gaze back into her glass, Hildie focused on placing the straws into her mouth.

"Hildie, answer me. Do you even have a room here?"

It seemed like forever before the girl spoke. "Will you still let me eat the spaghetti if I say I don't?"

"Of course."

"Then . . . I don't."

"Where are you staying?" Emma asked, her mind racing with a hundred different answers that might come next. But she never even imagined the one that finally did.

"In the chair room."

After a moment, she repeated it, just to make sure she'd heard her right. "The chair room?"

"Yeah. The place where they keep all the tables and chairs and stuff."

"Well . . . why . . . What are you doing in there?"

Then came the standard eleven-year-old reply. "Nothin'."

"Hildie. Where do you live?"

"I told you. In the chair room."

"No. I mean, normally. Where do you live normally?"

"Nowhere."

Their eyes locked, and Hildie was the first to blink. Emma cocked her head and scratched it. "What do you mean, nowhere?"

"I mean nowhere. Are you dumb or something?"

Emma swallowed around the lump in her throat. "Hildie, you can't always have been homeless. Where did you live before the chair room?"

The girl's eyes glazed with emotion as she looked up at Emma. "Are you going to make me leave? Because I can't go back where I was before."

"Where was that?"

"A shelter in Atlanta."

"Is that where your parents are now?"

"Nah. My dad left when I was two, and my mom died last month."

Emma's chest ached. "Hildie, I'm so sorry."

"They wouldn't let me stay in the shelter once she died."

"That's when you came here?"

"Yeah, my mom read to me about this place from the newspaper." The girl's brown-gold eyes turned dark and flashed—only for a second—with golden shards of pure pain. "We looked at the pictures from when it opened. They did a big thing on it in the Sunday *Journal* with color pictures and everything."

"I remember."

Emma struggled to keep her emotions in check, but she wanted to just let loose and let the tears flow.

"My mom loved all that glamorous stuff. So after that, we'd watch the leftover papers for news on what was going on. There were weddings and birthday parties, and the pictures of all the great food . . . well . . . you know. We even took the Marta train out here to see it in person once. So when I got really hungry, I figured this would be a good place to come. So I did."

Emma pictured the young girl making her way all the way from downtown Atlanta out to Roswell, and finding her way to the hotel. Her heart broke just a little.

The waitress had barely set the plate in front of her before Hildie snatched a knot of garlic bread from her plate and stuffed it into her mouth.

The moment the waitress left Emma's salad and moved away, she leaned forward and asked, "How long have you been hiding here, Hildie?"

"I don't know," she managed through a full mouth. "A long time."

"Like a week?"

"More like three, I guess." She stabbed a meatball and poked it into her mouth.

"And you've been hijacking room service carts all that time?"

"Some," she muttered over the meatball. "Sometimes I sneak into one of the big rooms after a party. I really clean up on those nights! Your wedding cake, by the way, is the best ever. I especially liked when you made the one out of cupcakes. I got five of 'em that night."

Emma shook her head and closed her eyes for a moment. When she opened them again, Hildie swallowed and stared at her soulfully.

"Emma, are you gonna send me away?" She could hardly answer. "Because I got no place to go. And I won't bother anyone here, I promise. It's like you won't even know I'm here."

"Well, we're not going to do anything right this minute," she finally replied with a forced smile. "You have spaghetti to eat."

Hildie grinned from one ear to the other. "Thanks," she said, and she dug her fork into the mound of spaghetti and began to twirl it. Suddenly, the girl jerked upward, and she gasped.

"Uh-oh."

Emma tipped her head and followed the direction of the horror in Hildie's eyes. Jackson stood just behind her chair, his arms folded, his brown eyes flashing with very serious curiosity.

"Hi," she said as she rose to her feet and touched his shoulder. "Jackson, I want you to meet a new friend of mine."

"This is the guy you're going to marry?" Hildie asked her. "Are you kidding me?"

"No, I'm not kidding. This is Jackson Drake, my fiancé. And the owner of this hotel."

Hildie groaned and fell back against the chair, her face parallel to the ceiling as she said, "Nice to make your acquaintance. *Again*."

"You two have met?" Emma asked. Tugging on Jackson's arm, she added, "Come and sit down."

"Yes, we've met," he said as he slipped into the chair beside Emma. "Sort of. She was a hurricane that nearly bowled me over in the elevator one day. So your family is still staying at the hotel?"

Hildie's eyes darted toward Emma's for a moment before she ignored Jackson's inquiry and returned her attention to the plate of messy pasta before her. Emma handed her a napkin and nodded toward the smear of tomato sauce on the girl's cheek. Hildie wiped it grudgingly, glancing quickly at Jackson as she did.

He looked at Emma and asked, "So how do you and Miss Hurricane know one another?"

"We've run into each other a couple of times, and tonight I invited her to have a bite with me."

Jackson arched an eyebrow as he asked, "Is that so?"

"Well, thanks for the grub," Hildie chimed in. "I've got to be going now."

She'd just made it to her feet when Emma raised her hand and ordered, "Freeze!"

Tossing her head backward in dramatic fashion, the girl groaned. "Oh, come on."

"Sit down and finish your dinner," Emma commanded, and Hildie reluctantly tossed herself back into the chair.

"What, you're going to rat me out to The Man or something?"

"*The Man* is a wonderful, very understanding person, Hildie."

"I'll bet," she grumbled. "Go ahead. Tell him. And let's just see how understanding and wonderful Prince Charming turns out to be. My money is against it."

Tips for Calming the Nervous Bride-to-Be

In the months before the wedding, the bride may experience feelings of anxiety, coupled with a sense of bewilderment brought on by the overwhelming amount of details on her to-do list.
The typical stresses of ordinary life may even become magnified for her.

Here are a few simple suggestions to help her focus on one checklist at a time for a more satisfying wedding experience:

❖ Help the bride compile an organized list of duties.
Note: If she has hired a wedding planner, this list will be provided to her.

❖ Remind the bride often that she is about to marry the man of her dreams,
and the wedding is just the party that will kick off what's really important: The Marriage.

❖ Create a peaceful environment in which to help her make the decisions facing her.

For instance:
• Limit the planning sessions to people who make the bride feel safe and nurtured
• Choose soothing music as a backdrop
• Light aromatherapy candles
• Prepare a light snack for her in the afternoon to increase her energy
• Keep lots of bottled water on hand to ensure the bride is hydrated and focused
• Help deflect daily non-wedding-related stress inducers

8

*H*ildie, this is Fee. She's my right-hand man when it comes to baking all the wedding cakes and tearoom cookies. Fee, this is Hildie. Would you mind letting her help you prep the trays for tomorrow?"

"Sure."

Jackson marveled at Emma's sense of calm; it appeared to transfer to the young girl. She seemed to be in her element immediately as she exchanged some odd form of handshake with Fee and climbed up on the stool next to her at the worktable.

"This has got to be the coolest job ever," she told Fee, grinning at the rows of flower-shaped cookies set out before them.

"Dude. You have no idea."

Emma took Jackson's hand and led him into her office. He sat down in one of the two chairs crammed into the space to the side of the door, his knees touching the back of Emma's desk.

"You really need a bigger office," he observed.

"Jackson." Emma's way of bringing him back to the issue at hand.

"Sorry. So she's been stowing away here at the hotel?"

"She was living in a shelter downtown with her mom, but a month or so ago her mom died, and Hildie ran away before they could get her into foster care."

"And she ran away to . . . The Tanglewood? How does something like that happen?"

"Oh, Jackson," Emma said, caving in a bit as her face contorted and her brown eyes melted like a pan of chocolate on the stove. "Her mom read to her out of the newspaper about the opening, and they even rode Marta out here to have a look. We've worked so hard to paint this place as a magical environment, and I think Hildie bought into that. She came here looking for some magic."

Jackson reached across the desk and stroked Emma's hand. "I'd say she found a little of it in you," he said. "Just like I did."

Emma pushed up a smile as tears spilled from her eyes. "She doesn't have anyone, Jackson."

"Well, Emma, let's be sensible about this. We can't just take her in like a stray cat."

"I know, but we can show her a little love and give her a warm bed to sleep in until we can contact social services, can't we? It's not like they'll be around to answer their phones at this time of the evening."

"So what are you thinking?"

"I'm going to take her home with me."

"Emma, I don't know if—"

"Jackson," she interrupted. "You know I love you. But there's nothing you can say to change my mind, so let's not waste the energy arguing, okay? I'm going to take her home, get her into the bath, wash those filthy clothes of hers, and set her up in my guest room. Maybe just for a night or two, until we can find her a better option."

For just a minute, Jackson wondered if this was Emma's payback for his making the decision about selling the hotel without her permission or input. But on second thought, no; he knew her far better than that. This was simply Emma being Emma, reaching out to someone who'd touched her heart, providing what she could to make the situation more bearable for her.

"Do you want me to come with you?" he asked, resigned. "Help to get her settled or something?"

"No." Emma grinned at him, kissed the tip of her finger, and pressed it against his cheek. "I'm just going to take an aspirin and sit here for a minute. You kiss me goodnight and go home. I'll see you tomorrow."

Jackson rounded the desk and took Emma into his arms. "Another headache?"

"Just a little one."

They shared a deep kiss before he told her, "I look forward to the night when we don't have to go our separate ways."

"We've somehow managed it for this long," she reassured him, tucking her head underneath his chin. "We can stay strong another few weeks, can't we?"

"Speak for yourself," he whimpered.

Emma giggled, throwing a soft little punch against his ribs. "Man up, Drake." Lifting her head and looking solemnly into his eyes, she promised, "I'll be worth the wait."

"I have no doubt."

৩৶

"Here, put this on when you come out of the shower," Emma said, handing Hildie a T-shirt bearing the Nike slogan *Just do it* she'd found in her drawer. "I dried it on the hot setting, and it's been too small for me ever since, but I didn't have the heart to throw it out."

The girl held up the shirt and grimaced. "You some sort of athlete or something?"

"Me?" She chuckled. "No. I just like to run."

"I never understood people who run just for the sake of running," Hildie observed. "I only run if I'm being chased or really want to get somewhere."

"Well, I run for those reasons too. It's just sometimes the somewhere I really want to reach is a certain spot on the trail. Or the five-mile mark."

"Hmm." She thought it over for a moment before adding, "I can see that. I guess."

"There's soap, shampoo, and conditioner on the window ledge. I want you to use them all. Okay?"

"Are you saying I smell?"

"I'm trying *not* to say that. So don't make me, all right?"

Hildie laughed and nodded. "Okay."

"I put clean towels on the counter," Emma called after her.

As soon as the bathroom door clicked shut, Emma picked up the mound of clothes Hildie had pulled out of the one small duffle bag she'd retrieved from "the chair room" where she'd hidden it. Two pairs of pants, three T-shirts, one pair of socks, and three panties; this stinky mess was pretty much all the girl had to her name.

She pulled open the door to the laundry room and started the load of clothes, wondering what in the world she would do with Hildie once she cleaned her up and gave her a good breakfast in the morning.

"Daddy?" she asked as soon as her father answered the phone. "Did I wake you?"

"Am I really that old that you worry about waking me at nine thirty at night?"

Emma snickered. "Sorry."

"What's cookin', Emmy?"

"I've had the most extraordinary day."

It took a full fifteen minutes to tell about her meeting with Hildie, the discovery of her dire circumstances, and Emma's desire to do something to help without having a clue what that would be.

"You'll have to call social services," her dad stated. "The system is no doubt a scary place for a young girl, but it's the first step toward finding her a good foster home, and maybe even getting her adopted."

"That's what I want for her," Emma replied. "A family."

"Your mother does some charity work with one of those organizations. Homeless Children's Fund, or Save the Homeless Kids, something like that. I'll talk to her in the morning, and maybe we can get you a contact, someone to call to help the girl out."

"Thank you, Daddy."

"I love you, sweet girl."

"Love you, too."

Emma placed the phone in its dock just as Hildie emerged from the hall, drowning in the too-big T-shirt, most of her hair wrapped in a terry cloth towel.

"Was that Prince Charming on the phone? Calling to see if I'd made off with the silver or something?"

Emma chuckled. "No. That was my father."

Hildie's eyes grew somewhat hazy as she considered the words. "That's nice. You have a dad to call you up and say he loves you." After a moment, she added, "What's that like?"

"It's pretty great," Emma replied with a grin. "Most of the time. Other times, family isn't really all it's cracked up to be. Grab my comb from the bathroom counter and come over here. I'll help you with your hair."

"Thanks, but I know how to do it myself."

"Just get the comb and sit your fanny down in front of me."

Hildie shrugged and retrieved the comb. Emma tossed a cushion to the floor and pointed at it until the girl plopped down on top of it.

"Sheesh. Bossy, aren't you?" Hildie observed.

"Yes."

Emma pulled the towel from Hildie's head and tossed it to the floor beside her. The tangled mop of wet curls fell over the girl's small shoulders, and she cried out as Emma tried to pull the comb through.

"Ease up on the pulling!"

"Oh, suck it up," Emma teased, as she gently worked at the tangles, one section at a time.

"Hey, you know, I really like your friend at the hotel. Fee."

"Oh yeah? She's pretty great, isn't she?" Emma asked.

"I like her tattoos. And that little diamond in her nose."

"Fiona is one of a kind."

"Is that her whole name? Fiona? I like that."

"What about you?" Emma inquired. "What's Hildie short for?"

"You'll laugh."

"I won't."

"Yes, you will. Everyone does."

"I'll bet I can guess," Emma sang.

"Nope. You can't."

The comb made it through the first section of hair, and Emma moved on to the next.

"Hildegarde."

"Eww. No."

"Hilda?"

"No."

"*Hildarette?*"

They both laughed at that.

"What's your whole name? Is it just Emma, or is that short for something?"

"Oh no you don't," Emma cried. "Not until you tell me yours."

"Well, you're never going to guess, so I might as well tell you."

"You might as well."

When she delayed, Emma yanked playfully on her hair. "Come on, *Hildarama*. Fess up."

Hildie clicked her tongue and sighed. "Brunhilda."

"Brunhilda," Emma repeated. "Oh, dear."

"I know. Awful, isn't it?"

"Well . . . that's a pretty big name to lay on a little baby."

"Don't I know it. My mom's parents were German. It's big in Germany, I guess. It's supposed to mean 'ready for battle' or something."

"Well, that describes you perfectly, Brunhilda."

"Don't call me that, okay?"

Emma chuckled. "Okay. Sorry."

"Your turn."

"Emma Rae."

Hildie thought it over, tried it out once. "Emma Rae." With a slight shrug to one shoulder, she gave her approval. "I guess that's pretty good."

"I live with it."

"I know what you mean."

⤳

Jackson stalked into the office, then nearly screeched to a halt. He'd expected to find Bree—*like the cheese*—sitting behind

Susannah's reception desk. Instead, an orange-haired elderly woman with thick glasses looked back at him.

"Hello," she said. "You must be Mr. Drake?"

"Jackson. And you are?"

"Mavis Duncan," the woman replied. "At your service."

"Where's Bree?"

"Is that the other secretary? I guess she quit. The service sent me instead."

Jackson stared at her just long enough to be rude. "Oh," he finally replied. "Are you . . . finding everything okay?"

"Just dandy. Two messages next to your phone, and a cup of hot apple cider on your desk."

"Hot . . . what?"

"Cider."

"I just like coffee. But thank you for—"

"No," she said, and she blinked her large eyes behind the haze of the thickest lenses Jackson had ever seen. "Oh, no. You won't be drinking coffee anymore, Mr. Drake. Jackson."

He snickered. "Oh, Mavis, I think I will."

"No, no," she answered. "Do you have any idea what coffee can do to your body? Too much of it increases your loss of bone mineral density. Too much caffeine speeds up osteoporosis. Oh, I could go on all day. But while I'm here, you won't be drinking any more—"

Jackson split her words right in two as he closed the door to his office behind him and headed straight for the phone to dial the number from the card Susannah had tucked into his business-card holder.

"Yes. Miss Delbert, this is Jackson Drake at The Tanglewood Inn. I know you're a friend of Susannah's, and you've been trying to place someone to take care of things while she's out of town."

"Yes, Mr. Drake. Please call me Cheryl. I'm very sorry about Bree. But how is Mavis working out for you?" she asked.

"She's not, Cheryl."

"Oh. I'm . . . sorry."

"You'll take care of that for me, won't you, Cheryl?"

"Yes, sir, I'll get right on it."

"Good. And I'd like her replaced with someone relatively normal, Cheryl. Can you do that for me?"

"Yes, sir."

"Very good. I'll let Mavis know that she can be on her way now."

Jackson breathed in deeply as he hung up the phone. He leaned back into the chair and released the breath slowly, his eyes closed. The moment he'd expelled the last of it, he rose to his feet and closed the gap between the desk and the door. He took another deep breath as he opened it.

"Mavis?"

"Yes, Jackson?"

"Thanks for coming in. But you can go now."

"I beg your pardon?"

"No need. But you should go. Right now. Thank you."

He closed the door, but then waited and listened. After a long moment of silence, he heard Mavis grunt as she rattled her belongings together and stomped out of the office.

"Couldn't I come and live with you?"

Fee's eyes popped wide, and she glanced at Emma in distress.

"Hildie, I know this is a little scary for you," Emma said softly, "but my mother knows this woman very well. Mrs. Troy is going to take very good care of you until they can place you in a safe foster home."

"But why can't I just go home with Fee?" Hildie's chestnut eyes flashed with fear, and she turned toward Fee. "I won't be any trouble, I promise. I'll be good as gold. You'll see. I can do it."

"Look, Hildie," Fee said on a sigh. "I like you just fine. Actually, you're the nicest kid I've met. But Sean and I live in a pretty small house. I don't know where we'd put you."

"I'm little. I don't take up much room. What about you, Emma? Couldn't I live with you?"

Emma scuffed a stool up next to Hildie's and sat on it. Taking the girl's hand and shaking it, she said, "You know, I think it's great that you relate to Fee this way. And you know I'm just crazy about you."

"Then why can't—"

"Because we need to do this the right way. There are families out there who are completely set up for someone like you, Hildie. Places where you'll have your own bedroom, and you'll go to school, and you'll come home to someone who can help you with your homework. Mrs. Troy is going to find you the perfect place."

"Right," Fee chimed in as she removed her apron and laid it across the edge of the table. "You'll get three hot squares and the whole family deal. It's important for a kid your age."

The girl's eyes brimmed with tears, and she glared at Emma. "I hate you," she snapped. "I wish I never met you."

She suddenly tore out of the kitchen, leaving the door flapping behind her.

"Want me to go?" Fee asked with a nod.

"No. I'll go," Emma said as she checked her cell phone. "But if Mrs. Troy comes while I'm gone, text me?"

"Here!" Fee called after her, and she rushed to the doorway and tucked a napkin-draped pecan tassie into Emma's hand. "They're her faves."

"How do you *know that?*"

Fee shrugged and pushed her black glasses up the bridge of her nose. "She helped me prep the tearoom trays. We bonded. Maybe it will help you lure her out."

"What, like a hungry cat?"

"Yeah. Like that."

Emma shrugged and turned to leave.

"Be careful you don't get mauled. We've got a party of eight for tea at noon."

Tearoom Pecan Tassies

Preheat oven to 375 degrees.

Tassie shells:
1 cup softened butter
6 ounces softened cream cheese
2 cups all-purpose flour

Pecan filling:
1 egg, beaten
1 teaspoon vanilla extract
A pinch of salt
¾ cup light brown sugar
¾ cup chopped pecans

Required: 12-cup pan designed for miniature muffins

Beat butter and cream cheese until creamy.
Add flour in four parts, blending smoothly each time.
Pinch off pieces of dough (about the size of a
pecan in the shell).
Press dough into bottom and sides of miniature muffin tins.

Mix filling ingredients together.
Pour into prepared tassie shells, about two-thirds
of the way full.

Bake for 20-25 minutes.

Cool completely while still in the pan.

9

I've looked everywhere, and I can't find her."

Jackson watched Emma pace in front of the window. She didn't lose it very often, but when she did, pacing was usually involved.

He noticed the paper napkin cupped cautiously in her hand.

"What have you got there? Is that one of those pecan pies you make for the tearoom?" he asked, nodding toward the tiny pastry in her hand. "Is it for me?"

"It's for Hildie, Jackson. Focus."

"Did you check the storage room?" he suggested, diverting his attention from the pecan delicacy calling his name. "Isn't that where she likes to hide?"

"That was the first place I looked. I've been all over this hotel and—" The jingle of her phone stopped her, mid-word. She looked at the screen and groaned. "And now Mrs. Troy is here to pick her up, and I've lost her. I've lost Hildie, Jackson."

He got up and went to her, placing a firm arm around her shoulder. Both of them stood there silently, looking out over the sunlit town of Roswell.

"She'll turn up," he whispered as he pulled Emma closer. "Ask Fee to send the woman up here to my office, and we'll have a discussion about what comes next."

Emma tipped her head, looked up at him, and sighed. "You're a very calming influence. Are you aware of that?"

"It's a gift," he teased.

"Well, it's a good one." Emma dialed a number on her cell phone as she asked, "Where's Bree this morning?"

"Who?"

"Bree. The girl filling in for Susannah."

"Oh," Jackson groaned, turning back to his desk and flopping down into the desk chair. "Bree-like-the-cheese left me after her first day."

"Why? What did you do?" His objection waylaid by the phone in her hand, Emma blurted, "Fee. Will you ask Mrs. Troy to come up to Jackson's office, please? . . . Thanks so much. Let me know if you see Hildie." She pressed the button to end the call and picked up where she had left off. "If you call Cheryl Delbert, I'm sure she can get someone over here."

"I did that. She sent Mavis."

"Mavis? I didn't see anyone at the desk when I came in."

"No. I sent Mavis over to Bree's house."

"You did?" One corner of her mouth twitched as she arched an eyebrow and looked at him. "She was that bad?"

"Worse."

"Are you sure you're not just looking for Susannah, Jackson? Because anyone and everyone will pale by comparison if you—"

"She told me I wasn't going to drink coffee anymore, Emma."

"She what?"

"Yeah," he said, and he shook his head and chuckled. "She brought me apple cider instead."

"Did she say why?"

"Oh, yes. She was very clear about that."

After thinking it over, Emma asked, "Was it good? The cider?"

He wondered if she might be joking. "I don't know."

"You didn't taste it?"

"No, Emma," he chided, semi-horrified that she would ask. *Really? Did I taste it?*

"You don't have to get ornery with me, Jackson. I just wondered. I mean, honestly, it wouldn't kill you to drink a little less coffee now and then."

Jackson straightened and stared at her until she flinched.

"Fine. Sorry. Poor you. Cider. Are they going to send someone else over?"

He narrowed his eyes and continued to stare her down for a few beats before he shook his head back to the moment. "Yes."

"Well, chin up, Jackson. I'm sure this one will be a regular coffee-drinking joe who types a hundred words per minute and rivals Susannah in every way. You know, I'm having lunch with my mother and Aunt Sophie today. Maybe one of them can fill in."

She grinned at him, and his lips had just parted with a retort when a soft knock sounded at the office door and a smartly dressed African American woman stepped in.

"Mrs. Troy?" Emma greeted her. "Thank you so much for coming. I'm Emma Rae Travis, and this is the owner of the hotel, Jackson Drake."

"The hotel is lovely," she commented, shaking their hands. "I almost don't blame the child for wanting to call it home. Where is she?"

Emma chuckled. "That's the question of the hour. When I told her you were coming, she took off again, and we haven't been able to locate her."

"Ideally," she replied. "We'll evaluate her, investigate whether there are any other family members willing to take on her care. If not, we'll try to place her."

"How long will all that take?"

"There are a lot of variables, Mr. Drake. I can't be certain."

"And in the meantime? Where will she stay?"

"We have emergency shelters where we place children such as Hildie. If we can't place her in a foster home, we also have some transitional living programs that we can look at."

"These emergency shelters," Jackson said. "Are they safe?"

"We make every effort to protect and care for our children."

"I'm sorry. Emma has really taken a liking to this girl, and I know these are the questions she'd ask if she were still in the room."

"I understand," Mrs. Troy assured him. "Every year, there are more than a million and a half children in this country who join the ranks of runaways and the homeless. Hildie is categorized as an unaccompanied youth, which means a child under the age of eighteen who is on her own without at least one parent or older sibling. In an urban environment like Atlanta, you can imagine the challenges we face trying to provide even very basic needs for kids like Hildie. That being said, we do have programs in place to help us with our efforts."

"That's good to know," he said.

But would it be good enough for Emma? Jackson couldn't be sure.

⋙

"Hildie?"

The girl spun completely around from the waist up, her chestnut eyes sparkling with confusion, fear, and something else besides.

"Emma Rae!" Aunt Sophie exclaimed from her spot on the floor next to Hildie. "Have you met this remarkable young girl? Her name is Hildie. Isn't that delightful?"

"I have met her," Emma said as she scooped Sophie under the arms and helped her to her feet. "But neither of you should be sitting on this cold floor, Aunt Soph. There are five hundred chairs in this room. I want you both to sit down on a couple of them."

She dragged over a ladder-back dining chair with a thick upholstered seat and helped her aunt down to it. When Sophie appeared settled, Emma turned back toward Hildie.

"Honey, I'd like you to come and talk to Mrs. Troy with me. Just hear her out, okay?"

Hildie remained cross-legged on the floor, her chin pressing against her chest as she shook her head adamantly.

Emma squatted down beside her and rubbed Hildie's shoulder. "You're kind of running out of options here. And I'd like to see you get a few of them back."

When she lifted her head, the girl's face glistened with fresh tears. "Nobody's going to want me, Emma. People want babies. I'm eleven. All my bad habits are already starch-pressed in."

"No!" Sophie cried from behind Emma. "That's not true. You come over here and sit by me. Right this minute."

Emma looked on, amazed, as Hildie hopped to her feet, scraped a chair toward Sophie, and obediently sat down next to her.

"If nobody wants you at age eleven," Sophie said, "does that make me completely discardable at fifty-two?"

Emma suppressed the chuckle rising in her throat.

"You're only fifty-two?" Hildie asked, suspicious.

"Well. No," she admitted. "But I feel fifty-two, so why can't I just stay there?"

Hildie giggled. "No reason, I guess."

"Anyway, do you think I'm discardable, Hildie?"

"Of course not. But you're different than me."

"None of us are different. Not one of us!"

Emma hadn't seen her aunt so worked up in years. The lines around her eyes stretched longer as she narrowed her eyes and looked at Hildie with a serious and steadfast glimmer.

"Every one of us is flesh and bone and spirit. It doesn't matter about our age or the color of our skin or where we live or what we like to eat. We're just plain flesh-bone-spirit. Not one of us is expendable. Not one of us is without worth to other human beings." Sophie snatched Hildie's hand and held it to her heart. "Those other people want babies. Good for them! But somebody wants a free-thinking eleven-year-old with a crazy hive of beautiful hair, without a single allergy to anything at all."

Sophie looked at Emma with a glint in her gray-blue eyes. "Emma Rae, did you know that this child doesn't have a single food allergy? Not even to peanuts! That's quite an accomplishment in this day and age, don't you think so?"

Emma nodded, holding back the thump of emotion rattling her heart. "I do. That's kind of amazing."

"Emma Rae has diabetes," Sophie told Hildie. "Her little body doesn't know how to create insulin, so she doesn't process sugar the way she should. Do you think that was easy on her mama?"

Hildie shook her head tentatively.

"No. But Emma Rae was just the child Avery and Gavin were meant to have, diabetes and all. In just that same way," she said, jiggling the girl's hand, "you're just the child someone else is meant to have. But you need to let them look for who that is."

Hildie gazed at Sophie, her face awash with a smooth combination of disbelief and hope.

"Maybe they're no good with babies. Or they can't stand to change a dirty diaper. Or they have no patience for a toddler who doesn't understand a word they tell them. But an eleven-year-old with an active imagination and a lick of sense? Well, that's just the right child for them, these people somewhere out there in the world. Do you understand me, Hildie?"

She shrugged slightly and replied, "I guess so."

Emma knelt down in front of Hildie and gave her a warm smile. "But how will they find you if you don't let them know you're here?"

Hildie sighed and tilted her head backward, staring at the ceiling.

"Just come and talk to Mrs. Troy, Hildie. Give her a chance to find you a better situation than hiding in this room and stealing leftover food. Somewhere out there is a home with your name on it. I just know it."

Sophie slipped her arm around the girl's shoulder and squeezed her. "My Emma Rae is the most trustworthy person you'll ever know. You do what she tells you."

"She's waiting for us in Jackson's office," Emma said as she rose to her feet and extended her hand. "Let's go talk to her." Hildie just sat there for what seemed to Emma like several minutes. Waving her hand, she grinned. "Yes? Come with me?"

Hildie groaned softly before taking Emma's hand. "Yes. All right."

As they hit the door, Emma turned back and extended her free hand to Sophie. "Come on, Aunt Soph."

Once they left the storage room and entered the hall, she leaned in toward her aunt. "How is it that you always seem to end up in just the right place at just the right time?"

"Jesus takes the wheel, Emma Rae. I just ride along."

"Well, it's freakish . . . But I love you for it."

"Yes. I know," Sophie said as she smoothed her silver hair. "Perhaps Hildie can come and meet your uncle Tuck. He was orphaned at a young age, too."

Uncle Tuck died when I was nine, Emma thought. But she didn't remind her.

⌘

Emma cradled Isabel in her arms and swayed from side to side in front of the large glass door overlooking Sherilyn's back yard. Andy tossed a ball across the length of the grass, and their dog Henry barreled after it.

"So what's going to happen to her?" Kat asked about Hildie.

"She finally agreed to go with Mrs. Troy, and hopefully they'll place her in a foster home so she can get her land legs again. I'm just praying it's somewhere warm and safe and dry, you know?"

"Emma, your tea is on the table," Sherilyn told her as she sat down. "Come and join us."

"I will," she sang softly. Gazing down at the baby in her arms, she grinned. "I'm just having some alone time with my girl, Izzy."

The baby's eyes eased open at the sound of her name. The long, dark lashes surrounding her bluish eyes fluttered, and they came to rest on the top of her cheek as she drifted back to sleep. Emma planted a tender kiss on her head before tucking the baby into the bassinet next to Sherilyn and sitting down with Sherilyn and Kat at the dining table.

She sniffed the tea steeping in a large flowered mug in front of her. "Mmmm. Thank you, Mommy. This smells like heaven."

"No more *Mommy* for the moment," Sherilyn teased. "Right now, let's talk wedding."

A surge of adrenaline pulsed through her and Emma grinned joyously. "Okay, let's."

Kat flipped open Sherilyn's pink laptop on the table before her. "We went over the details before you got here," she told Emma. "And I think we have all of the bases covered, but let's just run through it one time with you."

"Okay, shoot!"

"The invitations have been mailed, and we've already received nineteen RSVP cards back. So that's just fifteen outstanding. We'll give them another week, and I'll make phone calls to confirm the rest."

Sherilyn nodded as Kat swiped the mouse and moved down the list on the screen before them.

"The flowers are all ordered and confirmed," Kat stated. "Also confirmed are six chandeliers for the trees in the courtyard, twelve floor-stand candelabras—"

Just about the time Emma's eyes began to glaze over, Sherilyn interrupted. "No. No. Stop. Too much information for Em's brain. Let's just go over the basics with her, and she'll leave the details to us."

"Thank you," Emma said on a sigh.

Kat chuckled and returned her attention to the screen of Sherilyn's laptop.

"Music?" she asked, and Sherilyn nodded. "Ben Colson has confirmed for the reception."

"Oooh, goodie!" Emma cried.

"And we have a string quartet for the ceremony," she continued. "We've reviewed the menu with Pearl, reserved the honeymoon suite from the day prior until the following day, confirmed the photographer and Pastor Miguel for the ceremony, and we have Andy set to go with Jackson for their tuxes on Thursday night."

Emma leaned back and watched Kat and Sherilyn as they put their heads together and whispered over some detail looming on the flickering computer screen.

"Yes. I took care of that today," Kat said softly.

"Excellent!" Sherilyn beamed. "Check it off then. Emma, did you put the license somewhere safe?"

"Check."

"And you've picked up the rings from the engraver?"

"Check! Well. Jackson picks them up tomorrow."

"Perfect."

"Good grief," Emma said on a sigh as she observed them. "You two could rule the entire world with nothing more than a laptop and a credit card."

"Emma," Sherilyn said with a sudden stern look in her eye. "Tell me you've narrowed down the cake."

"Well, I thought I had."

"Emma Rae! Kat and I have taken care of every minute detail aside from the wedding cake. Please. Decide."

"It's not that easy," Emma defended herself to Kat. "It would be like you picking just the right jewelry for your own wedding, with all of your past creations to choose from!"

"We keep hearing this argument out of her," Sherilyn told Kat with a grin. "But still no cake."

"Soon," Emma vowed. "I promise."

"Ooh!" Kat exclaimed, and she shared a feline-that-ate-the-canary grin with Sherilyn. "Emma, I have something for you."

"You do?" Emma set her teacup on the table and smiled. "Do tell."

Kat reached into her bag; produced a large, forest-green velvet box with a brass-hinged lid; and slid the box toward Emma. "If you don't like it, please don't feel obligated to wear it. But I created it with you in mind."

Emma's heart fluttered softly as she eased the lid open. Inside, resting on a nest of pale ivory satin fabric with the striking logo of Kat's new jewelry design firm on the inside of the lid, sat an exquisitely simple ivy-patterned rhinestone headband.

"I tried to use the design of the flower and vines on the cap sleeve of your gown," Kat told her. "And if you look very closely, the center of a few of the flowers are dotted with very pale amethyst gemstones to tie in your lavender-blue hydrangea."

Emma's hand floated to her heart as she took a closer look. She'd never seen anything quite so beautiful, and the afternoon sun caused the array of stones to sizzle before her. The thought that Kat had designed it specifically with her in mind . . .

"Isn't it amazing, Em?" Sherilyn asked her. "It's so understated and elegant. Not like those huge tiaras so many southern brides seem to wear. I was thinking that, since you've chosen such a delicate veil, and you said you wanted to wear your hair up, it's going to really look stunning."

"It's perfect," Emma said on a sigh, and when her eyes met Kat's glistening brown ones, a single tear escaped and streamed down Emma's cheek. "Kat, I can't believe you did this."

"You've become such an important part of my life," Kat told her with emotion. "Everyone at The Tanglewood has. I would never have met Russell, or jumped off the ledge from being Audrey's assistant to creating my own line of jewelry . . . So many wonderful things have happened to me because of you and Jackson and your beautiful hotel."

And at that, Sherilyn burst into tears and bolted from her chair.

"I'm going out to check on Andy," she called over her shoulder as an afterthought before rushing out the door.

"Did I say something wrong?" Kat asked.

"No. Jackson did."

Kat chuckled. "But Jackson's not here. What did he say, and when?"

"He said yes when asked what Sherilyn believes to be a truly horrible question."

"Which was?"

"'Will you sell this hotel?'"

Kat gasped. "No."

"Afraid so."

"Well, no wonder she's crying. I think I might cry, too."

"Oh, good. That makes it official. You're one of us now, Kat."

Tips for Combining a Tiara and Veil

When wearing the hair down:

✤ Hold the comb attached to the veil upside down, with both the veil and the blusher pulled back.

✤ Rotate the comb forward and slide it into the hair with the concave side facing the scalp.

✤ Slide the tiara onto the head at an angle and adjust it so that there is no gap between it and the veil.

✤ If the tiara has pin loops, secure it with bobby pins to hold it in place.

When wearing an updo:

✤ The tiara or headband should be placed in front of or against the bulk of the hair.

✤ Attach the veil behind and underneath the bulk of the updo, and be sure that the tiara connects to the edges of the veil, leaving no gap in-between.

10

"If everyone has a glass of something, I'd like to propose a toast."

Jackson's arm rested loosely around Emma's shoulder, and he looked down at her and smiled as she beamed at her father. Gavin stood at the other side of the room from them, glass in hand, waiting for the rest of the guests to join the circle.

"Tonight," Gavin said, "two families come together in anticipation of the questionable blessing of being bound together for life because of these two."

Avery jabbed Gavin's rib with her elbow as she shook her head. "Really."

"Well, come on, Avery," he teased. "You don't think these people would actually *choose* us if they had their choice, do you?"

"Don't be silly!" Madeline chastised with a sweet smile. "We're *three-illed* to consider y'all *fam-ly*."

Jackson surveyed the room amidst the hum of the *ooohs* and *ahhhs* of the guests' reactions. His oldest sister, Georgiann, looked radiant as she leaned in close to her husband, gripping middle sister Madeline's hand. Norma, the youngest of the Drake sisters, crinkled her nose as she laughed at Gavin's joke and shared a smile with her husband, Louis. Miguel and his wife—Jackson's niece—rounded out the Drake side of the well-wishers gathered in Norma's parlor.

The Travises were well represented by Emma's parents and her aunt Sophie, who stood just to Jackson's left, clinging to his arm and seeming extraordinarily present-minded at the moment. Sherilyn, Andy, Fee, and Sean, also stewards of the Travis clan, joined the circle, glasses in hand. The room brimmed with one cohesive family unit of well-wishers and support, and a hot ember of emotion flickered in Jackson's chest.

He leaned over and kissed Sophie's cheek with a tender peck. "We're so glad you're here, Sophie," he told her, and she nuzzled against his arm.

"As Emma and Jackson approach their upcoming nuptial—" Gavin continued, "and at long last, I might add—I think every one of us in Norma Jean and Louis's gracious home offers them prayers of hope and encouragement toward a marriage built on our shoulders, the people who love them the most."

Emma bookended Sophie's affection by squirming against his other arm, and Jackson kissed the top of her head and breathed in the clean vanilla scent of her brown hair.

"To Jackson and Emmy!" Gavin exclaimed, his glass high in the air, and the others chimed in with their own good wishes for the happy couple.

"Thank you, Gavin," Jackson said, lifting his glass toward his future father-in-law. "And I want to assure you that I'd choose you if given the choice."

"Fortunately, no one gave it to you." Gavin guffawed, and Avery nudged him again, shaking her head and laughing. "You just take care of our Emmy, Jackson, and we'll be square."

"I promise."

Emma turned her full body toward Jackson and slipped one arm around his neck. "Kiss me," she breathed, and he did. When they parted, she held her eyes shut for a few seconds before they fluttered open. "Oh, you're so good at that!"

"You still want to marry me, then," he surmised.

"Who said anything about that?" she teased him. "But I never grow tired of your kisses. Isn't that enough?"

"Not quite," he answered, and he kissed her again.

The metallic jingle of a bell rang softly in his ears, originating from the brass bell in Harriet's hand.

"Dinner is served," the uniformed fixture at Norma's home informed them.

"Thank you, Harriet," Louis replied.

"All right, you two!" Gavin exclaimed. "There will be time enough for smooching later. Jackson's sister has put together a feast fit for kings. Let's all indulge, shall we?"

Jackson offered his arm to Sophie, and he walked her into the dining room, followed by Emma on her father's arm. When he pulled out Sophie's chair and waited for her to sit down, she paused and looked up at him with a meaningful countenance.

"We'll talk privately later, Jackson," she whispered. "All right?"

"Of course."

"Do you have to go so soon?"

"Vanessa's with the baby," Sherilyn stated, and that was enough for Emma. Despite the fact that she'd somehow managed to raise Andy, Emma suspected that his mother's experience with babies included a nanny or two. "But we had a great time, Em. I'm very happy for you."

"Even though I'm marrying the enemy?" Emma asked her with a grin.

"Even though . . . You look tired."

"I am. I'll call you tomorrow."

"Love you," Sherilyn offered with a hug. "Where is the enemy, anyway? I want to say good night."

"Out on the veranda with my aunt Sophie. Their heads have been together for quite some time."

"I won't interrupt then," she said. "Just tell him for me."

Once she'd walked Sherilyn to the door and shared an embrace with Andy, Emma set out for the veranda.

"What are you two whispering about out here?" she asked as she joined them.

"Never you mind," Sophie told her. "You don't have to know everything about everything, Emma Rae."

"I don't? Because it feels like I do."

Her aunt smiled at her as she struggled to stand up. Jackson helped her to her feet, and she kissed his cheek when he bent toward her.

"I'm going to ask Sissy to take me home," she announced. "I'm tired now."

"Well, thank you for coming, Aunt Soph. It wouldn't have been a celebration without you."

"I could have sworn you two were already married," she muttered on her way into the house.

"Wait, you mean we're not?" Jackson teased, and he wrapped his arms around Emma's waist and drew her close to him.

The two of them stood there for several minutes, looking out at the midnight-blue sky beyond the lawn and falling under the spell of the flickering canopy of silver stars overhead.

"When I was a kid, I thought the sky was like a tent over us," she told Jackson. "And since the sky was so many millions of years old, I figured it must be wearing thin. Proven, of course, by the stars, which were just pinholes of light shining through the worn fabric from the other side."

"Not very scientific," Jackson observed. "But quite creative."

"Do you think Norma would get her feelings hurt if we cut out?" she asked.

"No, why?"

She took a deep breath and then leaned into him as she exhaled. "I don't know. I'm just so tired all of a sudden."

"Let's go, then."

Jackson took her hand and led her into the house. Guests milled about the dining room and adjacent parlor, and Emma simply allowed Jackson to lead her past them.

"Emma's worn out," he announced. "I'm going to get her home so she can get some rest."

"Oh, all right," Norma sang. "You get a good night's sleep and you'll be right as rain tomorrow."

"Thank you so much for tonight," Emma told her. "I'm so happy you're going to be my new sister."

"It's not new at all," Norma said as she hugged her and swayed her from side to side. "We've been sisters since the day we met."

"We're going to hit the road as well," Gavin told them.

While Gavin helped Sophie into her coat, Avery appeared at her side and smoothed the hair away from Emma's face with a gentle hand.

"You're a little pale, dear," she said, taking hold of Emma's hand. "Is there anything I can get you?"

"Eighteen hours of uninterrupted sleep?"

"Can you ease up a little, maybe sleep in late tomorrow?"

"No, I've got a full schedule from 9 a.m. and on through the day," she replied with a sigh.

"Jackson," Avery said as he stepped up beside them. "Emma Rae is pale, and her hands are a little clammy. Is your blood sugar low, sweetheart?"

"I don't know how it could be, with everything I ate tonight," Emma told her. "But I'll check my glucose level as soon as we get into the car."

"Jackson, you'll watch her closely, won't you?"

"I will, Avery."

It seemed like a long path from the good-nights to the passenger seat of Jackson's car, but when she finally reached it, there was no mistaking her sense of relief. After Jackson rounded the car and slid behind the wheel, he picked up her purse and handed it to her.

"Is your meter in here?"

"Yes."

He flicked on the overhead light while she pulled out the small blue case that held her supplies.

"So what was that talk about with Aunt Sophie?" she asked him as she pricked her finger.

"Oh. She'd like me to lobby for her as your maid of honor."

Emma giggled. The small screen flashed with the number: 109.

"It's a little low after such a big meal," she said. "But I don't think it's worth worrying over. I guess I'm just really, really tired."

"How about we ask Fee to handle things in the morning? You have a good healthy breakfast and come in later."

"No, Jackson, I can't do—"

"Yes, you can. And you will, Emma."

"Hey," she said with a sigh as she leaned her head against the car seat and closed her eyes. "You're not the boss of me."

"Well, actually, I am."

"Oh. Right."

Emma set her cup of tea on the table and slipped down into her favorite perch, the brown leather easy chair that had once sat in the corner of her father's library. From the arm of the chair she grabbed the coral throw Aunt Sophie had crocheted and wrapped it around her shoulders before picking up the cup and taking a sip of chamomile tea.

The soothing scent took her back. Chamomile. Her mother's lifelong answer to anything that ailed a child . . . a girl . . . a woman. This morning, she'd turned to the old friend when, after nine hours of sleep, she awoke still feeling tired and out of sorts.

The newscaster had announced that this would be one of the last chilly mornings before the Atlanta area peeked through the window at spring. Although she'd been holding vigil for spring ever since she and Jackson had set their wedding date, Emma acknowledged that she might actually miss crisp mornings like this one. If she felt better, she'd go for a run. Instead, she opted for chamomile tea while she awaited Jackson's arrival.

The thought of him sent her hand instinctively into her hair, raking through it with her fingers. She returned the cup to the tabletop, then grabbed a gray scrunchie from the drawer and combed her messy hair back into a neat ponytail. She rummaged deeper into the drawer until she found a tube of tinted lip balm and quickly applied it. Truth be told, she wasn't sure she could eat anything; but the fact that Jackson had called earlier and offered to stop by and cook for her brightened the morning considerably.

She picked up the cup again, holding it between both of her hands and pressing the warmth against her face. From the dinner at Norma's to Hildie's well-being to the wedding cake decision that still eluded her, the anxious hum of Emma's thoughts bounced her around like a ride in the back of a pickup truck on a bumpy country road. Then came the unexpected pothole of adrenaline as her mind crashed into the imminent sale of The Tanglewood.

Just about the time she began to question how Jackson could have come to such a decision, his familiar three-part knock sounded at the door. She carried her teacup with her and tightened the coral throw around her shoulders as she padded in stocking feet across the soft rug to answer the door.

"Morning," she said and kissed his cheek.

"How are you doing?" he asked as he closed the door behind them. "Do you feel all right?"

"I do. Just a little tired."

"Emma."

The serious lilt to his voice made her turn back and look at him. "What?"

"This is more than a little tired."

"What do you mean?"

His answer came in the form of action as he took the cup from her and placed it on the table, guiding her with his free hand toward the chair. "Sit down."

She obeyed, but she couldn't help herself from laughing. "Jackson, are you preparing me for bad news? Because really, unless it impacts the next forty-eight hours or so, I'm not sure I want to hear it."

Jackson knelt down on the floor in front of her and took both of her hands in his.

"Didn't we already do this? I think I said yes."

"Hush."

Emma blinked hard, arching both brows. "Hush?"

"Yes. Hush."

Hush. This must be earth-shaking, she told herself. *Better brace yourself.*

"No sugar-coating, no smart retorts, no denials," he said by way of instruction. "I want to know what's going on with you. Right now. Straight out."

"Jackson, I don't know what you mean. Really, I don't."

He sighed. "Emma, you're not right lately."

"Thank you."

"Are you aware that your hands are moist and it's fifty degrees outside? You're pale, you're exhausted, and how many headaches have you had in the last couple of weeks?"

Emma didn't speak for a long moment as her mind raced over the recent past.

Maybe he's right? I haven't been feeling . . .

"I don't want you to fight me on this, Emma. Please. Call your doctor and make an appointment."

She sighed and lifted Jackson's hands to her lips and kissed one of them.

"I will."

"I'm going to make us some breakfast. You make the call."

Jackson rattled around in the kitchen behind her while Emma pressed number 6 on the speed dial.

"Hi, Stephanie. It's Emma Travis."

"Emma, how are you doing?"

"Well, that's why I'm calling. I think I need to see Dr. Mathis. Just for a check-up. I'm not feeling quite right."

"How's your glucose?"

"It's running a little low most of the time. Not in the danger zone, but lower than normal. And I've been having a lot of headaches."

"Feeling tired?"

"Exhausted," she replied.

"Let me check the schedule. Can you hang on?"

"Sure."

While the tinny hold music clanked in her ear, Emma strolled toward the kitchen. She sat on one folded leg at the dining table and grinned at Jackson, who was draped in a white apron and whisking a bowl full of eggs.

"Emma, we have a cancellation at three thirty this afternoon. Do you think you can make it?"

"Today?" she said with a cringe, but Jackson nodded vehemently with that *I-mean-business* stance of his. "I'll make that work, Stephanie. Thank you. I'll see you then."

"Good girl," he said as she disconnected the call. "I think that deserves a veggie scramble and wheat toast, don't you?"

"Can I have jam on the toast?"

"A little."

"All right, then, I accept my reward, and I want to thank all the little people who made this breakfast a reality . . ."

"Wiseacre," he remarked, shaking his head and grinning.

After breakfast, Jackson washed the dishes while Emma called Fee to give her a heads-up.

"I need to see the doctor, and they have a cancellation this afternoon, so I won't be coming in today after all. Can you cover for me?"

"Sure. You don't do that much around here anyway," she teased, her dry wit shining through.

"Well, I figured as much."

"Hey. Are you sick?"

"No, not sick really. I just want to see Dr. Mathis and get checked out."

"Glad to hear it. You haven't been yourself lately."

"Really? You've noticed it, too?"

"Oh, yeah. I think this is a good move."

Emma swallowed around the lump in her throat. "Call me if you need me?"

"Yep. What about you? You need anything?"

"No. Jackson is here now, and I think I'm going to take a nap after he heads for the hotel."

"A nap. Dude, can you save me some of that?"

"I'll seal it in Tupperware for later."

"Awesome."

She laid the phone down on the table and turned back toward Jackson as he removed the apron and dried his hands on it.

"My hearing is doing something funny," he told her. "I thought I heard you say you were going to take a nap."

"No, no," she said, shaking her head. "You heard right. I thought I just might."

"It's a little hard for me to picture," he said, taking her hands and guiding her to her feet. He wrapped his arms around her waist, clasping his hands behind her, then smiled down at her. "Emma Rae Travis . . . taking a nap. Next thing we know, lions will lie down with lambs, and dogs and cats will run and play together. And then the global anarchy."

"Let's not go that far, bud. It's just a little something new I thought I'd try and see what it's like."

"Be sure and let me know how it works out for you," he said and kissed her. "I have meetings with the lawyers all afternoon, but I can probably get away around six. I'll pick up some dinner and head over here, if you're in the mood."

"That sounds good. I'll call you after my appointment."

Emma watched Jackson as he descended the stairs and headed for his car. His long, lean legs needed half the strides that she required to close the gap between the front door and the street.

I love everything about that man, she thought as he slid behind the wheel. He looked back and waved at her one last time before pulling away, and a flock of butterflies swirled around inside her as he did.

Although she meant to take that nap she'd touted, when she reached the bed and noticed the sketch pad leaning against the bottom shelf of the nightstand, Emma couldn't help herself. She pulled it out, grabbed the small box of colored pencils sitting next to it, and began to draw.

Biting her lip, she lost herself in the mission of putting the cake in her head to the sketch pad: three simple squared tiers, a rich purple fondant with thick lavender ribbons at the base of each of them, perhaps some of those sugar trumpet lilies Fee had recently mastered.

The bottom layer quilted with pearls . . . The middle tier ruched . . .

Classic. Easy. Just like the love she shared with Jackson.

Classic and Simple

11

"Emma, I'm not going to mess around," Dr. Mathis said as she rolled the leather-cushioned stool in front of her and sat down. "I don't like what I'm seeing here. Your glucose is too low, and Stephanie noted that you've had symptoms for at least two weeks."

"Well, I wouldn't say—"

"You're two months overdue for your blood work, but the headaches alone should have been a good indication that you needed to come in. And it's no wonder you have headaches. Your blood pressure is sky-high."

Dr. Mathis began scribbling on her prescription pad as she continued, "I want you to go in to the lab first thing tomorrow and do a fasting blood test. While you're there, we'll get a urine sample." She tore off the sheet and handed it to Emma. "And I want you to slow down."

A burst of laughter popped impulsively out of her throat. *Slow down.*

"Emma, this is serious. Type 1 diabetes is nothing to take lightly. We'll know more once I get a look at your lab results, but I suspect we're going to find that your glucose levels have been spiking due to stress. You're only taking notice of the low swings because they cause the most profound symptoms. But those headaches and the high blood pressure indicate to me that your levels are hopping around. You need to pay attention to your body, Emma. Take it easy."

Emma surprised herself when her eyes brimmed with tears.

"What's going on in your life?" the doctor asked, squeezing Emma's hand. "Not the everyday, short-term stress points, but the chronic ones. I know you're getting married soon."

Emma nodded. "In a few weeks."

"But I was married at The Tanglewood myself," Dr. Mathis said with a smile. "I imagine Sherilyn is handling just about every detail on your behalf."

"Well, she is. I mean, she and Kat together. Sherilyn just had her baby, so . . ."

"Oh, that's great! Give her my best, will you?"

Emma nodded again, and a lone tear escaped her eye and streamed down her cheek. "And there's the usual stuff at the hotel, except for . . . well . . . there's this little girl who's been stowing away there . . . and I can't decide on a wedding cake no matter how hard I . . . and . . . and Jackson is selling the—"

She couldn't go on. Emotion rose in her like hot lava from the inside of a volcano, and she began to cry. The Ugly Cry, as Sherilyn always called it, the one where your face contorts and tears flow in spurts, and you have to work really hard to stop the sobs from turning into wails.

"Oh, sweetheart," Dr. Mathis cooed, and she rolled closer, wrapped her arms around Emma as she convulsed with weeping, and just hugged her. "I think we've hit the iceberg, haven't we?"

Emma nodded, somewhat frantically, but she didn't pull out of Dr. Mathis's soothing embrace for another couple of minutes.

"Listen to me, okay?" the doctor said, taking Emma by the shoulders and looking into her eyes. "You are in a dangerous area at the moment. You need to get a handle on your reactions to what's going on around you. I know it's stressful. But you're going to have to insist on some quiet time for yourself, you're going to have to watch your diet and get some extra sleep. Are you taking your supplements?"

Emma nodded.

"Good. And I want you to try some deep breathing techniques. Stephanie will give you a pamphlet."

Emma couldn't help but chuckle. Deep breathing wasn't going to—

"Emma." Dr. Mathis tightened her grip on Emma's shoulders and smiled. "The bottom line is this: Our stress hormones were designed to help us deal with short-term stressful situations. But when things start to cave in around us, we freeze a little. We can't fight, and there's no flight. What we naturally do is stew in our own juices, which can cause chronic issues that affect our health and wellness. In a diabetic, those effects can be catastrophic, and we don't want that. I need you to promise me you're going to slow down and take care of yourself."

"I promise."

"I'd like you to take these for a while," she said as she released Emma and turned back to the counter to retrieve her prescription pad. "It's a low dose of blood pressure medicine so we can get that back in check. Do you need something to help you sleep?"

Emma cringed a bit and shook her head. "No. I don't want to."

"Okay. If you change your mind, and you're not getting the rest your body needs to carry you through, I want you to call me."

"I will."

The smile melted from Dr. Mathis's pretty face, and she turned serious again. "No joke, Emma. The time to get this situation in check is *now*. Are we clear?"

"Yes. Very."

"And I want to see you again in two weeks to discuss your lab results and see how you're doing. Make the appointment today, and keep it, Emma. I can't help you unless you let me."

"I know. I'll do it. I promise."

She tried to hide the tentative tone in her voice as she made that promise because, in light of the reality that had become her life, Emma knew how difficult it might be to keep it.

<hr />

Jackson unfolded the turkey wraps from the wax paper and set them on plates, holding his tongue until Emma finished telling him everything that had transpired with Dr. Mathis. She poured tea over ice and brought the glasses to the table.

"What's in the containers?" she asked as she set the glasses down.

"One is pasta salad," he told her, retrieving napkins from the buffet drawer. "The big one is hummus with celery sticks and baby carrots."

"And turkey wraps with sprouts and veggies?" she said on a chuckle.

"I know. I may have gone overboard with the healthy dinner thing," he admitted. "But I'm worried about you, Emma, and, as it turns out, with good reason."

She stepped up behind his chair and wrapped her arms around his neck, kissing the top of his head.

"This just confirms to me that I'm doing the right thing by selling the hotel," he said, and she circled him and sat down in the adjacent chair. "You and I have been on a fast track ever since the day we met, before the hotel even opened, Emma. After the sale, we can take a whole year and live out the dream we've been talking about for months."

"Move to Paris?"

"Yes. I can write, and you can take those classes you want to take. On the off days, we can sleep in late and go for walks, really settle in to marriage. How many newly married couples have the opportunity to live like that?" She shrugged in response. "And while we do, you'll work on lowering your blood pressure and taking care of yourself for a change."

"You mean live like that, while you take care of me." Her distaste for surrendering to this rang unmistakably in Jackson's ears.

"That, too," he said with a smile. "There's nothing I'd rather do with my time."

"Oh, Jackson."

Her deep sigh drew his full attention, and he wondered what might come next. When she didn't elaborate, he jiggled her hand playfully. "Oh, Jackson, what?" he asked her.

"I don't know. When I think of walking away from The Tanglewood, it tears me up a little inside. The place is our home. Those people are our family."

"And they'll still be our family, whether we own the place or just look in on it every now and then."

"But how will we look in on it from Paris?" she asked, and a mist of emotion sharpened the brown of her eyes.

"It's not like we'll be gone forever, Emma. We'll be back. Atlanta is home to both of us. But The Tanglewood isn't part of a package deal. It's not all or nothing."

She sighed again, and Jackson felt the weight of it just behind his heart.

"You feel this strongly about it?" he asked her. "You don't want me to sell?"

Emma closed her eyes and massaged her temples. "That's not for me to say. I know that, Jackson. I just can't wrap my brain around . . . leaving it all behind."

"I spoke to the attorneys at length today, Emma."

"I know. The deal is already under way. I get that," she told him. "I do. It was your decision to make, and you made it with our future in mind. It's just—"

"You don't want to go to Paris," he completed for her.

"No! I do want to go. You and me, and all the time in the world to get lost in one another, in a beautiful city. Of course I want that! How crazy would I have to be *not* to want it?"

"Pretty crazy."

"I know. But The Tanglewood . . ."

"What I was going to say before is that I spoke to the attorneys. I've made it clear that every member of the executive staff stays in place. That includes Sherilyn and Fee. Morelli's is still in place. Nothing changes, except that you and I won't be in the business mix anymore. Fee will step up and take ownership of the tearoom. They're all going to be fine, Emma. I wouldn't do this if I wasn't sure of that."

"I know you wouldn't," and she reached across the table, taking his hands between both of hers.

"And there's a new bottom line now that we didn't have before," he added. "You are under the gun from morning to night, and your health depends on us taking these measures because . . . when the phones are ringing and the brides are crying and Sherilyn is flitting in and out with all of her own challenges, you know you won't amp down. It's not in you. I know it's not."

He saw it in her eyes. She knew it, too.

"The best thing that's ever happened to me is finding you, Emma. We have an opportunity of a lifetime here, and now your life also depends on us taking it. It's as if God handed us this gift of an open door at just the right time. Are we going to refuse it?"

There it was again; one of those heavy, anxiety-riddled sighs of hers. He could hardly bear their massive bulk on his heart.

"They will all be here when we come home," he promised. "But we'll be stronger and happier and refreshed, ready for the chance to find new doors to walk through."

She smiled at him, and Jackson took his turn at sighing. His, in relief.

"If you tell me that you don't want me to sell, Emma, I won't sell."

Her eyes brightened with surprise, and she stared hard at him. "Do you mean that?"

"Of course I mean it. I just want to make sure you're not asking me to change directions because of other people. If you want me to cancel the deal, it has to be because you choose The Tanglewood over Paris. And that's fine with me. But what isn't fine with me," he said, leaning toward her for emphasis, "is your failure to step back from some of the craziness. Because that's not an option, Emma. You *have to* take care of yourself."

"I know," she breathed, rubbing her forehead. "I know you're right."

After a long moment, Jackson touched her cheek, and Emma looked back at him and smiled.

"It's in your hands right now, Emma. I haven't signed anything yet. It's not too late to pull out of the deal. But on Friday, I *do* sign the papers, and it *will* be too late. We have a few days. Whatever you want, we'll make it work. What do you really want?"

"You want to sell and go to Paris for a year," she stated.

"Sure. But in the long run, I don't care where I'm your husband, as long as I am, and as long as you're taking care of yourself so you'll be around for the lifetime I plan on spending with you. I've lost one love in my life, Emma. I'm not equipped to lose another."

After a few seconds thick with hesitation and angst, Emma fell back against the chair and groaned.

"I've made a decision!" she suddenly exclaimed. "I have decided that we are going to eat this pleasant and healthy dinner you've brought along, and we are not going to think about The Tanglewood, or anyone or anything associated with it, for the rest of the night. Just one evening, un*Tanglewooded*. What do you say?"

"I think it's a brilliant choice. Now please pass the hummus."

"You've got it!" she declared, plopping the container down in front of him.

"And after dinner, I challenge you to a Scrabble match."

"I accept," she replied. "Special rule: No hotel-related words allowed."

"I'm in," Jackson replied with a grin.

"Is *spa vacation* one word, or two?"

ᚱᚲ᠑

"Oh, Daddy, I'm so conflicted."

"I can see that, Emmy. What can I do to help?"

"You're doing it," she said with a weak smile. "Just listening, not judging." With a broadened grin, she added, "And I know that can't be easy for you."

Gavin's brow furrowed, and he asked, "Am I really that judgmental? That's how you see me?"

"No!" she reassured him as she rubbed his arm. "Not judgmental. Large and in charge."

"Well, that I am," he conceded.

"Where's Mother, anyway?" she asked, pouring a second cup of tea.

"Your aunt isn't doing very well. Avery's taken her over to the hospital for some tests."

"Daddy, why didn't you tell me that when I first got here? What's wrong with Aunt Sophie?"

"She's been very lucid this last month or so." He took a long draw from his cup of coffee before he continued. "But this week has been very different. She's drifted substantially, and your mother is concerned."

"What do you mean?"

"Well, she stayed the night here at the house over the weekend, and in the morning we found her sleeping outside on the veranda."

"Oh." That didn't sound so awful.

"Wearing my old combat fatigues."

"Oh! From the attic?"

He nodded. "She'd gone up there and rummaged around in the boxes."

"That could have been dangerous."

"You haven't seen anything until you've seen your aunt Sophie in full fatigues and combat boots."

Emma tried not to snicker, but the visual crept up on her.

"Mother must have been beside herself."

"Well, actually, she took it all in stride when she found her like that, even when Sophie insisted on lobster and grits for breakfast. There was quite the fallout when Avery tried to dissuade her, but your mother remained pretty calm."

"Really?" Emma exclaimed with a grin. "That surprises me, for some reason."

"Yeah, she did very well until yesterday."

"Do I want to know what happened yesterday?"

"The assisted living nurse phoned to say that Sophie had taken a fall."

"What?"

"She's fine," he reassured her. "Nothing broken, nothing bleeding. But your mother is worried."

"Now I'm worried, too."

A dozen scenarios wound their way around in Emma's mind until they tangled into a knot and she groaned loudly in the effort to escape.

"Just take it easy, Emmy. There's no need to panic. She should be home within the hour, and I'm sure she'll tell us that everything is just dandy."

"Daddy, how can Jackson and I pick up and move to Paris for a year with everything that's going on? Sherilyn's just had her baby, and she wants me to get to know her. Fee might not even want the added responsibility of taking on my job. And if they bring in someone new, how can I be sure that they'll appreciate her for everything that she is? I mean, she's very easy to misread on first impression."

Her father quirked a smile without comment.

"And now Aunt Sophie is having trouble. If I went to Paris and something happened to her—"

"Jackson is right about one thing," he interrupted, and he tapped the top of Emma's hand. "You can't make a decision based on anyone or anything else. You and he need to consider what's best for your future together and make a solid decision based on that alone."

"But what if being with our family and friends *is* what's best for our future?" she said with a sigh. "I mean, what are we, really, without the people we love?"

"You're going to be married. Whatever else there is, that trumps everything else."

Emma sighed. "Good advice, Dad. You could be the next Dear Abby."

"There's a thought."

She popped with laughter. When a decision had to be made, a talk with her father almost always made her feel lighter somehow. He hadn't really given her any sort of answer to speak of, but she still appreciated the sense of well-being that came from a father-daughter summit.

"Do you mind if I hang around until Mother comes back?"

"Not if you don't mind occupying yourself while I head to the study to make a few phone calls."

"Not at all."

Gavin kissed his daughter's cheek before he left, and Emma took her tea out to the sun porch. She snuggled into the cozy chair in the corner and propped her feet on the ottoman as she tore the bandage from her arm where they'd taken blood that morning. She tossed it into the small wicker trash can as she fondly recalled the Ethan Allen excursion with her mother when she'd bought the furniture for the sunporch.

A chair made from wood and woven sea grass seemed to Emma like an odd choice, considering the regal nature of the rest of her mother's furniture, but two Catalina chairs upholstered in wide gray and white stripes with matching ottomans, and a simple table between them—a flared white iron base with a distressed wood top in the shape of a full-petaled daisy—set just the right tone for the small, glass-enclosed sitting room. It had become Emma's favorite in her parents' Atlanta home.

As she sipped her tea, she'd just begun to consider heading to the kitchen for a quick microwave warm-up when she heard the garage door. She quickly grabbed her cup and headed into the kitchen just as Avery came inside.

"How's Aunt Sophie?"

Her mother tilted her head and tried for a smile. "We have to wait for the results of the tests they put her through this morning," she said as Emma helped her out of her coat. "But she fell sound asleep just moments after I got her settled back in her little apartment."

"Can I make you some tea?" Emma offered. "You look like you might be exhausted, too."

"Oh, that would be lovely, Emma Rae. Thank you."

"Why don't you go out to the sunporch and relax? I'll bring it along."

Avery kissed Emma's cheek, set her purse on the counter as she passed, and headed off to heed Emma's suggestion without another word. It took all of five minutes to steep a couple of cups of tea and place a few butter cookies on a china plate, but by the time Emma reached her mother, Avery had curled into one of the Catalina chairs and drifted off to sleep.

Interesting Ways to Incorporate Family Members into the Wedding Celebration

❖ The Unity Candle, consisting of two taper candles and a pillar candle, can be a wonderful way to involve the parents of the bride and groom, or even a favorite aunt or treasured grandparents.
After the bride and groom light the pillar candle, the family members are given the taper candles and they light them from the flame on the pillar to symbolize the new union.

❖ A rose ceremony, in which single roses are given to the mothers of the bride and groom, is a touching way of showing them how valuable they both are to this new relationship forged from them both.
An alternative to this is giving single roses to a group of family members you wish to incorporate in a meaningful way. During the ceremony, these people are asked to bring the roses, one at a time, and place them in a vase between the bride and groom. This symbolizes the support they offer the new couple as people they can turn to in the hard times and a foundation of prayer for the new union.

❖ "A threefold cord is not easily broken" is a verse out of Scripture that can be the basis for a segment of the ceremony. Three strands of string or rope attached to a metal ring are braided by a beloved family member, symbolizing the union of the bride and groom, with God in the middle of their marriage.

12

$\mathcal{J}$ackson checked his watch as he exited the elevator and made his way down the corridor. He might just have time to call and check on Emma before his conference call, if he hurried.

An odd scent accosted his nostrils as he closed in on his office.

"What is that?" he asked right out loud as he paused to sniff the air.

Musky. Sweet . . . heavy!

He'd just turned the corner and stepped into Reception, when he stopped in his tracks. Seated behind Susannah's desk, an unfamiliar woman smiled at him. Long, straight, bleached hair past her shoulders, and he wondered if her very suntanned face gave a fair representation of middle age or whether all that sun had created the premature cowhide texturing of her skin.

She rose to her feet and extended her hand to him across the desk, the butterfly sleeves of her paisley smock grazing two full rows of framed photographs arranged on the desktop.

"Mary Troutman," she offered. "I'm the new temp. You must be Jackson Drake."

He shook her hand weakly as he looked around the office. A long blue scarf draped the window, and two smaller versions capped the beaded shades of the floor lamps in opposite corners. A large stuffed elephant stood guard over the credenza, and a plant with enormous green leaves occupied a woven basket next to the desk where the trash can used to sit.

His nostrils stung again, and Jackson looked around. "Mary? What is that smell?"

Her over-whitened smile widened as she nodded at the brass incense burner tucked into the corner of Susannah's completely unrecognizable desk. Her sharp-pronged red fingernails bordered on dangerous as she pointed at it.

"Patchouli," she said, as if imparting some universal wisdom. "I love that you responded to it, Jackson. Patchouli usually appeals to the enlightened. It's especially effective before meditation to ground and center the mind. Its fragrance heightens strength and passion."

Jackson massaged his temple for a moment before he told her, "Mary, I don't think my particular response to it is what you hoped. It actually gives me a bit of a headache. That being said, lit substances like cigarettes and patchouli . . . not allowed here at The Tanglewood. So I'll need you to put that out."

"Oh." Mary's leathery face fell a little. "All right. The good news, Jackson, is that the scent will linger in the area for up to twenty-four hours!"

"That's the good news?" he muttered on his way into his office.

He pulled his cell phone from his pocket and opened up a text box as he lowered himself into the chair.

I think I'm asleep. Please call and wake me. Quickly.

A moment later, Emma replied. *Day's going that well, is it?*

You wouldn't believe me if I told you.

Aunt Sophie fell. Mother took her to the hospital.

Jackson stared at the message for a moment before picking up the receiver of his desk phone and dialing.

"Tell me what happened," he said the moment Emma answered.

"The assisted living nurse found her and called my mother. She took her over to the hospital, and they ran a battery of tests. Aunt Sophie seems fine, no broken bones or anything, but Mother says she's a little disoriented and out of sorts."

"That's a shame," Jackson answered. "Is there anything I can do?"

"No, I don't think so. I'm going over to visit with her in a bit to see for myself."

"Give her my love?"

"Of course," Emma replied. "So what's your nightmare?"

"A middle-aged hippie sitting at Susannah's desk."

"Oh, no. Another bad one?"

"Emma," he whispered into the phone, cupping the mouthpiece with his hand, "she's kind of scary. She's got scarves hanging everywhere, a stuffed elephant on the table, and she's burning incense."

"Incense!"

"Yes," he vowed. "She must have rented a U-Haul truck to get it all up here! A little over-the-top for a temp job, wouldn't you say?"

"What kind of incense?"

He thought about it for a few seconds. "It starts with a *p*."

"Patchouli?"

"It frightens me that you know that."

Emma's laughter rang like music in his ears. "Dinner tonight?" she asked him.

"Can't. I've got a late meeting, and Miguel organized a basketball game tonight at the rec center."

"Oh, that's right. I forgot. I'll see you tomorrow, then?"

"I'll call you in the morning."

"Well, call my office because I'm coming back to work tomorrow."

"Emma, you can take a couple more days, you know. I'll put in a good word for you with the owner."

"Oh, don't bother. That guy is a piece of work," she teased. "And you won't want to get too close, anyway. I hear he smells like patchouli."

❧

Her aunt didn't respond well to sugar these days, so Emma had carefully chosen treats from the tearoom shelf with the lowest sugar content and packed them in a small pastry box tied with white string. Shortbread cookies, zucchini bread, and just two brownie bites—minus the frosting.

"No latte cookies?" Sophie asked as she peered inside. "I love those little chocolate-dipped delights."

"None on hand," Emma told her with an apologetic shrug. "But I think you'll find something in there that you like."

"I adore everything you bake. You know that."

Emma slipped out of her sweater and draped it across the back of the chair at the small dinette set in the corner. Slipping her arm through her aunt's, she led her to the sitting area by the window and helped her into her favorite chair before sitting down across from her.

"I want you to tell me how you're feeling, Aunt Soph. You gave us all quite a scare."

"Did I?" she asked, and her lovely eyes glazed over a bit. "What did I do?"

"You fell. You don't remember?"

Sophie squinted slightly, and Emma watched her scan the air for some memory of her accident. At last, she simply shrugged and shook her head. "I think you must be mistaken, dear heart. But thank you for worrying about me. Your aunt Sophie is just fine. No need to fret."

Emma reached over and stroked the paper-thin skin on the back of her aunt's hands. "You're a treasure to me. You know that, don't you?"

"And you to me," Sophie responded. Her eyes lit up as an idea occurred to her. "Can you stay for dinner? They're serving pot roast in the main dining room downstairs. Helen says it's the kind with the little red potatoes and baby carrots with rosemary. That sounds much better than anything I could make for myself, don't you think?"

"I think it sounds scrumptious!" Emma exclaimed with a wide grin, broadened just for her aunt. "I'd love to be your date."

"I just need to take a little nap before we head downstairs. Is that all right, dear?"

"It's quite all right. I can use a little quiet time myself. Let me help you to your bedroom."

"No, no. I'm fine right here in my chair," she said. "If you'll just help me put up my feet."

Emma nodded, and she nudged the ottoman toward her. With extreme care, she gently lifted Sophie's legs, one at a time, until she felt certain of her aunt's comfort. Easing her head forward, Emma nudged a small pillow behind her neck and spread a daisy afghan over her body.

With a kiss on the woman's cheek, Emma whispered, "I love you so much, Aunt Soph. Sleep well."

"Wake me in an hour? I want to get downstairs before all of the pot roast is gone."

"One hour," she promised with another gleaming smile, again widened for Sophie's benefit.

While her aunt dozed, Emma padded into the bedroom, gathered a small mound of dirty clothes into a laundry bag, and tugged on the drawstring to close it. She tossed it to the floor beside the door so she wouldn't forget to take it with her. Gathering half a dozen bottles of prescription medicines from the shelf in the bathroom, along with a large plastic pillbox with section dividers for each day of the week, Emma spread it all out on the bed.

She proceeded to replenish the box for the coming week as her thoughts bounced around like a large rubber ball . . . from the whimsical cake in the shape of a teapot she planned to start the next day . . . to Fee and Sean's ongoing hunt for a house big enough to consolidate his workout equipment and the contents of Fee's massive closet . . . to poor Jackson's administrative assistant train wreck of one animated disaster after another.

Audrey would return to town next week, hopefully with J.R. in tow. She wanted to talk to him about the cabinetry work he'd done in Anton Morelli's kitchen. If he had some time available, she'd love to have him take a crack at her office.

Her thoughts flash-froze.

Will I still have an office long enough to care whether it's got built-in shelves and cabinets?

Emma's heart began to race again, the way it did every time she thought about leaving the hotel behind. Moving to Paris with Jackson induced a swoon every time she considered it. But selling The Tanglewood, moving to another country—even for just a little while—and saying good-bye to their friends and family . . . to Aunt Sophie! How on earth would they ever manage it?

When the time came to wake her aunt, Sophie simply nuzzled deeper into the afghan and sighed. Emma phoned Helen, the nursing assistant assigned to her aunt, and asked that a dinner plate be sent up for her later rather than disturbing her now. Helen agreed, and they had a brief chat about Sophie's medications, her follow-up medical appointments, and her recent mental decline.

"She's in no way completely diminished," the woman reassured her. "But I have noticed a decline in the last week or two."

"You'll keep a careful watch on her for us, won't you?"

"Of course, Ms. Travis. You know I adore your aunt."

"Well," Emma said with a smile, "she's hard not to love."

Instead of heading home after she kissed Sophie's forehead and tiptoed out of her apartment with the laundry bag slung over her shoulder, Emma decided to stop by the hotel for a bite to eat. If she felt like it, maybe she'd get a head start on tomorrow's teapot cake, if Fee hadn't already begun to construct it.

The instant she passed through the lobby doors, however, Emma's focus on what she might order for dinner shattered into shards that spun in several different directions. While Anton Morelli's voice in broken Italian bellows ebbed and flowed from his kitchen, a diminutive man in an expensive suit argued with the front desk manager about his bill. On the other side of the glass doors, the courtyard hummed with well-dressed guests milling about under the twinkling white lights strung through the tree branches as two violinists set the mood with beautiful classical music.

"Dude, what are you doing here?" Fee asked as she and Kat raced past her. "There's a cake emergency in the Victoria. Be right back," she tossed over her shoulder as they passed the front desk and turned the corner, bound for the Victoria ballroom, where Diane and Raymond Butler had scheduled the celebration of their twenty-fifth wedding anniversary.

Emma realized that she hadn't moved an inch. She just stood there, in the middle of the hotel lobby, her feet firmly cemented to the glossy floor as the world inside those glass doors buzzed around her. The goings-on at The Tanglewood seemed like a ballet to her now, choreographed dancers moving to and fro, never quite intersecting with the others, but always threatening to do just that.

"Emma *Raaa-eee*." Madeline's unmistakable southern drawl tugged Emma's attention toward the restaurant and she noticed that Jackson's middle sister seemed to be floating as she approached. "What are you doin' here, *sugah*? I thought I heard you were out of the line of *fi-ah* for a few days."

"Oh, I'm returning tomorrow," she told her. "But I thought I'd come in to have a look at the schedule and see if there's anything I need to know for the morning."

"Have you had your supper yet? Would you like to join Norma and me? Come on into Morelli's and have something to eat with us, *sugah*."

"You know, I saw Kat and Fee fly through here a minute ago. I think I'm going to hang out in the kitchen until they come back so I can find out what's going on."

"Oh, are you *shu-ah*?" she sang.

"Yes. But give my love to Norma."

"I'll do that, honey."

Madeline turned and headed back to the restaurant, and Emma remained planted, still somewhat lost in the evening dance of The Tanglewood.

"Miss Travis, good to see you." . . . "Oh, hello, Emma. How are you?" . . . "Emma, did you get my e-mail? I'd like to talk to you about moving the Hendrix bridal tea out of the courtyard and into the Desiree room on the thirtieth."

She blinked her eyes, and the glaze of emotion resolved into a few lone tears that wound down her face. Suddenly, Emma inhaled sharply and wheeled around, heading straight for the front door. Fee called out to her just as her hand touched the large brass handle.

"Hey, wait a minute. Where are you going?"

Emma quickly wiped her face with the back of her hand and sniffed. "Sorry. I have something I have to do," she called out as she hurried toward the door.

"I just wanted to tell you I finally got Anton to part with his recipe for—"

"I'm sorry. I'll see you in the morning, Fee. We'll talk then."

"—that fudge of his," Fee finished, but the words dropped to the ground as Emma took off at a full run toward her car before the door had even closed behind her.

Anton Morelli's "Secret Million-Dollar Fudge"

4 ½ cups granulated sugar
2 tablespoons butter
¼ teaspoon salt
1 12-ounce can evaporated milk
12 1-ounce squares semi-sweet chocolate
12 ounces chocolate chips
1 pint marshmallow cream
1 cup chopped walnuts

Grease a 12x8x2-inch pan.

Boil sugar, butter, salt, and milk for 6 minutes,
stirring constantly.
In a large bowl, pour boiling mixture over
the remaining ingredients.
Beat until chocolate is melted and the mixture is smooth.

Pour into a greased 12x8x2-inch pan and cool completely.
Let stand for several hours before cutting into squares.
Store in a sealed container lined with wax paper.

13

'That's unexpected news, bro." Huge droplets of sweat fell from Sean's bald head as he shook it. "Does Fee know?"

"I think so. I mean, I know it's radical, but I think it's the right thing," Jackson replied, as Miguel tossed him a bottle of water before joining him and the others on the floor.

Andy, Miguel, Jackson, and Sean leaned against the wall like a weary line-up, exhausted after two hours of nonstop basketball with their buddies from Miguel's men's group.

"Emma and I have been talking about this for months now," he said, pausing to pour a stream of cold water down his throat. "It was just a pipe dream, really, until Rod called and made the offer. There's some famous pastry school that accepted her last year, but she never went. So we go, we live in Paris, she attends those classes, I work on the book I've been spouting about for two years now—"

"You're gonna write a book?" Sean interrupted. "What, like a novel?"

"Nah. A how-to kind of thing about building a business from the ground up."

"Yeah, well, there's not enough of those out there," Sean quipped, and Jackson gave him a quick punch on the arm. "Sorry, man. I'm just joking."

"And Emma hasn't been feeling so great lately," Jackson told them seriously. "I'm worried. I mean, she's got three strikes against her anyway with the diabetes, but her doctor told her the other day that she either slows it down or her body is going to slow it down for her."

"I had no idea," Miguel commented.

"She's funny about that stuff," he said. "She doesn't like anyone to think she's *less than*, you know? She works hard to keep up with it, but lately . . ."

Jackson's words trailed off when the gymnasium door exploded open, banging against the wall behind it. They all leaned forward and looked toward the back of the gym as Emma barreled in and ran toward them.

"Emma?" Jackson exclaimed, jumping to his feet just in time to catch her as she thudded into him. "What is it? What's wrong? Is it Sophie?"

"No, no," she cried, breathless. "I have to talk to you." She folded in half, her hands propped against her knees, as she tried to continue. "I have to . . . talk . . . right now, Jackson."

"Okay. Relax and catch your breath. Do you want some water?"

"No," she replied, still struggling to regulate her breathing. "On second thought, yes."

He retrieved a new bottle from the cooler, twisted off the top, and handed it to her. She downed about half of it before speaking again.

"I'm . . . sorry," she said with a sheepish, uncomfortable stab at a smile when she noticed the others. "I interrupted. Sorry, guys."

"It's fine," Miguel said as he stood. "We were just heading in to the locker room anyway. You two stay here and talk."

Sean and Andy took the cue and got up as well.

"Hey, Emma," Andy said, and he patted her arm as he passed her.

"Hi."

"'Sup?" Sean commented as well.

"Let me know if you need anything," Miguel added, and the three of them filed across the court and through the door.

"Oh, Jackson. I am so sorry."

"For what?" he said with a smile, taking her hand. "Let's sit down and breathe for another minute. Then you tell me what's got you so worked up."

In the short walk to the bleachers, a dozen scenarios burned the fire line inside Jackson's mind, but he couldn't seem to land on any one of them for more than an instant. They sat down, and Emma perched on the edge of the bench like a nervous bird on a wire.

"Tell me," he said.

She looked down at the floor for a long time, and when she lifted her head again and gazed at him with deep regret in her stormy brown eyes, tears cascaded down her face in full streams. Jackson's heart began to race, and his palms went cold and sweaty. Emma never exhibited this kind of behavior. She normally managed to keep pretty even-keeled under the most stressful situations, except for the pacing. He determined that this must be something truly horrible if she hadn't thought of pacing.

And suddenly a notion dropped on him. Gently at first, like an irritating feather tickling the inside of his nose. Then harder, with a thud that continued to press in.

No, he prayed. *That can't be it . . . Oh, Lord, don't let her take off that ring and hand it to me.*

"Jackson," she chirped through the emotion blocking her throat. "I'm so sorry."

Where is this coming from? . . . No, it can't be . . . Don't say it, Emma. Please.

"My heart has been so heavy over this. The burden is just . . . Well, I've never felt anything so deeply, so . . . And the thing is, I can't even explain it to you. Not really."

Dear God.

"But you know how, sometimes, you just know that you know something?"

His chest ached. He sniffed back a mist of emotion gaining a chokehold on him, and he nodded. "Yeah. I think so."

"Well, it really hit me hard tonight, and I'm so certain."

He narrowed his eyes and rigidly turned toward her. Staring her down and steeling himself for her answer, he rasped, "Go ahead, Emma. Tell me."

"I hope you'll understand."

"Just say it."

"Please don't do it, Jackson."

He swallowed. "I'm sorry. What?"

"Don't do it. Don't sell The Tanglewood."

It took half a minute for his heart to start beating again. But when it did, Jackson blew out a huge puff of air he hadn't realized he'd been holding. And then he started to laugh. Hysterically. And he grabbed her—his beautiful *fiancée*—and he clutched her to him until she probably couldn't breathe. The relief washed over him in icy waves.

"Jackson?" she asked, her voice muffled against his chest as he held her there. "Umm, Jack-son?"

"Sorry," he said, releasing her for a moment, but then snagging her back again and embracing her with everything he had.

"Are you all right?"

"Yes," he declared. "I'm perfect."

⌒⌒

"What did you think I was going to say?" Emma asked him as Jackson continued to rock her back and forth as he held her in a vise grip. "Are you sure you're all right?"

"Yes. I told you, I'm perfect."

"Well, I already knew that," she teased. "But really . . . you're killing me."

"What?" He drew back and looked down at her. "Oh. I'm sorry." Shaking her shoulders with both hands, and looking like some kind of crazy person, he repeated, "Sorry."

"So?" she asked, folding her leg beneath her. "What do you think? About not selling."

"And you can't explain to me why you feel this way."

"I really can't," she told him as she pulled her hair back into a sloppy ponytail and secured it with a scrunchie from her pocket. "I was just standing there in the lobby, Jackson. Your sister was there, and Fee and Kat raced by, and Roy in Accounting, and . . . well, I just knew I couldn't give up my life there. *Our life* there."

Jackson nodded thoughtfully. "I still have the same concern, Emma. Your health, the stress levels—"

"Jackson, a day will never come when there will be no stress in our lives. In Georgia or in Paris, or in Bora Bora! I'm still going to have to figure out how to manage it. But if I have the choice, I want to learn to manage it here, with our friends and our family and my brides and . . . and . . ."

He pressed his hand lightly over her mouth. "Stop talking," he whispered, and Emma chuckled. "Can you do that?"

She nodded, her grin pressing against his fingers.

"Everything all right in here?" Miguel called to them from the door. "I'm getting ready to lock things down."

"Can you hold up on that?" Jackson asked him, still staring into Emma's eyes. "Can you stick around for a few minutes, Miguel?"

"Of course." He crossed the gym and stood over them as Jackson removed his hand from Emma's mouth. "What's up?"

"Emma and I would like for you to pray with us. Can you do that?"

"Did Noah build an ark?" Miguel joked.

"We have a big decision to make," Jackson explained, "and we can't make it on our own."

"You're very wise. Let's take it higher then, shall we?"

Emma sighed as Miguel joined them on the bleachers, reaching for her hand, then Jackson's. Thirty minutes later, the three of them parted ways in the parking lot on the promise that Jackson and Emma would sleep on it overnight and see where their hearts led them.

Emma felt a truckload lighter as they walked along, Jackson's arm loose around her shoulder. Her cell phone rang, and she reached into her purse.

"Fee," she told him as she opened it. "Yeah, Fee. What's up?"

"You ran out of the hotel like a bat from you-know-where. You okay?"

"I am," she said with a sigh. "I just needed to see Jackson."

"Are you with him now?"

"Yes, why?"

"Can the two of you come over to our place?"

"Sure. I guess so."

"It's important, Emma."

"Okay. We'll be there in fifteen minutes."

Always the Baker, FINALLY the Bride

She ended the call and looked up at Jackson. "Can you follow me to Fee and Sean's? She says it's important."

He nodded and pulled her in for a kiss before heading toward his car. "Lead the way."

⟡

The emotions of the day had swung from one extreme to another, and Emma paused to stretch after she pulled up in front of the tiny cottage that used to be known as Sean's house. Since Fee and her closet had moved in, Emma and Jackson had taken to just calling it The Closet

She met up with Jackson at the edge of the driveway, and he extended his hand and clasped hers. When Sean opened the door to greet them, his eyes seemed unusually wide, with large, dilated pupils.

"Thanks for coming," he said, rubbing his dark, bald head.

"What's the story?" Jackson asked as they stepped inside.

"You need to see for yourself," Fee told them, leaning against the arched doorway to the kitchen. "But first, we want you both to know that . . ." She darted an excited glance at her smiling husband before continuing. " . . . we bought a house tonight!"

"Fee, that's awesome!" Emma exclaimed.

"I just saw you at the gym two hours ago," Jackson said, shaking Sean's hand. "Why didn't you tell me?"

"They just accepted our offer a little while ago," Fee answered for him. "We can hardly believe it. We close in thirty days!"

"My little Fiona," Emma said, snaring her by the shoulders and pulling her close. "A home owner."

"Dude. Shut it," she said with a grin, squirming out of Emma's embrace. "We're pretty stoked. It's more than twice the size of this place, and it has . . . *wait for it!* . . . two walk-in closets! Count 'em. Two."

Emma glanced around at the neatly piled boxes providing a full border to the room. In the small dining area, the table had been pushed into the corner so that two jam-packed rolling wardrobes could squeeze in. Wire shoe racks hung over the bathroom and bedroom doors, and the door on the coat closet couldn't even be closed for all of the garments poking out of it.

"I love my girl's individuality, don't get me wrong," Sean told them. "But all this gothic, steam punk, and buckled jazz takes up a lotta room."

"And now we'll have it," Fee told him with a smile. Turning to Emma, she pulled a very serious face "Look, something else happened tonight, and you need to tell me what to do."

"What do you mean?" Emma asked, glancing at Jackson for a quick moment. "What happened?"

Fee nodded toward the hallway leading to the one bedroom in the house. "Have a look."

Emma felt tentative as she made her way into the hall and turned the knob on the bedroom door. She looked back at Fee, who nodded, and she opened the door.

Curled into a small ball of wild hair and fair skin, wrapped in a black shirt about thirty sizes too big, lay a sleeping Hildie.

Emma's focus darted behind her to Fee.

"How did this happen?" she whispered.

Fee nodded back toward the hall, and Emma followed her, pulling the door so that it only remained ajar by an inch.

"She showed up at the hotel earlier," Fee said softly. "She came into the kitchen looking like she'd been through the war. You didn't answer your phone, and I didn't know what to do, so I brought her home with me. I gave her some dinner, forced her into the shower, and put her clothes in the wash."

"Sounds familiar."

"Dude. What should we do?"

"I'll call Mrs. Troy in the morning. Do you want me to take her home with me? I've clearly got more room than you guys do."

"Nah. We'll work it out. But calling the kid police . . . won't that just put her right back where she's so miserable?"

"That's the law, Fee. I don't really think we have a choice here."

"There's gotta be something."

"Well, if you can think of it, let me know. Right now, the only thing I know is that she needs a family, and Mrs. Troy seems to be the only link to making that happen."

When she turned around, Jackson stood behind her, and he placed a hand on Emma's shoulder.

"Hildie?" he asked as he peered through the open crack in the bedroom door.

She nodded. "She showed up at the hotel tonight, and Fee brought her home."

"You should have seen her, Jackson," Fee told him. "That little chick has been through it."

"I'd say she has," he commented.

"We'll figure it out in the morning," Emma told them, leading the way back to the living room. "I'll call Mrs. Troy first thing, and I'll let you know what she has to say."

"I hate going that route," Fee admitted.

"We have to make sure her needs are met, baby," Sean said.

"But if they were being met, she wouldn't have come running back to us."

"We have to work with what we've got," Emma told them. "And unfortunately, the foster care system is what we've got."

After a moment of silence between them, Fee sighed. "That stinks."

"It sure does."

Jackson walked Emma to her car and opened the door for her. Before she slid in, he wrapped his arms around her and pulled her close, kissing her softly on the neck.

"Anything you need?" he whispered.

"At the risk of sounding a lot like Sherilyn," she teased, "what I'd really like . . . what would make me feel infinitely better . . ."

"Chocolate?" he asked.

"Nah." She grinned up at him before pulling a very serious face. "Cake!"

༒ঌৎঌৎঌৎঌৎঌৎঌৎঌৎঌৎঌৎঌৎঌৎঌৎঌ

Five Important Tips for the Diabetic Bride Who Wants to Eat Cake on Her Wedding Day

If you've been diabetic for a long time, you know that there are certain things you can do to incorporate treats into your diet. By carefully managing nutrition and exercise in the weeks leading up to the big day, you can safely indulge in the wedding cake.

1. Keep a journal of your food intake for two weeks prior to the wedding, carefully monitoring carbohydrates. Typically, 35-40 carbs per meal is safely consumed. By adjusting your intake at mealtime, you can lead up to a dessert allowance.

2. Use wisdom in the amount of low- and non-calorie sweeteners you use as well. Be certain to read labels on these items, always remaining aware that they do not necessarily equate to fewer carbohydrates. Packaged snacks labeled "No sugar added," for instance, are not free of carbohydrates. Every carb should be counted and assessed in the weeks leading up to the wedding.

3. Include your daily glucose levels in your journal so that you can easily compare the types of carbohydrates consumed with spikes in glucose numbers. For instance, some diabetics tolerate carbohydrate consumption better when it is combined with a protein; others may do better to reduce carbs at mealtime and spend their carb allotment on a sweet, stand-alone snack.

༒ঌৎঌৎঌৎঌৎঌৎঌৎঌৎঌৎঌৎঌৎঌৎঌৎঌ

Pay close attention to portion sizes. For instance, a piece of fudge can be thoughtfully incorporated into your daily menu as it consists of only 15 grams of carbohydrates; however, the portion size is only one square inch.
5. Step up your physical activity in the weeks before the wedding. Exercise is an effective tool in burning calories as well as maintaining blood sugar control.

14

The shadow of Emma's sweet face moved over him before Jackson had even opened his eyes that morning. And now, sitting behind his desk, his eyes closed again and his folded hands pressing against his face, Jackson still couldn't shake the sight of her, rushing across the gym toward him, thudding against him, crying and pleading with him not to go through with the sale of the hotel.

He'd had the same desperate feeling a dozen times since Rod had issued the unexpected and lucrative offer, feeling like a bit of an emotional pendulum, swinging from *Yes, of course!* to *No, how could I?* with little actual provocation. But now . . .

How could he say no to Emma?

They had prayed with Miguel before leaving the gym the night before, and they had promised one another they'd sleep on it and see how they felt in the morning. The only thing Jackson had felt completely certain of upon waking, however, was that Emma had asked him not to sell, and he couldn't bear the thought of refusing her anything. Since they'd settled into their relationship, Emma had never been one to ask for much beyond the basics: loyalty, truth, maybe a little extra understanding on the rougher days.

At the same time, Jackson couldn't help counting off the list of things they'd give up if they decided not to sell The Tanglewood. And the list grew pretty lengthy.

No living in Paris for a year, he thought. Which meant none of those cooking classes for Emma, and no leisurely writing time in Jackson's future. He'd had such clear visions when they began dreaming their dream . . . images of early morning walks, wardrobes consisting of jeans and tennis shoes, a laptop and too many cups of coffee at charming French cafés.

Profound financial security. The deal Allegiant had offered exceeded Jackson's wildest dreams. Neither he nor Emma actually hurt for money or worried about the specifics of their future, but with this deal . . . they would find themselves set for life. In such a precarious economic climate, a guy couldn't discount the importance of that kind of security.

Continued stress for Emma.

And that final point poked him in the chest with a sharp finger. She had no intention of slowing down, no matter what she promised him, and probably herself. It wasn't in her chemical makeup to cut back on hours, delegate some of the load to others, or generally shift her focus to looking after *herself* for a change. But if she didn't, the ramifications could be staggering. And one thing to which Jackson would never surrender: *Losing Emma*. They had to realistically consider her unique challenges as they constructed the plans for their future. Selling the hotel and moving to Paris for a year to regroup might just have been the only solution to that particular challenge.

Jackson groaned softly and leaned back into his creaking chair.

Waiting for an answer to all of this, he thought. *Any time now, Lord.*

"Excuse me. Mr. Drake?"

He jerked toward the door where a young woman stood facing him. Her hair snagged his immediate attention; about seven different shades of brown, all of it slicked into short, spikey little pigtails. She wore about six pounds of glittering bangle bracelets, earrings that dragged over the slope of her shoulders, black trousers and a zebra-print blouse that tied above the waist, revealing just the slightest peek of skin at the midriff. He figured her klunky black shoes added about five inches to her diminutive height.

"Are you Jackson Drake?" she asked him.

"Yes. Can I help you?"

"I'm Lauren Franks. Your temp?"

His heart sank just a little. One more in the long line of oddballs, none of whom could ever replace Susannah. He wanted to ask her if she was even old enough to hold a full-time job but decided against it.

"There's a blue binder on the desk, Lauren," he told her. He paused, then added, "At least I think it's still there."

She turned back toward Reception and nodded. "Yes, it's there."

"All of the notes are there for the day-to-day duties. Have a look through it, and let me know if you have any questions."

"Okay," she said, and her bright smile caught him a little off guard. "Can I get you some coffee first?"

The corner of his mouth twitched slightly, and he turned it into a smile. "No. But thank you."

"Door closed or open?"

"Closed. Thank you."

"Sure thing."

Jackson leaned back in his chair again and scratched the side of his jaw. She had seemed almost normal there at the end.

Dare to dream, he told himself.

Even if just for an hour or so, before Lauren Franks fired up the hibachi on her credenza or strung colored lanterns around the reception office.

⤟⤞

The subject line simply stated, "Hey."

J.R. had always been a man of few words, but this took the cake. Emma opened the e-mail and scrolled.

Audrey doesn't want you to worry about the delay in her return. We should roll in on Thursday. She has a very fine excuse, btw. See attached.

She'd only just begun to wonder about Audrey's return that morning when one of her brides mentioned faulty tailoring on her bridal gown. They'd tentatively scheduled a final fitting for that afternoon, but it looked like J.R.'s e-mail changed that plan.

She clicked on the attachment, and a beautiful image filled the screen: a sweeping panoramic background . . . sunrise—or sunset?—beyond a stunning green hilltop . . . Audrey wore an exquisite beaded dress and held hands with J.R. as she faced him. J.R.'s uniform had always been jeans, a dark T-shirt and a leather jacket; however, in the photo he wore what appeared to be a tuxedo without the tie.

Emma leaned forward, scrutinizing the photograph. They weren't just holding hands, after all; they were . . . *exchanging rings!*

J.R. and Audrey . . . got married!

Emma popped to her feet and clanked open the door to her office. Fee jumped at the clatter and dropped the piping bag she was holding.

"Dude. What the hey?"

"Come in here, Fiona. You've got to see this!"

Fee peeled the plastic gloves from her hands and tossed them to the stainless steel tabletop before following Emma into her office.

"Look at the monitor," Emma urged. "You've got to see this."

Emma remained in the doorway, watching with breathless anticipation. Fee adjusted her square glasses and cocked her head slightly as she gazed at the screen.

"Is that—?"

"Audrey and J.R.," Emma finished for her. "They got married!"

Fee slowly dropped to the desk chair and clicked the mouse for a zoomed-in look at the image on the screen. "I'll be."

"I know! They'll be back in two days. We have to give them a party!"

Fee rushed past her. "I'll call Carly," she said on her way out the door. "You call Sherilyn."

Emma had only just settled behind her desk and reached for the phone, when it rang. She sighed, snatched the receiver and answered.

"Emma Travis."

"Hello, Emma. This is Delores Troy."

"Mrs. Troy!" she exclaimed, quickly changing gears. "Are you calling about Hildie?"

"I am. I wanted to let you know that I've found a very good new placement for her. A young couple out in Buckhead. They have two children, the daughter just a little bit older than Hildie."

"That's . . . wonderful."

"I think it's going to be a good fit for her. I'll drive her over there this afternoon."

"I'm so happy about that," Emma told her with a sigh. "Thank you for letting me know."

"Hildie is here in my office," the woman added. "She'd like to speak to you, if you have the time."

"Of course!"

"All right. Hang on for just a moment."

Emma held her breath as she waited, wondering if Hildie might try to solicit her help to form a plan of escape.

"Hey, Emma."

"Hi, Hildie. Are you all right?"

"I guess."

"Mrs. Troy says she has a great place for you. I hope you're excited."

She sighed. "I guess."

"Hildie," Emma said. "Try to go into this with the anticipation of meeting some great people and getting a whole new start. Can you do that?"

After a long pause, the girl repeated her mantra. "I guess."

"Pretty soon, you'll be in a new school and meeting other kids your own age. It's going to be an adventure, Hildie." For nearly thirty seconds, only the rumble of Hildie's breathing sounded on the line. "I hope you'll call me, if that's allowed. Let me know about all of your new friends, and about the family? . . . Will you do that?"

Another noisy silence followed. "Yeah. I guess. Is Fee there?"

Emma craned to look into the kitchen. "No, she stepped out. But I'll tell her you asked about her, Hildie. We both think you're just going to thrive with this new family."

"Yeah. Okay. See ya."

And before Emma could say another word, Mrs. Troy came back on the line.

"I'll keep you posted, Emma."

"Thank you so much."

An unexpected wave of sadness washed over Emma as she hung up.

Eleven years old. Such a young age to have to develop a game face.

The kitchen door whooshed open and clacked back and forth behind Fee as she breezed through it with Kat in tow.

"I can't believe she didn't even tell Kat!" Fee exclaimed, squeezing into one of the two chairs jammed against the back of Emma's desk. "They only just called her this morning. Can you believe that?"

"I sort of had a suspicion," Kat said as she took the other chair. "She was very tight-lipped about this trip to Vegas. She only said she could hardly wait to catch up to J.R., but there was a little something more. I could see it in her eyes."

Emma chuckled. "Well, at least they didn't get married in one of those Las Vegas quickie places."

"No," Kat said, pulling up the same photo on her phone that J.R. had sent that morning. She angled the device toward them as she grinned. "This looks fairly well planned with that gown, a reverend, and a hilltop at sunrise."

"Her dress is beautiful," Emma noted. "Is it one of her designs?"

Kat nodded. "She told me this morning that they only decided to do this two weeks ago, and she designed and made the dress herself, in the midst of everything else she had to do."

"Well, it's exquisite," Emma told them.

"Speaking of dresses," Fee interjected, "weren't you supposed to have the final fitting of yours today?"

Emma shrugged one shoulder and smiled. "They'll be back on Thursday and we'll reschedule."

"I've never seen anyone take a wedding in stride the way you do," Kat observed.

"Everything but the cake," Fee added.

"Not yet?" Kat asked Emma.

"I'm having a little stress over the final version of the cake. But everything else is in your capable hands, and those of my matron of honor."

"Sherilyn's beside herself with excitement. She's personally handling every last detail."

"While you bust your bundt cake here at the hotel," Fee added with a chuckle.

"I actually don't mind," Kat told them. "It's nice to have a change of venue and shift gears for a while. I don't have another show until the end of the year, so it's kind of like cleansing my palette before I move on to the next course."

"Maybe that's what you need, Emma," Fee suggested. "A palette cleansing."

"How would I do that? We have six weddings, an anniversary, and a bachelorette party between now and my wedding. Cleansing my cake palette seems a little unlikely with all of those cakes and pastries I'm responsible for." She jerked her head back and chuckled. "Oh! And now a party for Audrey and J.R. that we need to plan and execute in just a couple of days."

"That's why God sent me," Fee said with a sly grin, looking at her over the top of her square black glasses and wiggling her eyebrows. "You've got me and half a dozen interns to rely on. Take it easy for thirty seconds or so, huh?"

Emma narrowed her eyes at her friend and clicked her tongue, ignoring the arrival of the four interns they'd requested to prep for Susan McBain's bachelorette party. "Have you been talking to Jackson?"

Fee's gaze darted away as she replied, "Maybe."

"I knew it."

"But he's right, you know. You need to slow down."

"I'll add that to my To Do list right now, Fiona." Pretending to tap at the keyboard on her desk, she sang, "*Slooooow dooooown*. Got it!"

"Is designing your cake on there?" Fee asked. "Because if it's not, you know, maybe you should add that, too."

"Get out of my office."

Kat giggled as she followed Fee into the kitchen and closed the door to Emma's office behind them.

Typing a text with both thumbs, Emma shook her head at them.

Guess who got married.

A few seconds later, Jackson's reply jingled at her. *Did I sleep through our wedding? Sorry about that, kid.*

Audrey and J.R., smarty pants. E-mailing you the photo now.

His response took a couple of minutes. *They look happy.*

Don't sound surprised. That's why they call it wedded BLISS.

Emma awaited his reply, but impatience finally took its toll and she picked up the phone and dialed. An unfamiliar voice greeted her.

"Tanglewood Inn, Jackson Drake's office."

"Hi. Who's this?"

"This is Lauren Franks, Mr. Drake's assistant."

"His assistant. Really." Emma grinned. "Well, Lauren, this is Emma, Mr. Drake's fiancée. Is he available?"

"Certainly. Hang on one moment, please, and I'll put you through."

She sounded like a high school student!

"Sorry. I got sidetracked," Jackson said the moment he picked up the phone.

"It's okay. You have a new assistant?"

"Oh. Lauren."

"Another temp?"

"Yeah."

"How does she stack up?"

Jackson chuckled. "Pretty well if you stand her next to the others. I mean, she's letting me drink coffee, so that's something. Hey, great news about Audrey and J.R."

"Yeah, we're going to put together a small party for them when they get here in a couple of days."

Jackson's pause pinched her.

"Hey," he said softly. "Can you come up to my office for a few minutes?"

"Sure. Want something yummy?"

"*You* are my something yummy."

"No, I mean a cupcake. We've got the interns icing a whole kitchen full of them."

"Well, you know I'm not refusing."

Emma giggled. "I'll bring one for Lauren, too."

"Oh, well, you'd better hurry then."

"Why?"

"I'm just thinking about my track record of late. If you take too long, she might be gone by the time you get here."

"I'll be right up."

Emma greeted the interns, then grabbed two of the finished cupcakes from one of the trays as she passed it.

She called out over her shoulder to Fee, "I'll be with Jackson for a few minutes."

"Hey!" Fee exclaimed as she reached the door, and Emma turned around to see her placing cupcakes on a massive acrylic stand. "How about a wedding cake made out of cupcakes, huh?"

Emma stared her down for a moment.

"Completely unexpected, right? Fee continued. "Very non-traditional. What do you think?"

"I think I'm headed up to Jackson's office. See you in a while."

On the ride upstairs, Emma leaned against the elevator wall and stared at the cupcakes she held, one in each hand.

A cupcake wedding cake, she thought, and she tipped her head to one side as she imagined it. *Not com-pleeetely out of the question, I suppose.*

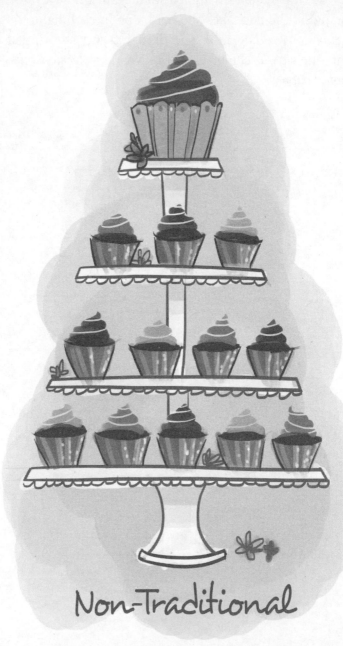

Non-Traditional

15

$\mathcal{J}$ackson nodded and wished a good morning to several Tanglewood employees as he made his way through the lobby toward the elevator. He thought about stopping in the kitchen to see Emma, but he recalled that she had mentioned a breakfast appointment at Carly's to discuss the cake for Audrey and J.R.'s reception, and to get a peek at their new baby. Carly and Audrey had been best friends since they were kids, Jackson thought he remembered, but now—since Audrey had married Carly's husband's brother—they were family.

The glass-encased elevator groaned as it came to a stop on the fourth floor. Jackson turned the corner and headed to his office to find young Lauren seated behind Susannah's desk, wearing a bright copper, cropped sweater that skimmed a massive brown leather belt with a crescent buckle. She wore her short hair pinned upward into an organized, if slightly wayward, mess. She hopped to her feet the instant she saw him, revealing a peek of skin beneath the short sweater when she did. The girl seemed to really enjoy showing her stomach to the world.

"Mr. Drake, I am so sorry. I tried to—"

The roar of several voices accosted him all at once from the doorway to his office, slicing Lauren's apology right in two. His sisters Madeline and Norma, a seething Sherilyn, and a stone-faced Fee—all of them talking at once.

"It's all right, Lauren. Don't worry about it. If you're here long enough, you'll realize sometimes there's nothing you can do to hold back Hurricane Tanglewood."

She sighed and sat down again. "Let me know if you need anything?"

"It's going to be all about the cleanup crew afterward, I'm afraid," he told her.

He pecked Madeline's cheek as he passed through the fray and headed for his desk.

". . . unreasonable . . ." ". . . thinking clearly . . ." ". . . unstoppable . . ."

"Hey!" he bellowed, punctuating it with the loud *Smack!* of his briefcase against the desktop. They all snapped to instant silence and stared at him with wide eyes. "All right, then. I can't hear a word any one hen is saying when you cluck like that. Pull up some chairs, have a seat, and tell me what you're all worked up about."

Fee stepped into action first, dragging two chairs from the round table in the corner to the edge of his desk and lining them up next to the two already there. Jackson sucked in a sharp, deep breath as they all sat down and faced him.

"Let's try this one at a time," he suggested. "Madeline, would you like to go first?"

"Oh, well, thank you, Jack," she drawled. "But I think Sherilyn would be best suited to speak for us all since she's the one who organized this meetin'."

Sherilyn. Well, that explains a lot.

Emma's best friend since her college days, Sherilyn Drummond lived up to the fire of her red hair. When she felt strongly about something, she let a person know it. And since the sale of the hotel seemed to be her *cause du jour* these days, Jackson prepared himself for what would surely follow.

"All right then. Sherilyn, the floor is yours. Lay it on me."

She swallowed hard before she began. "Jackson, we mean no disrespect."

All evidence to the contrary.

"It's just that we're all taking the sale of The Tanglewood kind of hard. We feel like you made a decision based on profit margin, rather than taking the feelings of the people most impacted into consideration."

"I can assure you—"

"Jackson, honey," Madeline said with a gentle smile, "you offered the floor to Sherilyn, *sugah*. I think it's quite rude to interrupt."

He tried not to laugh right out loud. "You're right. I apologize. Go ahead, Sherilyn."

"Thank you," she said, and she cleared her throat. "I just felt like we should point out to you that, although you own the hotel and have every technical right to make decisions without our input . . . well . . . You've created a family here, Jackson. We're more than your employees. We're a *family*, and I just feel—*we just feel*—a little like orphans suddenly with the family home being sold out from underneath us. Don't get me wrong here. Emma told me how you're fighting for each of us to retain our positions and all that, and I know we all really appreciate that . . . but it's about more than a job for us, Jackson. It's the whole . . . *atmosphere!* . . . that you've created here at The Tanglewood. That can't be recreated under corporate ownership, you know? And I just . . . well, I appreciate you hearing me out."

The corner of Jackson's mouth twitched a little, but he held back the smile trying to push through.

"My turn?" he asked her, and he looked to Madeline for confirmation. She gave it to him with a sweet nod.

He propped his elbows on the desk and clasped his hands as he leaned forward and gazed into Sherilyn's bright turquoise eyes.

"I know you don't think I'm listening, but I hear everything you've said. Surely you've gotten to know me well enough to know that I value the family feeling of this place as much as you do. Do you have any idea how proud I am of what we've built here?" Sherilyn lifted one shoulder in a reluctant shrug. "You people mean the world to Emma and me. But there are outside factors that don't have anything to do with you, details that can't be ignored, and that is what has spurred the decision to sell."

"Can you tell us what those are?" Norma inquired.

Jackson found himself locked, eye to eye, with Fee, and he barely caught the minutest trace of the shake of her head.

"I don't think we need Jackson to do that," she said, never breaking eye contact. "I thought the goal here was for him to hear us out, and I think he's done that."

He wanted to kiss her for that, but, knowing Fee, he thought better of it.

"I just think it will help everyone better understand the thought process behind this enormous decision," Norma remarked. Leaning toward her brother, she added, "Just for a little closure."

"No!" Sherilyn said, and she stood up. "No, I don't want closure. I want you to change your mind! I mean, come on. You're selling The Tanglewood? Really?! Why would you do something like that? Why would you build something so phenomenal and unique, and then just . . . just . . . toss it out there to the highest bidder? Jackson, I don't understand. You just can't do this."

Jackson got up and rounded the chairs occupied by Norma and Madeline. He took Sherilyn by the shoulder and turned her around to face him. Looking her squarely in the eyes, he smiled. "We haven't signed anything yet." She perked up considerably, and he pressed his hand against her shoulder. "Wait. Listen to me."

"Okay," she conceded. "Sorry."

"We haven't signed anything yet, and we won't until Emma and I are both convinced that this is part of the overall plan for our lives. We're talking and we're praying, and I give you my word, Sherilyn, that we are not making this decision lightly just to sell to the highest bidder. But we have to make a choice that is right for our future together. Can you understand that?"

She gave him a defeated shrug before the surrender: "Yeah."

"And you know us both. You know we couldn't decide to do something so drastic without taking every one of our friends and family members into consideration, right?"

She looked down at her white, lace-embroidered tennis shoes with the shiny pink laces and nodded.

"Can you trust me with this?" he asked

Her long pause seemed pregnant with reluctance. "I want to," she finally told him. "I just can't let it go. I can't stop thinking that—"

"How about this, then," he interrupted, placing a finger under her chin and raising her face toward him. "Can you trust God with it?"

She winced.

"Can you believe that we are praying for an answer and that we won't do anything until we get it?"

"What are you waiting for, Jackson?" she asked him in a soft, emotional voice. "I mean, what's God got to show you beyond the impact that this place has had on countless lives? I married Andy here. Fee wouldn't even have met Sean if not for The Tanglewood! And Audrey and J.R. . . .There's a magic about this place the way it is, Jackson. Don't throw that away."

"I'm not throwing anything away, Sherilyn. I can promise you that. But there are other things to consider. And we're in the process of considering them. Just give us the space to do that, will you? Can you trust us enough to simply pray that we're led in the right direction, and accept that sometimes things have to change? Not always. But sometimes."

Sherilyn pulled away from him and sat back down in her chair.

Jackson returned to the other side of the desk and sat down. "Is there anything else that needs to be said?" he asked them, looking from one to the next in anticipation.

"I think Sherilyn has spoken well for us all," Madeline told him. "I appreciate you giving us your time and your ear, little *bruthah*."

"Can I just add one thing?" Norma asked, and Jackson gazed at her as she, the youngest of The Hens, as he had taken to calling his older sisters, brushed her sandy hair away from her face and her hazel eyes flashed.

"Of course."

"We've talked often about how you bought this hotel with Desiree in mind."

The unexpected mention of his late wife's name pricked his chest.

"You say all the time how it was her dream, her vision. But I'd just like to point out that, although that may have been the catalyst for buying The Tanglewood, it's absolutely become something else entirely. Somewhere along the line, this place turned into your dream, Emma's dream, Sherilyn's dream, and on and on. It's become a bit like lightning in a bottle, hasn't it?"

Jackson chuckled. "Yes, it has."

"So just consider that when you and Emma make your final decision, will you?"

He smiled at her. "We will."

"That's all we can ask, then."

And with that, the group of them stood up, and so did he. Madeline hugged him, and then Norma did as well. Sherilyn stepped up in front of him, her arms limp at her sides.

"Thanks for listening," she offered, and he pulled her into an embrace, kissing the side of her head.

Before they left, Fee touched his arm and gave it a squeeze. Jackson thought that might have been the most affectionate she'd ever been toward him.

"Keep us in the loop, at least?" Sherilyn asked him from just outside his office door.

"You know we will."

They filed through Reception and into the hall like a band of half-hearted warriors returning from a battle they weren't quite sure they'd won. Jackson remained in the doorway to his office, against the jamb.

"Can I get you anything?" Lauren asked him. "Coffee? A stiff drink?"

A loud laugh belted out of him at that. "I like you, Lauren."

The girl's face lit up as a bright smile beamed from it.

"Two coffees would be great," he told her. "One for me, and one for Emma."

"Yes, sir!"

Jackson returned to his desk and grabbed his cell phone.

911, he typed into the text box. *Drop everything and come to my office?*

A few seconds later, the reply jingled.

Consider everything dropped. On my way.

~❧~

"It's hard to believe we have to take these measures to find thirty uninterrupted minutes to be together," Jackson said as they climbed the Vickery Creek trail to the top of the knoll.

"And we had to leave the hotel and both of our houses to get it," Emma said with a giggle, and she reached over and grabbed his hand. "So tell me what you're thinking now . . . about the sale of the hotel."

Jackson sighed. He'd wanted to talk to her about the sale of the hotel since the morning after their prayers with Miguel. But interruptions and distractions had abounded and, now that he had her alone and they were free to talk, he suddenly felt uncertain.

"To tell you the truth, Emma, I'm still a little conflicted."

"Oh." From the sound of that one single syllable, he guessed that Emma didn't have lingering concerns.

They reached the top of the ridge where the access trail dead-ended into a separate two-mile trail navigating around the circumference of the beautiful knoll. Jackson started toward the second part of their usual hike, and Emma followed quietly. They didn't stop again until they reached the first scenic ridge on the north side overlooking the gorge formed by Vickery Creek. They both instinctively paused to take in the view.

After a moment, Emma released his hand. "I'm not," she said, and Jackson looked at her squarely.

"You're not, what?"

"I'm not conflicted."

Jackson sighed. "No?"

"I don't want to give up the life we've made, Jackson."

"To a large degree, I don't either," he admitted.

"Then . . ."

"I don't want to give you up either, Emma. I want you to be healthy and strong, and for the first time I'm starting to realize that your pace at the hotel negates that."

"It doesn't negate it, Jackson."

He closed his eyes for a moment and swallowed hard. "The fact that you say that tells me you're not taking to heart the warning the doctor gave you."

"I am," she said, and she took both of his hands and squeezed them. "I promise, I am."

"Then what's going to change, Emma?"

"Well, I've been giving that a lot of thought," she said, releasing his hands and moving to the edge of the ridge. "I thought maybe I could hire another pastry chef to work with Fee and me, someone to share some of the responsibilities."

"You think Fee would be okay with that?"

"I think she'd relish it," she told him. "She's so great with the interns, scheduling them and training them. I think she'd be happy to have some more help."

Jackson smiled. *Well. That's a start.*

"And I have my follow-up with Dr. Mathis in a few days. I thought I'd ask her to recommend a nutritionist. Someone who can help me monitor my diet and make some changes that will help my blood pressure readings."

"Really?"

"Yes," she said, and when she turned back toward him, he noted the unusually serious expression on her lovely—but somewhat pale—face. "I'll do whatever it takes to get and stay healthy, Jackson. But I don't want t—"

A crack of thunder cut her word cleanly in two. They only had a couple of seconds of eye contact before a bolt of lightning struck in the distance, the dark sky opened up, and a massive torrent of rain dropped down over them.

"Really?" he asked the sky. "Really!?"

"Ohhh!" Emma squealed, and Jackson snatched her hand. "Let's make a run for the car."

She kept up with him, stride for stride, as they backtracked. "Be careful at the turn," she shouted. "When it rains, it gets—"

And with that, Jackson's shoe hit a patch of slick mud and he went flying face first down to the sloppy trail.

"—muddy," she said softly as he hit the ground. "Are you all right?"

He barely heard her over the thunder of the downpour, but he nodded as he slicked his drenched hair back from his face with a grubby hand. Despite the bleeding scrape on his left elbow, Jackson knew the worst of the damage had been to his ego.

"This is ridiculous!" she shouted at the rain. "Can you believe this?"

Jackson made it to his feet, and by the time they got under way again, a solid sheet of sideways rain limited visibility to just a few yards ahead. A greenish tint reflected from the sky, and the wind wailed so fiercely that he could hardly hear the *plop-plop-plop* of their synchronized footsteps as they tromped down the hill.

He wiped his eyes with the back of his muddy wrist as they reached the bottom, and Emma growled as she lunged past him toward her car. She'd already unlocked the door and slid behind the wheel of the bright red Mini Cooper by the time he reached the rear bumper.

Jackson folded up like an accordion fan to get himself into the car, grumbling as he clanked the door shut behind him. "This car of yours!"

"I like this car."

"Yes. I know you do. But where are the other eighty-six clowns going to sit?"

"Oh, stop it, Grumpy."

"I'd be a lot less grumpy if you had a normal-sized car, Emma. This isn't exactly practical when you're about to marry a man who's six feet tall!"

"Well, you don't have to ride in it, you know. We could have taken your car."

"What's wrong with a couple having two life-size cars, instead of one regular and one child-size?"

Emma turned and glared at him. "What are you mad at, Jackson? The size of my car, or the fact that I disagree with you about the sale of the hotel?"

Both, he thought. But he didn't say so.

"Just drop me at home so I can shower and get out of these filthy clothes, will you?"

"Gladly!" she snapped.

But when she turned the key . . . nothing.

"Uh-oh."

She turned it again. Still nothing.

Jackson's heart stopped for a moment. "Emma?"

After a long pause, she asked, "Do you belong to Triple A?"

"You mean you don't?" he exclaimed, and Emma tossed her head back against the headrest and groaned.

"Is there anything I can say or do that's right today, Jackson?" she asked him.

"Yes. You can tell me you brought your phone."

"You mean you didn't?"

Emma's Special Creamed Raspberry Cake Filling

1 ½ cups frozen raspberries
1 tablespoon corn starch
¼ cup sugar
⅛ cup sweetened condensed milk
2 tablespoons fresh lemon juice

Combine all ingredients in a small saucepan.
Stirring constantly, bring to a boil over medium heat.
Stir until thickened to desired consistency.
Cool completely before spreading onto cake.

Raspberry cream filling works best
between the layers of a chocolate fudge cake.
It can also be used to fill a vanilla bean layer cake.

16

"It's a shame Russell couldn't make it. I know how close he is to J.R."

Kat's sunshiny face melted into a stormy one as she nodded at Emma. "I know. I'm really starting to miss him."

"Do you think he'll be able to make it to our wedding?" she asked, her arm tucked into the fold of Jackson's.

"I don't know yet. He'd hoped the movie would have wrapped by now, but he's got a very interesting director on this one. They're already a week over schedule with no signs of progress."

Jackson laughed. "I wonder if Russell has anything to do with the delays."

Kat grinned as she playfully smacked Jackson's shoulder. "Hey, now."

"Well, come on," he said on a chuckle. "He's not exactly the most focused individual I've ever met."

"Here they come!" Audrey's best friend, Carly, waved her arms at them as she stepped away from the ballroom door and pushed a basket filled with bright red rose petals toward Kat. "Is everyone ready? Do you have your rose petals?"

With a squeal muffled through the hand clamped firmly over her mouth, Carly looked like she might jump right out of her skin as everyone held fistfuls of petals at the ready.

The well-wishers moved into place around the two-tiered, raspberry-filled marble cake Emma had just finished a couple of hours earlier. Emma took the opportunity to straighten the topper Carly had found: a grinning bride and groom onboard a motorcycle. Fee had used edible gold leaf to paint the bride's hair platinum blonde to better reflect Audrey, but the groom on the front of the bike wore a leather jacket and looked every bit the part of J.R. Hunt.

"Dude. Don't fuss," Fee whispered as Emma adjusted the topper one last time.

She cast a smile up at Jackson before glancing around the room at all of their friends: Sherilyn and Andy; Fee and Sean; Carly and her husband, J.R.'s brother Devon; Kat; even Audrey's former client Lisette and her handsome husband had managed to attend the last-minute celebration. Lisette was the bride who'd been the catalyst for Audrey's new life as a plus-size fashions designer, and Audrey's size 14 evening gown had scored a major hit on the runway for Riley Eastwood's label. Emma knew Audrey would be thrilled to see Lisette again.

Kat, the only single in the room, leaned into Fee and whispered something to her that elicited a chuckle. The two of them had become great friends, and Emma noted that they couldn't have been more different if they had worked at it. A surge of emotion moved through her as she realized how many of those in the room were among the people that she held most dear.

"Okay, okay, everyone ready?" Carly exclaimed softly, and she shoved the door open.

J.R. and Audrey stood just outside the door, and J.R. had just reached out for the handle when the door popped open on its own, so his hand remained frozen in midair. Both of them looked as if they'd been shot at, and Audrey's porcelain face broke into a knowing smile when she saw Carly waiting for her inside the English Rose ballroom.

"*Sur-priiiiise!!*" their friends shouted, and each of them tossed handfuls of rose petals at the newly married couple.

Audrey brashed the petals from her hair as she grabbed Carly and tugged her into an embrace. "You said it was a party for Emma and Jackson!" she cried. Then to Kat, over Carly's shoulder, she added, "But I had a feeling."

"Well, we had to celebrate," Kat replied with a giggle. "Let's see the rings."

Audrey beamed as she fanned her hand around the semicircle of onlookers, and all of the woman ooohed and ahhhed over the striking band of diamonds. Emma looked at J.R. just as he reluctantly waved his hand one time to display a dark Tungsten carbide band framed in platinum. A tough ring for a tough guy. Emma thought it completely suited him.

"Beautiful," she said as Audrey's hand reached her, and she picked a rose petal from the shoulder of the striking military-style jacket embellished with silver chains and buckles that Audrey wore over black jeans.

Audrey's amber eyes wandered over to the cake display, and she laughed. "Where on earth did you get that topper?"

"Carly found it. Darling, isn't it?"

"J.R., look at that! We're on top of an Emma Travis cake!"

"Immortalized," J.R. remarked, and he leaned in to plant a kiss on Emma's cheek. "Now we've made it."

"It's a beautiful cake, Emma," Audrey told her. "I can't wait to see yours. What's it going to look like?"

Emma cringed, and Fee let out a cackle.

"Better to avoid that subject," Sherilyn warned.

"Oh." Audrey grinned at Emma. "Okay, then!"

J.R. embraced his brother Devon and muttered something quietly. Devon's eyes lit up as he grinned and nodded. "It's all good," he replied. "I've got my girl by my side, and a baby waiting at home. Now my wandering brother is settling down. I couldn't ask for anything more."

"Well, maybe one thing more," Carly teased. "Your wandering brother and his wife could settle permanently right here in Atlanta."

Audrey and J.R. exchanged meaningful glances before looking back to Carly and Devon.

"No way," Devon declared. "Bro!"

"Yep. The movers arrive with my things next week," J.R. announced. "We've rented a storage locker for it, and we'll both be living in Audrey's Buckhead loft until we can find a house out here toward Roswell so we can be close to all of you."

Several sets of eyes bore down on Jackson at that, and Sherilyn was first to pipe up. "Well, you might want to rethink that. It seems The Tanglewood is changing hands very soon."

"What?" J.R. exclaimed as Sherilyn's eyes misted over with tears. He immediately looked to Jackson for confirmation. "You wouldn't, right?"

"It seems that he would," Sherilyn remarked, leaning in to Andy's side.

Jackson squirmed a little next to Emma, and she spouted, "Why don't we keep on topic here! Let's pour that cider and toast the happy couple."

"I think we can tell them," Jackson said, smiling at her. "Don't you?"

"If you're sure."

Jackson extended his arm toward Sherilyn. "Come over here, Red. I want you right next to me when we give y'all the news."

Sherilyn raised one eyebrow and her gaze darted to Emma. It only took a nod for Sherilyn to rush to Jackson's side, and he placed an arm around her shoulder and pulled her in close to him.

"Emma and I decided to turn down the offer on the hotel," he said, and before he could take a follow-up breath, Sherilyn snaked her arms around his neck and squealed over the cheers and clapping hands around them.

"Wait, wait a minute! What about your year in Paris?" Fee asked. "And the whole idea of kicking back and taking life a little slower for a while?"

"Well, we can't very well leave the country for a year now," he said. "But we're hoping for a delayed honeymoon to France at some point toward Christmas."

Fee countered with a half-glare at Emma over the top of her rectangular black glasses. After such a long time, Emma could read Fee like a familiar book.

"I'm going to take steps to relieve some of the stress, Fiona. For both of us. And you'll like this part of the plan. After the wedding, we're going to hire another pastry chef. And I'm going to cut my schedule back a bit."

J.R. looked from Audrey to Emma. "What'd I miss?"

"Emma has been having some health challenges," Jackson told them, and Sherilyn leaned around him and gawked at Emma.

"What kind of health challenges? Why haven't you told me this?"

"Can we please just stay on point here?" Emma asked them with a laugh. "We are keeping the hotel, we're hiring some additional staff, and we are here to celebrate the marriage of two of our dearest friends!"

Sean handed Emma and Jackson glasses of sparkling cider that he had quietly poured, and he returned to Lisette for another couple of glasses that he then handed over to Sherilyn and Kat. When everyone had a glass in their hand, Carly stepped forward.

"Audrey has always been family to me," she said, and Audrey smiled at her. "But now she's actually my *sister-in-law*! And I couldn't be happier. Aud and J.R., you were so meant to be. I think everyone saw it, even before you did. And though we would have preferred a wedding here in town with all of your friends in attendance, I think I speak for everyone here tonight when I tell you that we wish you every happiness, every blessing, and every joy." Raising her glass, she added, "To Audrey and J.R."

Flutes clinked and good wishes flowed, and they all drank to the future happiness of yet another happy couple brought together under the roof of The Tanglewood Inn.

❧

"I hate to interrupt," Lauren said softly, and Jackson looked up to find just her head poking through the slightly open door.

As Rod continued his noisy diatribe on the other end of the phone, Jackson mouthed, "What is it?"

"It seems some hotel guests are trapped in the elevator."

Jackson waved his hand at her to draw her closer, and he plucked a business card from the messy Rolodex on his desk. "Call them, ask for Bobby," he whispered. "Tell him it's an emergency."

Lauren grabbed the card and hurried from the office, closing the door behind her.

"Rod, Rod, come on," Jackson exclaimed. "I have an emergency here. Gotta go, buddy."

"Don't you dare hang up on me, Drake. We're going to hash this out right now."

"There's nothing to hash out, Rod. I've made my final decision. I'm sorry. If Allegiant still wants to franchise, I'm in. But I'm not selling this—"

"You know they want the whole caboodle. They're not gonna go for it, Jack."

"Then I think the deal is off the table."

"Jack. Jack, you gotta be kidding me."

"Look, I'm sorry," he said, sincerely. "I've talked it over with Emma and we just don't think—"

"What, she's not even your wife yet and she's calling the shots?" Rod snapped. "Maybe I should have taken the meeting with Emma instead."

"Maybe so," Jackson replied calmly. "Or at least included her, because we come as a package deal. She wants to stay, and so do I."

"No one said you couldn't stay, Jack."

"Rod, look. I have hotel guests incarcerated in one of only two elevators in the hotel. I gotta go."

"No! Look, Jackson, we can talk about this . . ."

"Sorry, Rod. I really am."

And with that, Jackson disconnected the call. At first, he thought he heard Rod continue to rant after he hung up . . . until he realized the rant emanated from the hallway.

"Where is it? Where is Jackson Drake's office?"

Jackson popped up from his chair and rounded the desk. As he stepped out into Lauren's office, an angry man stormed through the door, his bulging eyes seeming to make an entrance before the rest of him.

"You Jackson Drake? The owner of this hotel?"

"Yes, I am. If you're here about the elevator, we've called the—"

"The elevator," he repeated, running a hand through the few strands of hair on his head. "No, what's wrong with the elevator? I'm here because one of your maids stole from me!"

"I'm sorry, I—"

"That's right, you're sorry. Meanwhile, what good will your sorry do me at the big rock?"

"The . . . rock?"

"Oh, Mr. Drake," Frank, the front desk manager on duty, wheezed as he stumbled into the office behind the bug-eyed rock collector. "I'm so sorry." He leaned over slightly and pressed one hand against the doorjamb as he tried to catch his breath. "Did you know the elevator is out? I had to take the stairs."

"Yes. We're on it."

Jackson looked to Lauren, and she covered the phone receiver long enough to tell him, "Bobby is out sick. I'm on hold for his assistant."

His head spinning a little, Jackson looked back to the crisis at hand.

"I tried talking to this joker," the bald man spouted, pointing at Frank. "But he won't do a thing to bring the thief to justice. And I'll sue this place, Drake!"

"Mr. Schmidt," Frank interrupted, standing upright at last. "I had the housekeeping staff comb your room, and—"

"It's not in my room, I told you that."

"But it was. They found your camera under the bed, sir."

Schmidt looked for a few seconds like he might choke on his own tongue. Then he curled his face up and grunted. "Oh, sure they did. It was under the bed, was it?"

"If you'd like me to place your camera in the hotel safe for security's sake, I can certainly—"

"Not on your life, Joe. Besides, I need it today when we go to the rock."

Jackson glanced at Frank, who clued him in. "Stone Mountain."

"Ah," he said with a nod. "So where is Mr. Schmidt's camera right now?"

"We're holding it for you at the front desk, sir."

"I'll just bet you are," the man cracked, and he stomped out of the office.

"I'm sorry about that, Mr. Drake."

"It's fine. Let's comp the Schmidts for one night, Frank."

The manager tried to disguise his astonishment before shrugging. "Okay. I'll take care of it."

Just as Frank departed, Jackson's attention flipped over to Lauren as she jumped up from her desk, yanked a sterling silver cuff from her ear, pressed the phone to her head, and shouted, "Listen to me! We have people trapped in the elevator, and we cannot wait for someone to get out here. The Tanglewood Inn is a customer of yours, and Bobby has provided such stellar service that he's become a personal friend of the owner, Jackson Drake. I don't think he'll be too happy when I call him at home and tell him how you're mishandling one of his prime accounts, do you?"

Jackson arched both eyebrows and folded his arms as he observed Lauren in action.

"An hour?" she exclaimed. "I'm thinking twenty or thirty minutes, aren't you, Josh? . . . Good. I'll hold off on calling Bobby, but I want you to know I have him on speed dial and it won't take much of a delay to get me to hit that button . . . Yes. All right. I'll see you then."

She heaved a sigh as she hung up the phone and shook her head, replacing the ear cuff and raking back her multitoned hair. She started when she caught Jackson's gaze.

"Oh. I'm sorry. I just—"

"Lauren," he told her, "I think you and I need to talk later. You, young lady, are a force of nature."

Her worried expression ignited into a full-on grin. "Thank you."

"Now I'm headed down the hall to put out some fires. I sense a few more comp rooms in my immediate future."

❧❧❧❧❧❧❧❧❧❧❧❧❧❧❧❧❧❧

TO: Jackson Drake, Hotel Owner
FROM: Sherilyn Drummond,
Event Planning–Weddings

RE: Reminders

Hi, Jackson, it's Kat. Just a few quick reminders about the following.

✓ The final fitting for your tuxedo is scheduled for
tomorrow at 4:30.
Andy will meet you there for his fitting as well.

✓ I think you were supposed to pick up the
wedding bands from the engraver last week.
Sherilyn mentioned that you might need a reminder.

✓ I have the honeymoon suite booked for you
the night of the wedding.

And I did receive an e-mail confirmation yesterday from
the caretakers at the Travis family home in Savannah.
They will have the pantry stocked and the house ready
for your arrival the day after the wedding, staying for a week.
If there are any particular requests, just let me know
and I'll get the information to them.

Shout if there's anything additional you need. —Kat

❧❧❧❧❧❧❧❧❧❧❧❧❧❧❧❧❧❧

17

*O*h, Mother, there's no use telling her. She'll forget all about it tomorrow."

"I don't know," Emma's mother replied, shaking her head. "She's stayed with this for days now."

"Has she?"

"Yes, she went on about it for an hour over dinner last night, telling your father how thrilled she is that you've asked her to be your maid of honor. Then this morning, she insisted I take her to shop for a dress."

Emma couldn't resist chuckling. "I love her so much."

"And she loves you, dear heart. But will Sherilyn still love you when she gets to the ceremony to find your aunt Sophie standing at the front beside you?"

"I'll bet Sherilyn would hand her the bouquet!"

"Okey dokey, smokies!" Sophie called in a giddy voice from beyond the silk curtain of the dressing room. "Are you two ready to have a look-see?"

"We can't wait, Aunt Soph. Come on out!"

The attendant assisted Sophie as she stepped out and crossed to the center of the boutique sitting room. She gazed at the round pedestal for a moment before gripping the attendant's arm as if she were climbing a steep hill.

Emma hopped up and hurried to her, taking her other arm. The two of them practically lifted her aunt off the ground, and Sophie grinned from ear to ear from her perch atop the pedestal.

"Step back," she told Emma as she swept the full-length skirt of the pastel gown. "What do you think?"

"Well, I don't know, Aunt Soph," Emma said seriously, shaking her head. "If you don't mind upstaging the bride . . ."

Sophie giggled. "Oh, no one could do that, sweet girl."

Emma touched her aunt's hand and sighed. Muted watercolor flowers in yellows, pinks, and greens screened atop lilac satin created a stunning gown, and the rich lavender lace jacket with rhinestone buttons accentuated her aunt's fragile frame.

"You look exquisite," Emma told her aunt as tears glazed her eyes. "I'm so happy you'll be there with us."

"I haven't missed any of your weddings to Jackson, Emma Rae," she declared, and Emma chuckled.

"You're very faithful, Aunt Sophie."

"For the next one, I was thinking about a cathedral," she said, preoccupied with her reflections in the full-length mirrors. "That might be nice, don't you think?"

"I'm not really an ornate, cathedral-type of girl. But it sounds lovely."

"Well, we'll just have this simple one first and think about that next time."

Emma glanced at her mother, who sat regally on the jacquard-upholstered couch in the corner.

"Okay, Aunt Soph." Emma kissed her cheek before helping her down from the pedestal. "I think this is definitely your dress."

"I think so, too. Will it match the flowers?"

"Perfectly."

The attendant grinned at Emma before leading Sophie back toward the dressing room.

"Mother," she said as she sat down next to Avery, "don't look so worried. She's relatively healthy, and she lives in a constant state of bliss."

"Yes, she does."

"What more could any of us ask?"

Avery took Emma's hand and rubbed it. "You are a charming daughter, Emma Rae."

"Of course I am. We're a charming lot, we Travis women."

Her mother laughed and pecked Emma's cheek. "That we are."

❧

"Well, I just wanted you all to hear it directly from me." Jackson balanced his cell phone on his shoulder as he climbed out of his car and locked the door. "You'll share the news with the other hens?"

"Jackson! Don't call us that," Norma said on a chuckle.

He laughed in reply.

"I don't have to tell you how happy I am with your decision, but I just want to make sure you're happy with it."

He shrugged. "As happy as I can be when turning down a quick fortune."

"Oh, that wasn't the response I'd hoped for."

"I love The Tanglewood, Norm. But I love Emma more. She's tired—*really tired*—and I think I started to really invest in that dream we had of moving away for a year and just getting lost in each other and our marriage. Keeping the hotel makes that an impossibility, and it's always a little difficult to watch a dream swirl down the drain."

"You couldn't still go? Maybe orchestrate a team of support so you could still chase that dream?"

"Really?" he asked as he pulled open the door to the jewelry store. "Leave the day-to-day to . . . who? You? Are you volunteering?"

Norma chuckled. "Okay, I see your point. A little complicated. But you'll still go to France, Jack. Just not for a whole year, not without ties back to Georgia."

"Right."

"And you can live with that?"

"I can live with Emma."

"And that makes everything all right, doesn't it?"

"You know, it does."

The woman behind the glass counter of bling reminded Jackson of Susannah, and he paused to wonder when she might return.

"Listen, sis, I've gotta go. You'll spread the good word?"

"The minute we hang up. Love you."

"Love you, too."

Jackson closed the phone and placed it in the breast pocket of his suit jacket.

"Good afternoon," the saleswoman greeted him.

"Hello. I left two wedding bands to be engraved, and I'd like to pick them up."

"Certainly. Your name?"

"Drake."

"All right, Mr. Drake. Let me just look in the back room."

Jackson took the opportunity to browse the glass cases. Only two other customers occupied the store, a very young couple shopping for an engagement ring.

"Something reasonable," the potential groom whispered. "You know what I mean?"

"Yes, sir," the clerk assured him. "We have some very nice solitaires over here."

They walked past him, and Jackson's gaze landed on a display of pendants. One of them caught his eye right away, a small amethyst cross with two diamond wedding bands, entwined and laid over the cross.

"May I see this?" he asked the minute the saleswoman reappeared. "The cross, right there."

"Of course."

The woman, whose tag named her Veronica, reached under the counter. She produced the necklace and laid it on a flat display board covered with navy blue velvet. "It's stunning, isn't it?"

"It really is."

"It's a platinum setting with just under 1.5 carats of round amethysts, and another quarter carat of diamonds to form the wedding rings, on a beautiful 16-inch diamond-cut chain."

Jackson leaned down and took a closer look before lifting the necklace and dangling it from three fingers so that the light caught the stones. He peered at the price tag and deemed it worth the investment.

"I'd like to give this to my bride on our wedding day," he said with a smile. "Can you ring this up for me?"

"It's a lovely choice."

"And can I see the rings?"

"Well, actually, the rings aren't here."

Jackson blinked and swallowed hard. "What do you mean?"

"It appears that your fiancée picked them up two days ago."

"Oh." He chewed on that for a moment. "I thought that was my job."

"Maybe she was in the area? Thought she'd do you a favor?"

He chuckled. "More like she didn't trust me to remember."

Veronica grinned. "I wasn't going to say that. But I do meet a lot of brides and grooms."

"I guess you're somewhat of an expert, aren't you?"

"I'll ring up your pendant. Would you like it gift-wrapped?"

"No, thank you," he told her. "Just set it in one of your velvet boxes?"

"And what card would you like to use?"

Jackson pulled out his wallet and handed over his Visa. While Veronica finalized the purchase, he opened his cell phone and dialed Emma. It went to voice mail just as the saleswoman motioned to him to come and sign the receipt.

He tucked the phone back into his pocket as she said, "Your fiancée is sure to love this gift, Mr. Drake. She's a very lucky woman."

"I'm the one on the long end of this deal," he said, scribbling his name. "I just want to make sure she knows *that I know*."

Jackson got back to the hotel an hour before his next meeting, and he decided to take a stroll into Emma's kitchen and check in.

Fee stood at the end of a line of several virtual strangers stretched along the length of the worktable while two others, one of them an apron-clad guy with blue streaks in his hair, fussed with something in one of the ovens. He figured these were the interns Emma often spoke about.

"It's a delicate balance," Fee told them. "To get it just right, you have to—" She cut herself off as she noticed Jackson. "Hey, Jackson. Everyone, this is our resident big cheese. Jackson Drake owns The Tanglewood."

"Hello!"

"Emma and Kat are in her office," Fee pointed out, but he'd already seen them through the glass and started on his way toward them.

"Thanks, Fee."

Emma looked up when he opened the door, and Kat grinned at him. "Speak of the man himself."

"Am I interrupting?"

"It's wedding talk," Emma told him. "I think you can come in."

He sat down next to Kat. "Topic?"

"My aunt Sophie. She seems to be under the impression that she is the maid of honor for this, our umpteenth wedding."

Jackson chuckled. "And you want me to break the news to Sherilyn."

"No." Emma shot him a lopsided smile. "I'm asking Kat to order another bouquet so that I can make sure she has one, too."

"That's a nice idea."

"It is," Kat said. "So it got us to thinking about ways to incorporate a few of the family members. Emma has come up with a really lovely idea, and we're just working out the details."

"I'll leave you both to it, then. Just tell me where to be, and when. I think that's my role as the groom, according to Sherilyn. Correct?"

"Basically," Kat replied.

Jackson got up and started out the door, and then he paused. "Oh. Emma. Did you pick up the rings from the engraver?"

She groaned. "I knew you'd forget!"

"I didn't forget, *oh ye of little faith*," he defended. "I was just later than planned."

"But you have them now."

"No. You do."

"I don't."

"Yes, you do."

"Jackson," she said, standing up. "I do not have the rings."

"They told me you picked them up a couple of days ago."

"Well," she laughed uneasily, "I didn't."

Jackson and Emma both looked at Kat, and she jumped. "Well, I didn't either!"

Emma dropped slowly to her chair and stared straight ahead of her, at nothing in particular. After a moment, her hands popped to either side of her head, and she rubbed her temples. The action had become a recent cue for Jackson.

"Okay, okay," he said as he squeezed around the desk and grabbed her by the arm. He gently nudged her to her feet and led her toward the door. "Kat, you'll look into this for us, won't you?"

"Uh . . . yes! Absolutely."

"I am going to take this sweet girl to Morelli's for a snack and a nice hot cup of tea."

"Great idea."

"No, I . . ." Her objection fell to the floor, and she surrendered, allowing Jackson to lead her out into the kitchen.

Fee followed them to the other door. "Emma, I think Sharona is a good bet for the new position. Do you want to talk to her when—" She fell silent and looked up at Jackson. "Is she all right?"

"Talk to Kat."

His arm around Emma's waist, Jackson led the way to the restaurant and smiled at the hostess.

"Good afternoon," she said, straightening when she saw them.

"A cup of coffee and a pot of tea, Lucy? We're just going to take that table over there."

Emma sat down, and he slipped into the chair across from her.

"Are you breathing?" he asked, and she nodded. "Good. Can you speak?"

She blinked before narrowing her eyes and glaring at him. "Yes, Jackson. I can speak."

"Okay. Just checking."

"What do you suppose happened to our rings?" she asked. "It's not like we have the time to replace them before the wedding."

"We won't have to replace them. Kat's going to find out that they were just misplaced at the store, or accidentally given to another couple, *the Blakes*, who will be returning them to correct the mistake any time now."

"The Blakes?"

He shrugged. "Blake, Drake. You can see how it could get confusing."

Emma snorted and tapped his hand. "You're crazy."

"Maybe so, but at least I'm not Tom Blake, coming home with someone else's rings, right?"

She sighed, and a smile wiggled its way across her face. "Thank you."

"For what?"

"You know."

"Making you laugh?"

"Yes."

"Well, I'm a very funny guy, missy. You'll be laughing your fanny off for the next sixty or eighty years."

"Oh. Good," she said sarcastically before pulling a face and giggling. "Can I talk to you about the wedding?"

"As long as you don't say anything about the rings."

"I promise." She reached across the table and touched his hand. "I had this kind of cool idea about honoring our family members during the ceremony, and I want to see what you think."

She'd only just begun to explain when Kat appeared at the head of their table. Her frazzled expression didn't bode well for his attempts at alleviating the stress of the moment.

"Nothing?" Emma asked her.

"They've checked the back room, and the rings are definitely not just misplaced. They're not anywhere in the store."

"Oh, no . . ."

"But someone did sign for them two days ago, and she's going to fax the receipt over to me so we can see the signature."

"Okay."

"Stay calm," Kat said as Lucy delivered a tray of beverages to the table.

"We have that herbal chamomile you like," Lucy declared, and Emma gave her a smile.

"Is Pearl in yet?"

"Yes. She's in the kitchen with Mr. Morelli."

"Could you do me a favor, please? Ask her if she wouldn't mind making me another fruit bowl like she makes for me sometimes? It has grapefruit in it, and little graham crackers on the side."

"I'll ask her right away."

"Thank you, Lucy."

"Sure thing."

"Drink your tea," Kat told her. "Relax. By the time you're finished, I'll bet we'll have some answers."

"But did she say—"

"Emma," Jackson said, squeezing her hand, "you heard Kat. Relax, and she'll do the investigating for us."

The look on Kat's face as she left the table set the acid to churning in Jackson's gut, but he didn't let on when Emma glanced up at him.

"Everything is going to be fine. Finish telling me about your idea for the ceremony."

"Well, that tears it!" she exclaimed, leaning against the chair back with a sigh. "I've ruined you."

"What are you talking about?"

"You've got that look in your eye. The one we all get when we're trying to cut through my aunt's crazy talk without making her panic."

"Is it working?" he asked.

"Little bit. Yeah."

~~~~~~~~~~~~~~~~~~~~~~~~~~~~~~~~

Emma's Afternoon Fruit Bowl Snack

[Note. Also serves well with an omelet for a full meal.]

2 cups red grapefruit sections, chilled
1 banana, sliced
¼ cup walnut pieces
1 tablespoon fresh mint, chopped
1 tablespoon honey

Drain the juice from the grapefruit, setting aside
a small amount.
Combine all ingredients except the honey and the juice.
Stir the small amount of juice into the honey until
it looks like a glaze.
Toss gently, and drizzle the top with the honey
glaze mixture.
Serve in a chilled bowl.

~~~~~~~~~~~~~~~~~~~~~~~~~~~~~~~~

18

$\mathcal{K}$at rushed into Emma's office, preceded by the paper she waved frantically.

"Crisis averted," she declared, and she plopped into the chair across from Emma. "Our culprit is Sherilyn. She was afraid Jackson had forgotten, so she picked up the rings."

"You're joking."

"I knew the minute I saw the signature, so I called and verified with her. She has them in a very safe place, and Andy will pass them to Jackson."

"Thank the Lord!" Emma breathed, and she fell back against her chair. "Did she say why she didn't bother to let anyone know she had them?" Before Kat answered, Emma waved her hand. "Never mind. It doesn't matter."

The phone on her desk rang, and Emma groaned. "This thing hasn't stopped all day."

"I'll go," Kat said as she stood up.

"Thanks for letting me know," Emma said as Kat left. Snatching the receiver, she pushed a smile into her voice. "Emma Rae Travis."

"Emma, it's Audrey."

"Hi. How's married life?"

"So far, so good. Do you have a minute?"

"Sure," she lied. The truth was she didn't have ten spare minutes in the rest of the workday.

"You're going to get a call sometime this week from a woman named Valerie Platt. I told her about you over lunch today. She puts on a huge fashion event in Atlanta every year, and they're interested in having a specialty cake designed, as well as an enormous dessert table. I told her you are the only one she should talk to."

Emma's stomach dropped a little. "When is this event?"

"Not until late fall." *Thank God.* "The event gets a ton of press, and I thought it might be a nice opportunity for you."

"I appreciate that," she said as her head began to throb.

"I'm going to be there showing a spring preview for Riley."

"That's great."

"Anyway, if you have any trouble with her, or you need anything at all, give Billie a call and she—"

"Billie?"

"Oh. My assistant."

"I didn't know you'd replaced Kat."

"Kat is irreplaceable," she said with flourish. "But she left me no choice when she went out there and made a name for herself, the ungrateful thing."

Emma chuckled. "I know. She's that way."

"I stole Billie from Wes LaMont last year."

"Oh, that horrible designer who tried to steal your ideas."

"Didn't try, Emma. He succeeded. The good news is that his *Rubenesque* line has been a great big flop. Probably because he clearly couldn't stand the women he designed for. Anyway, just call Billie if you need anything, and I'll see you tomorrow."

"Tomorrow?"

"At Sherilyn's. Your slumber-shower." Emma's silence set Audrey to laughing. "Oh, Emma, you forgot all about it, didn't you?"

"Don't tell Sherilyn."

"I promise. Will I see you there, then?"

"If I have to crawl."

Just as she hung up, Fee stepped in and closed the office door behind her.

"I have a present for you."

Emma looked up, bewildered. "A present?"

Fee held up a small plastic box with a crooked bow taped to the top, which she slid across the desktop as she sat down. "Open."

Emma popped the lid and stared down at it. A large, strange-looking watch? "What is this?"

"A portable blood pressure cuff. You just strap it on like a watch, press the gray button, and it will tell you if you're about to have a stroke. Handy, huh?"

Emma couldn't hold back the string of stress-induced chuckles that bumped out of her. "A stroke, you freak? You're worried about my stress levels and my blood pressure, and you put that thought in my mind?"

"Shut it," Fee told her, and she stood up and leaned across the desk. "Let's take it out for a spin on its maiden voyage, shall we?"

Before Emma knew what happened, Fee had strapped the thing to her wrist and pushed the button.

"Stop it. I can do it."

"I'm sure you *can*. But *will* you?"

As the monitor ticked through the numbers, Emma smiled at Fee. "Thank you, Fiona. It's a very thoughtful gift."

"It is, isn't it?"

The moment the thing beeped at the finish, Fee accosted Emma's wrist and looked at the reading.

"I suspected as much."

"What? What is it?"

"164 over 99, Emma. This is way too high. What are your blood sugars doing? Have you had anything to eat?"

"Fiona, I know you're trying to help, but—"

"Just answer the question. Do you need something to eat?"

"No. I do not."

"What's your glucose?"

"An hour ago, it was 107."

"All right, then it's just your pressure."

"I started blood pressure meds recently. It really shouldn't be that high," Emma admitted, tapping the face of the wrist monitor.

"Smack it all you want. I don't think it's lying."

Emma's cheeks puffed with air before she blew it out and closed her eyes.

"Call your doctor, please."

Emma straightened, keeping her eyes closed. "I have an appointment with her tomorrow. Tell me about Sharona."

"Call your doctor, then I'll tell you all about how she's going to make your life much easier."

Emma opened one eye, and Fee pasted a huge mock-smile on her face.

"Call."

Reluctantly she picked up the phone and dialed.

"Stephanie? It's Emma Travis. Is Dr. Mathis still around?"

"She's with her last patient of the day, Emma. Is there something I can help you with?"

"I have an appointment with her tomorrow, so she may want to just wait until then. She put me on those blood pressure pills when I saw her last, but my reading is . . ." Looking at the face of the cuff, she read, "164 over 99."

"Eww."

"High, right?"

"Yes, that's high. Let me talk to her, and I'll call you back. Are you at home?"

"No. You can call my cell."

"Okay. Give me half an hour."

"Thanks, Steph."

Emma hung up the phone and glared at Fee. "Happy?"

"Giddy."

"Tell me about Sharona."

"She's top of her class at the institute, set to graduate in a couple of weeks. She excels in piping, fondant, and sculpting. Her sugar flowers are almost better than mine . . ."

"Wow."

"I said 'almost.'"

"Right. I got that."

"And we have a good working chemistry. I think the three of us could be a really good team, Emma."

"Okay. I'll talk to her. Will you set it up?"

"She's in tomorrow morning to help with the tearoom menu. We've got a group of twenty coming in at two o'clock."

"Did I know that?"

"Yes."

"Oh, good. Hey, while I'm thinking of it, Audrey has referred us to someone handling a big fashion deal in Atlanta in the fall." Emma checked the notepad next to her phone. "Valerie Platt."

"I'll be on the lookout."

"Speaking of which, did you know Audrey has a new assistant?"

"Billie. I had breakfast with her and Kat yesterday."

"You did?"

"Yeah. She's cool."

"How do you have time to have breakfast with people? It took me two days to schedule an argument with Jackson."

Fee cackled as she got up and headed for the door. "Last chance. Get you something to eat?"

"No. I'm fine."

"Wait for that call back from your doctor."

"Have you always been this much of a nag?"

"No. It's something new I'm trying."

"Well, I don't like it."

"Yes, you do. You just won't realize it until it wears on you a little more."

⁘

It looked to Emma like she might be the last to arrive at her own bridal shower, but her appointment with Dr. Mathis had taken far longer than she'd anticipated. They'd gone over the results of the labs, talked about adding a few supplements to her diet, and discussed possible nutritionists.

She pulled up in front of Andy and Sherilyn's house, hugging the curb while trying not to drive too far into the grass. Several other cars already filled the driveway and lined the street beyond the mailbox. As she climbed out of her Mini Cooper and grabbed the knapsack and purse from the floor, she spotted Andy making his way across the lawn wearing a funny pink bulging sack strapped across his chest.

"Is that my little Isabel in there?" she called with a grin as they closed the gap between them.

"Either that, or I need to go on a diet," he retorted, patting the sack where Isabel's diapered fanny pressed against it.

"That's a good look for you," she said with a nod toward the duck-covered diaper bag hanging from his shoulder. "Can I take a peek at her? I'll be quiet about it."

"Of course. And no need to be quiet. This little one could sleep through a Def Leppard concert."

"Tested that out, have you?"

Andy chuckled. "We're still on Seger. Working our way up the decibels."

Emma tickled Isabel's cheek with one finger and cooed at the sleeping baby. "She's beautiful, Andy."

"She's all Sherilyn."

Her heart squeezed a little at the genuine love Andy had for her best friend, and she clicked her tongue and smiled. "Has the party started yet?" she asked, and she tossed her knapsack over one shoulder.

"Has it ever. Go on in."

Emma adjusted the strap slipping from Andy's shoulder. "Are you running away from home for the night?"

"Giving my mother a little face time with her granddaughter."

"Send my best."

"Will do. Have fun."

Emma made her way to the front door and turned the knob. The moment it opened, Sherilyn stood there beaming at her.

"The bride is here," she called out over her shoulder before moving in for an enthusiastic embrace. "Let the slumber-shower commence."

"I love your husband," Emma said as Sherilyn placed a gawdy plastic tiara made out of rhinestones and pink feathers on her head.

"And now I love Jackson again, too."

Emma clucked at the joke. Jackson had returned to Sherilyn's good graces with the about-face on the sale of The Tanglewood. He could rest easy now, and all was right with the world.

Greetings crashed into and over one another as Emma stepped out into the great room, where most of her favorite females had gathered in her honor. Her mother and Aunt Sophie; Jackson's sisters Madeline, Georgiann, and Norma; Pearl and Fee; Audrey and Kat; and . . .

"*Hildie?*"

"Hey, Emma!"

"What in the world . . . ?"

"Fee asked me."

"And your foster family was good with it?"

"Yeah."

Fee shrugged casually. "I thought the kid could use a break from civilization."

Sherilyn laughed as she chided, "Are you saying we're uncivilized, Fee?"

"Yeah. A little."

A line of women took turns hugging Emma as she moved inside, dropped her bags, and sat down on the sofa next to Hildie.

"How's it going for you?" she asked, placing an arm around the girl's shoulder.

"Okay."

"Do you like your new school?"

"It's okay."

"Made any new friends? And *do not* say they're *okay!*"

Hildie giggled. "There's this one kid who's pretty cool. Her name is Bethany, and she's pretty good at skateboarding."

"Yes, and what about the family where you're staying? Are they *okay*, too?"

"They're all right. I mean, they sort of have the family thing down already, so it's like I'm trying to jam my squareness into their roundness, you know?"

"I think I do," Emma replied, grinning at Fee over Hildie's shoulder. "But give it some time. They're going to fall in love with you eventually, just like we did."

"Yeah, that's what Fee said."

"Dude," Fee added, ruffling Hildie's curly hair. "You've got lovable written all over you."

"Yeah," Hildie cracked. "I know."

Sherilyn cranked up the stereo on her way toward Emma, shaking her hips as she lip-synched along with Bob Seger's song, "Her Strut."

"Really?" Emma said dryly as Sherilyn danced in front of her. "This is what's ahead of me tonight?"

"We've already laid down the law," Norma announced. "Some of us have brought alternative music for after the shower, when the wusses in the room leave us behind and the slumber portion commences."

"My sister just called me a wuss," Georgiann remarked, and Avery touched her hand.

"It's all right. The non-wusses have to stay in sleeping bags while the wiser ones of us go home and sleep in our own beds."

"What is a wuss, anyway?" Sophie asked, and Emma laughed.

"It's a very, very wise person, Aunt Soph."

"Anyway, we've got a wide variety of music," Norma said. "From Brandon Heath . . ."

"I love Brandon Heath!" Kat exclaimed.

". . . to Casting Crowns . . ."

"My contribution," Pearl chimed in.

". . . and I think Fee brought some classic oldies, right?"

Emma knew Fee's musical tastes well. They'd spent many a late night in their kitchen, bopping around to the likes of the Kinks, the Temptations, and the Four Tops while finishing off a wedding cake or a selection of delectables for the tearoom.

"Excellent!" she said, and Emma jumped to her feet as she and Fee exchanged their traditional "secret handshake": Tap-tap of their fists, then both palms upright . . . two slaps given . . . two more slaps returned . . . a couple of quick hip bumps . . . and "Hoo-yeah!" in unison.

"Hey!" Hildie piped up. "I want to learn that. Do it again!"

Sherilyn shook her head at them. "While these two initiate Hildie into their secret club, I'll just tell you all about the food. There's every snack known to mankind spread out on the table. There's a giant lasagna in the oven whenever we're ready, and some garlic knots and salad. And Fee has made a very appealing assortment of cupcakes that she has arranged into a cake."

"You did?" Emma asked her. "When?"

"Let's just say I am sleep deprived, so nobody keep me awake with snoring tonight . . ." And nearly the whole group joined Fee in the chorus. ". . . *Nor-ma!*"

"What?" Norma cried. "I do *not snore!*"

Pearl bent double with laughter, and Norma smacked her arm.

"So, let's get some drinks and some snacks, and open some presents!" Sherilyn suggested. As they all moved into action, Sherilyn leaned close to Emma and softly told her, "I love this part."

"The gifts? Yes, I know."

"Grab a snack. I got you some of the crackers you like with those light cheese wedges."

"Thanks. What are you having?"

"What do you think? There are chocolate chip cookies on that table."

"Ah. Well, that answers that."

"Emma, I think your purse is ringing," Hildie announced before stuffing an entire cookie into her mouth.

Emma pulled her cell phone from the front pocket of her bag and opened it, grinning.

"Did you call to check on me?" she asked Jackson.

"I wanted to hit you before all of that estrogen left you crazy and curled up in a ball in the corner," he teased. "Are you having a good time?"

"I got here late," she whispered, turning away from the group. "But it would appear that they started without me."

"I'm sure you'll catch up any minute. How did your appointment go?"

"Good. I have the name of a nutritionist to work with. The labs were good, but my glucose is a mess. We've increased the blood pressure meds for just a few months, but she thinks I may live. At least through the wedding."

"Good to know."

"I was just headed to the snack table," she said on a chuckle as Sherilyn tugged on her arm. "It looks as if the Falcons will be stopping by. There's enough food to feed every one of them! What about you? What are you having for dinner?"

"Chinese. Sean's coming over."

"Oh, sure. Chinese? Talk about someone collapsing in a corner at the end of the night. Estrogen's got nothing on Chinese takeout, Jackson."

"Yeah. But in a good way," Jackson retorted. Emma laughed, and Jackson softened as he said, "I love you."

"I love you, too. I have to work tomorrow, but I'll see you tomorrow night."

"Emma?"

"Yep?"

"Relax tonight. Have a good time."

"With my girls around me? Of course."

Jackson chuckled. "G'night."

Pure and Uncomplicated

19

"What's that?"

Emma looked up at Hildie, standing over her and staring down at the paper towel laid out on the tabletop.

"Oh. I was inspired."

"To draw a cake?" Hildie asked her. "When there's cupcakes and cookies all over the place?"

"Yeah. Crazy, right?"

"Kinda."

"Well, I've been a little cake-challenged lately, and the wedding is almost here and I haven't been able to settle on one design. I spoke to my fiancé earlier, and I was thinking how easy it is to be with him, and . . ." She quickly scribbled the words *Pure and Uncomplicated* underneath the paper towel drawing before finishing with ". . . he inspired this."

"Looks weird."

Emma looked up at her and raised one eyebrow. "What do you mean? It does?"

"Well, yeah. Is that a tree growing up the side?"

She took a second look at the cake and grimaced. "No," she defended. "It's a . . . branch. You know, like—" Cutting herself off, she sighed and leaned back in the dining chair. "Yeah, maybe you're right."

"Okay, ladies," Sherilyn called out from the other side of the great room. "It's time for more games! Come on over here, Em."

"Oh, goodie," Hildie muttered dryly. "More games."

"I know, right?"

"If this is a slumber-shower, when do we get to slumber? I'm kind of over the games."

Emma broke into laughter. "Whatever the game," she announced, "Hildie's on my team."

∽✑∾

"I appreciate your coming over, buddy."

"Well, when you nixed Andy's idea of a bachelor party—"

"Andy's idea of a bachelor party," Jackson pointed out, "is a poker game with the baby in a carriage in the corner and Henry noshing on the snacks when we're not looking."

"True enough. Anyway, I figured Chinese was the least I could do on the night of the bachelorette deal," Sean told him as he handed over a quart container of shrimp lo mein. "You want moo shu?"

"Yeah."

Sean dumped a glob of the pork and egg mixture on a plate, topped it with a fork, and slid it across the slick table toward Jackson.

"You get egg rolls?"

"Dude," Sean said, sounding a lot like his wife. "Duh."

"I wonder if that will happen to me."

"If what will happen?" Sean asked, pushing a wax packet at him with an egg roll sticking out of it.

"If I'll start to sound like Emma, the way you sounded like Fee just now."

A bright-white smile wound its way across Sean's dark face. "Yeah. You'll wake up one morning, out of the blue, craving cake or something. It happens before you know it."

"I look forward to it," he commented.

"Got anything to drink?"

"Water," Jackson said. "Maybe a Coke or two."

Jackson dug into the meal while Sean grabbed a couple of bottles of water from the refrigerator.

"Yeah, I didn't really anticipate all the ways she would impact my life," Sean said. "Like that kid, Hildie. I just thought Fee was a little crazy and it might pass, but before I knew it, we were both invested. I almost hope we pull it off."

"Pull what off?"

"Oh. Yeah. We're trying to adopt her."

Jackson coughed on the lo mein noodle stuck halfway down his throat and gawked at Sean with bulging eyes. "What? You're what?"

"Yeah, we met with that caseworker woman . . ."

"Mrs. Troy?"

"Yeah. Troy. And she's helping us work through the system."

"Does Emma know?"

"I . . . I don't know. I just assumed Fee would have told her, but maybe not. She's pretty close to the vest with this thing. She seems like she's got a duck's back, but she's invested in this."

"And how do you feel about it?"

"I'm learning to love the kid, to tell you the truth."

"Have you spent any time with her?"

"Yeah, a little," Sean replied, and he paused to show Jackson another container. "Sweet and sour chicken?"

"Nah, I'm good."

"We took her to the Braves game. Man, the kid really loves baseball."

"And the foster family is okay with this?"

"Oh, yeah. The Rameys are great."

Jackson dunked an egg roll into plum sauce and took a bite, chewing on it while he also nibbled on the idea of Fee and Sean adopting Hildie. If Emma knew, she surely would have mentioned it. He hadn't realized he was staring until Sean's smile twitched.

"What, man?"

"Fee as a mom," he stated. "That . . . boggles my mind."

"Yeah. I hear ya. But I think she's better suited to it than you'd suspect."

After they ate, they decided to go around the corner to shoot a game of pool at the sports bar Jackson used to frequent now and then to watch a game with his buddies, the ones he hadn't seen or talked to for months on end. He hadn't been to O'Hara's since before the hotel opening.

Sean cleaned up in the first two games, but Jackson pulled out a win for the third. They each ordered something to drink and watched the end of a soccer game on the corner TV screen before heading out.

"So how was it?" Sean joked before heading for his car. "Better than a bachelor party, right?"

"Oh, yeah."

Jackson slapped Sean's arm as they shook hands, and he still wore the parting smile as he stepped back into his house. It had been a great night. He'd forgotten how much time had passed since he had made time for a simple night out with a friend. Sean was great company, and spending time with him made Jackson think about his old friend Decker Stanton. He wondered if Decker and Felicity had responded to the wedding invitation.

Without much forethought, Jackson grabbed his cell phone and dialed Decker.

"My caller ID must be on the fritz," Decker declared as he answered. "It says Jackson Drake is calling, but that can't be. He dropped off the earth months ago."

"The rumors of my disappearance have been greatly exaggerated," he cracked. Maybe Emma wasn't the only one who had gotten a little lost in her work at the hotel.

"Man, how are you? Felicity just showed me the invitation to your wedding. You're finally marrying that girl, are you?"

"I thought I might."

"Glad to hear it, bro. We knew the first time you brought her out to tailgate that she was the one. Took your guff and gave it right back to you."

Jackson laughed at that, and, after about fifteen minutes of catch-up on the phone with Decker, he headed for the shower, still thinking about that day. He couldn't remember whom the Falcons had played, but he vividly recalled Emma jumping out of her seat and doing a happy dance with his friends when Ryan threw a forty-yard touchdown play. He'd found himself thinking how Desiree hadn't cared one iota about football, and the comparison between the two women had shaken him to the core.

Who would have thought then that we'd end up here? he wondered.

The tumble down Memory Lane sent him to a crash landing at the bottom of that dream he and Emma had just given up—the one where they packed up their new marriage and took it to Paris for a spell. He never really thought of himself as much of a romantic, but the nights they'd spent fleshing out the details of that dream had made him feel like one.

Now, he just felt like a weary, clashing combination of disappointed dreamer and the luckiest guy on the planet.

~

As they watched the second movie of the night, Henry, Sherilyn's massive Old English sheepdog, nuzzled Hildie's leg while she rested her head in Fee's lap where they sat on the floor, Fee braiding the girl's long, curly locks. Norma, Pearl, and Audrey occupied the sofa behind them, and Kat sprawled on the floor at the foot of the coffee table.

Sherilyn and Emma had moved to the dining room, where Emma made notes on gifts and the people who had given them. Sherilyn pushed the bows they'd removed from each present through a hole in a thick paper plate to form a ribbon bouquet.

"You don't have to talk about it if it makes you uncomfortable," Sherilyn told her quietly. "I mean, Jackson was married before. And I know *you* weren't always celibate. So I just wondered, you know, how you've waited such a long time for the wedding."

Emma chuckled. "I don't know. We both kind of renewed our faith in God at the same time that we found one another. It just seemed like that was the way it was supposed to go somehow."

"Do you regret waiting?"

"Aside from the sheer torture of it?" Emma asked with a grin. "No. I don't think either of us does."

"Do you wonder if you'll be . . . you know . . . *compatible*?"

"I can honestly tell you, Sher, I haven't had a moment's thought about that. Jackson is . . . everything."

Sherilyn's hand went immediately to her heart, and she rolled her head down to her shoulder and grinned. "That's so great. They say it's all in the kiss. Is he a good kisser, Em?"

"The best. Seriously, I've never kissed someone where I felt it all the way to my toes, the way they do in the chick flicks they're watching."

They glanced over at the group of women in the living room, enthralled with big-screen images of Tom Hanks and Meg Ryan. Sherilyn giggled at Emma.

"Sometimes I look at Jackson," she continued, "and I can't believe he wants to spend his life with me. I'm the luckiest woman on earth."

"After me."

"Yes. After you."

"So I guess you're pretty disappointed about not going to Paris, huh?"

Emma sighed and tossed the pen down on the pad of paper. "Yeah. We'd been building on this pipe dream for so long, and then it was suddenly something that could actually happen. You don't get over it so fast when something like that evaporates."

"But you get to keep The Tanglewood," Sherilyn encouraged her.

"And I'm so grateful about that, believe me. Jackson changed his mind all because of me. I know he didn't do that lightly, and I don't *take it* lightly. But I can't help choking a little on the thought of us holding hands, walking along the Seine, or sipping coffee and eating croissants in some charming little bistro."

"Other than the geography, you can do all those things right here, can't you?"

Emma thought about it. "Sure," she conceded. "Still."

"I know." Sherilyn completed the ribbon bouquet and extended it toward her. "Here ya go! A memento of your slumber-shower."

Emma grinned as she took the bouquet. "Thank you, Sher. Really. For everything."

Sherilyn hopped up from her chair and dove at Emma, rocking her in an enthusiastic embrace. "I love you so much, you know."

"I know."

"Come on," Sherilyn said, grabbing Emma's hand. "Let's make popcorn. The next movie is bride's choice. After that, we'll let these losers sleep on the floor and we'll sneak upstairs and crawl into the cushy California king in my room."

"Well, that's not fair," Emma said, following her into the kitchen. "Is it?"

"Sure it is. You're the bride, and I'm the hostess who just had a baby not so long ago."

"Are you still working that angle?"

"Until it runs through the last fume of gasoline."

Emma chuckled. Surrounded in the safety net of her friends, she felt a little ungrateful at even the slightest trace of remorse in the decision she and Jackson had made. The Tanglewood and all of its accoutrements spelled security and love and professional fulfillment. As she stood at the microwave next to Sherilyn, waiting for the last *Pop!* from the bag of kettle corn, Emma basked in the sheer delight of marrying Jackson and settling into life with him and the hotel and everything that came with it.

"It's going to be a good life!" she exclaimed to Sherilyn.

When she plucked the steaming popcorn bag from the microwave and shook it, Henry jumped up from a deep sleep and trotted into the kitchen to check it out.

"Em, it already is a good life," Sherilyn told her. "It can only go up toward *great* from here!"

Giggling, Emma teased, "*Grrrrr-eat!* You sound like Tony the Tiger."

"Hey. I like Tony. He was my first boyfriend, you know."

"I remember the stories. And that ratty old stuffed tiger you used to keep on your bed."

"This, from the girl who fell in love with Race Bannon," Sherilyn returned as they headed into the living room to join the others, Henry close at their heels.

"Who's Race Bannon?" Pearl asked.

"The hot guy from *Jonny Quest*."

"Dude. You just called a cartoon guy hot," Fee said.

"Hey, Race was hot," Emma defended, plopping down between Audrey and Norma on the sofa. "An ex-secret agent with muscular arms and white-blond hair . . . bodyguard and friend to Dr. Benton Quest, the greatest scientific mind in the world . . . tutor to Jonny and his friend Hadji . . . and always saving their little dog Bandit at the last possible moment . . ."

"Are you people serious?" Hildie called out, her eyes still closed, not moving a muscle. "These are cartoon guys you're talking about?"

They all broke up laughing.

"Oh sure," Emma said, dipping into the bag of popcorn. "Laugh it up, haters. But Race is still the coolest guy on the Cartoon Network."

"Norma, be sure to warn your brother what he's up against, will you?" Sherilyn joked. "Race is a pretty tough act to follow."

"Yeah," Emma cracked dryly. "Not like Tony the Tiger."

"Oh, hush!"

"From the cereal?" Hildie asked as she pushed her way upright. "Really?"

"Well, who do you crush on?" Emma asked her with a grin. "Justin Bieber? All he can do is sing. He's not out there saving the world and making it a better place, like Race."

"Justin Bieber?" Hildie rejected. "Not likely."

"Who, then?" Kat asked her. "Whose picture will go up on your wall? Nick Jonas? Zac Efron?"

"Please."

"Hildie likes a higher class of heartthrob," Fee remarked.

"Like who?" Emma asked.

"Johnny Depp."

"Ooh, Fee! The same as you," Emma exclaimed. Turning to the others with a smile, she added, "Fee *ah-dooores* Johnny Depp."

"You do?" Hildie asked her, and Fee shrugged one shoulder and gave a nod.

"No one these days is as handsome as Robert Redford in *The Way We Were*," Norma told them with a swoon.

"Yeah, but if we're going back in the day," Audrey chimed in, "I think Humphrey Bogart was The Man."

"I like Clooney," Kat added as she plucked a handful of popcorn out of Emma's bag. "George is dreamy."

"I know who Sherilyn's crush is," Emma teased, and she sang his name. "Jon *Bon Jo vi*."

"Oooh, yeah," Norma said, nodding enthusiastically.

"Norma! You surprise me," Emma said with a giggle.

"Jon transcends generations, diversity, and tastes," Sherilyn pointed out as she stole a handful of popcorn. "He's been with the same woman for, like, thirty years, he's a philanthropist, and he's a gifted musician."

"And he looks good in jeans," Emma cracked.

"Well, there's that," Audrey quipped.

"You know who I think is cute," Pearl piped up. "Joel Osteen."

Silence boomed as the women exchanged curious glances.

"You mean . . . the *television preacher*?" Kat exclaimed.

"Yeah. I mean, he has such a nice smile."

"I don't think you're allowed to put Jon Bon Jovi and Joel Osteen in the same conversation," Fee pointed out. "It's in the Book of Isaiah somewhere."

"Who's your current-day Race Bannon, Emma?" Kat asked.

Emma pulled a very thoughtful face for a moment before singing, "Jack-son."

Groans, moans, and laughter all around inspired Henry to bark a few times to join in the fun, and the hum of idle chatter and the happy joking of Emma's friends morphed into a sweet melody for her.

These people, she thought, and she grinned and munched on popcorn as she looked around at them. *They're music to my ears.*

Interesting Wedding Trivia

❖ Although there is no law mandating that a bride must take the last name of her groom, over 70 percent of Americans polled think that she should.

❖ In many Eastern cultures, a white wedding dress is not worn because the color symbolizes mourning and grief.

❖ The wedding ring is placed on the third finger of the left hand because ancient cultures believed that the vein in that finger leads directly to the heart.

❖ The tradition of tossing rose petals at the bride's feet was derived from the intent of laying out a path toward a beautiful and prosperous future.

❖ The old adage "Three times a bridesmaid, never a bride" dates back as far as the sixteenth century. It was believed that if an unmarried woman had been a bridesmaid three times, she was doomed to remain single. However, if she served as a bridesmaid a seventh time, the spell was broken and she would at last be married.

❖ In Roman times, a small bun was broken above the bride's head at the end of the wedding ceremony, and during the Middle Ages the bride and groom would kiss over small cakes.
These traditions led to today's wedding essential: the wedding cake.

Note: Facts found at http://facts.randomhistory.com/interesting-facts-about-weddings.html

20

*E*mma's eyes fluttered open, burning as the morning sun poked at them from outside the window. She blinked several times to bring Sherilyn into focus on the other side of the bed. Instead, however, a large white blob looked back at her through a mop of unkempt hair.

"Morning, Henry," she muttered, and the dog panted at her. "Oh, man, Henry, did you ever hear of mouthwash?"

She turned and buried her face in her pillow and, as she did, something jingled. She jerked her head upright at the sound. Henry flinched at the same time, and the two of them lay there, face to face, eye to eye.

"What was that?" she asked him, but when she rolled over, the jingle sounded again, this time with the intensity of a clamoring alarm.

Clumps of silver sleigh bells were strapped to both of her ankles with elastic bands. As she moved, they clanked out a ballyhoo that sent Henry flying from the bed, out the door, and down the stairs.

Emma stood up and peered at herself in the mirror. In addition to the sound effects fastened around her ankles, she'd been wrapped in pink streamers and a bright feather boa, her messy hair held back by the previous night's plastic rhinestone tiara. She glared at her reflection for a closer look and discovered that block letters spelled out the word BRIDE in purple glitter on her forehead.

"Very funny, ladies," she called as she tromped down the hall to the stairs.

A stream of muffled giggles was the only reply.

"I scared the poor dog half to death, and that's on your heads," she continued as she descended the stairs. And through the hall she sang dry, one-syllable exclamations that synched with each jingling step. "Ha. Ha. Ha. Ha."

Sherilyn met her at the end of the hallway and handed her a steaming pink mug with a large purple flower on the side.

"English breakfast tea," she declared. "Cream, one packet of sweetener."

"Thank you," Emma replied as she took the mug. "Now help get me out of all of this."

"No," Kat said from the kitchen. "You have to wear it through breakfast."

"Well, at least let's tidy her up," Audrey suggested as she moved around behind Emma. "The loose tails of these streamers make her look like a mummy queen coming unraveled."

A sudden flash of light blinded her, and Emma blinked away the residual spots to find Sherilyn standing in front of her, camera phone in hand.

"Really?" Emma grumbled as she passed her by, Audrey scurrying after her, tearing off the ends of the crinkly pink streamers.

"For posterity," Sherilyn said with a grin. "Now what would you like for breakfast? There's a buffet fit for a bride on the counter."

Emma perked up as she inspected the various plates and bowls. She grabbed a large strawberry and popped it into her mouth. "Where are Fee and Hildie?"

"They had to go," Sherilyn told her. "Hildie has a soccer game today."

"Wow." Emma scratched her head beneath the tiara, making the tiara bounce up and down. "Those two are like peas in a pod, aren't they?"

She moved into the kitchen to check out the omelets Pearl and Kat turned out in a yummy assembly line. Norma rushed by with oven mitts on both hands and pulled a pan of fragrant cinnamon rolls from the oven.

"Oh, hey," Sherilyn said, tugging on Emma's arm. "Come sit down. I want to show you something."

Emma squeezed into the dining chair angled into the corner and folded one leg underneath her. Sherilyn scuffed another chair closer and held out her hand. A double ring box sat open on her palm, and Emma's heart began to race as she gazed at the familiar wedding bands.

"I picked them up for Jackson. Andy's going to take them to him, but I thought you might like to have a look first."

Emma smiled at her friend. "You scared us half to death, you know."

"I know. I'm sorry. I thought I was helping."

Emma snickered, then turned her attention to the rings. "They're beautiful though, aren't they?" Emma lifted Jackson's ring from the slot in the velvet box and examined the engraving on the inside of the band.

"I am my beloved's . . ."

Sherilyn plucked Emma's thin diamond band from the box and squinted.

". . . and my beloved is mine."

"I love that verse of Scripture." Norma had moved into the living room with a plate of food and sank down on the sofa. "Song of Solomon, right?"

Emma nodded, joining her on the sofa to show her the rings. "Jackson and I took that couples class at Miguel's church a while back. It was a study on purity and the sanctity of marriage. When we read that chapter, it just resonated for both of us."

Norma ruffled Emma's hair, then straightened the tiara on Emma's head as she grinned. Grabbing the end of the boa around Emma's neck, Norma wrapped it around herself so that it cloaked them both.

"I am so happy you've fallen in love with Jack," she said softly, and Emma dropped her head to Norma's shoulder. "You've changed him."

"Have I?"

"He's softer somehow, more in touch with his emotional side. And, of course, he's found his way back to God. That's all because of you, Emma."

"No, it's not," she said on a sigh. "And, you know, if I changed him, Norma, he changed me right back."

Norma squeezed her shoulder. "That's the way love works."

◈

Jackson had no plans to work on Saturday morning. In fact, he'd intended to just stop by his office for a few minutes to pick up his laptop after leaving it behind on Friday night, but the avalanche of paperwork beckoning his attention closed in on his sense of time. Two hours after he'd arrived, he was still sitting at his desk.

"Mr. Drake? I wasn't expecting you today."

He looked up to find Lauren standing in the doorway in tight jeans torn at the knee and a too-tight pink tank top over an even tighter black one. A large patch of exposed stomach poked out from beneath them, this time adorned by a full belly chain connected to her navel by a pierced ring.

"Yeah. You either," he replied. "What are you doing here?"

"Just as I was leaving yesterday, I got a call from Susannah Littlefield," she told him.

"Oh!"

"She's flying back to Atlanta today, and she's planning to come back to work on Monday. I wanted to make sure to clear things up so her desk is ready."

"Lauren," Jackson said, and his chair creaked as he leaned back into it. "Will you come in a minute? Sit down."

She ran a hand through her spikey hair and adjusted her butterfly barrette as she tentatively lowered herself into the chair across from him.

"What's your situation, Lauren?"

"My . . . situation?"

"Yes. Are you working as a temp for a reason? Are you looking for a permanent job?"

"I haven't been," she answered. "I kind of liked the flexibility of moving from one place to another."

"I see." Disappointment simmered inside him, and Jackson sighed. "A bit of a free spirit, then."

"Until I came here, anyway."

"Oh?"

"Well, I like it here, Mr. Drake."

"Jackson."

"The people are so nice, and I enjoy the work. It's something different all the time."

Jackson snickered. "And that's a good thing, huh, Lauren?"

She smiled at him and nodded. "For me, it is."

"Susannah Littlefield has been with me for many years," he explained. "Even before I bought the hotel. I don't know how to get along without her. But she plans to retire later this year, and I hope you might be interested in taking her place."

She looked stunned, a bit like a deer caught in the headlights of an oncoming car.

"Really?"

"Really. Is that something that interests you?"

She nodded, but no sound emerged from her open mouth. He could so clearly see the wheels turning in her head that he thought he almost heard the grind.

"That's a yes?"

She continued to nod, and then exclaimed, "Yes!"

"All right, then. Once Susannah gets back, I'd like to discuss it with her first. If she feels like it's a good fit as well, I'll contact the agency and talk to them about how to proceed. Then Susannah can begin training you, and you can stay on and work with her until she retires. How does that sound?"

Lauren stood up, looking down at him. "Thank you, Jackson."

"You're welcome."

He stood up as well, and then jumped a little when Lauren rounded his desk and plowed into him with a clumsy hug. "Really, I'm so happy to hear that you felt it too. The fit, I mean."

"Oh. Well. Good."

Just as he pulled back from her, Lauren placed her hand on his back—a little too low for comfort, in fact—and she . . . *squeezed*.

Looking up into his eyes with a strange and sultry smile, she cooed, "I just knew I wasn't imagining it, Jackson."

He narrowed his eyes and stared at her. It took about ten or twelve full seconds before it began to sink in, but then Jackson pushed away from the girl, fumbling as he quickly removed her hands from around his waist.

"Okay. Sit down again. Right now, over there. Sit down."

She shrugged, returned to the chair on the other side of the desk, and grinned at him as she wriggled down into it.

"Lauren."

He almost wanted to laugh, but he knew enough to realize how wildly inappropriate laughter would be in a situation like the one in which he was now stuck. He swallowed and took in a sharp breath of preparation.

"Lauren," he repeated.

"Yes, Jackson?"

"The fit I mentioned was purely professional. Do you understand what I mean?"

She thought it over and finally replied, "No. I don't think so."

"You realize I'm engaged to be married in a week, right?"

"Well. Yes. But when you said—"

"No," he interrupted. "Not at all. I meant that I thought you might fit here as my assistant, Lauren. Nothing more."

Again, she mulled over his words before responding. "Oh."

"So in light of what just happened, I think we can look at this as your last day here."

"What? Jackson, why?" she asked, fiddling with the chain around her stomach.

He sighed. "I think we both know why, but let me be clear. I'm flattered . . . and to be honest, a *little surprised* . . . but I can't hire someone who has feelings about anything other than doing a good job for me and for the hotel. Do you understand?"

"I . . . suppose . . ."

"So, thank you. And good-bye, Lauren."

"Good-bye?"

"Yes. Right now. Good-bye."

The girl stood up like a child who had just been sent to her room. She looked back at him from the doorway, and Jackson took care to keep his facial expression frozen and stern. But the instant after she'd grabbed her purse and marched out of the office, Jackson snickered unceremoniously.

"I just can *not* catch a break with assistants," he muttered, shaking his head before he laughed right out loud.

⤳❧

It took two full shelves to house all of Emma's prized recipes in their respective wooden boxes, labeled lovingly with a steady hand and a small bottle of white paint.

Cakes & Cupcakes

Pies & Desserts

Tearoom Fare

The laminated cards inside the boxes—many of them written in the shaky hand of her aunt Sophie or the round penmanship of her grandmother or scribbled by Emma and revised during trial-by-fire tests—were keepsakes that meant as much to Emma as that ring on her finger or her dad's favorite leather chair; in some ways, they meant even more.

Sherilyn had insisted that they be transferred to a computer disk in case of a disaster like theft or fire, but Emma still lovingly pulled out one of the acrylic display stands and attached a recipe card to it whenever she baked, even though most of them she knew by heart without even looking.

This new recipe, however, she had never used before. Aunt Sophie's Savannah Tea Cakes—cookies, in reality—had been staples of Emma's southern childhood. For some reason, they'd danced across her mind that morning when she caught a whiff of Norma's old-fashioned cinnamon rolls, and she arrived at the hotel intent on pulling the recipe card and putting together a test batch.

The tearoom had been scheduled for a party of twenty-six the following afternoon to celebrate the ninetieth birthday of Ellen Caldwell. The traceable Caldwell lineage reached back to the Civil War, and the family boasted Atlanta residence from then until now. In light of the fact that the tearoom had been chosen for the celebration, Emma thought the birthday girl would surely appreciate traditional southern fare such as Aunt Sophie's tea cakes. If they turned out well, she might pack up a few and take them with her to Sophie's when she went over later that day.

The original version of Nat King Cole's song, "Unforgettable," played on the small, bright-red radio on the recipe shelf, and Emma hummed along above the whir of her favorite commercial stand mixer.

Relaxation took many different forms for different people—for instance, her mother liked to paint; Aunt Sophie crocheted; Sherilyn munched on chocolate—but as for Emma . . . she spelled relaxation with a simple four-letter word.

B.A.K.E.

The textures, sounds, and fragrances of a baker's kitchen came together to form the ideal playground. Emma couldn't comprehend the thinking of anyone who didn't appreciate the seductive and attractive language of baking.

She dumped the soft, wet dough from the mixing bowl on the floured worktable and formed it into a large disk with her hands before transferring it to a sheet of plastic wrap. As she lovingly tucked away the edges, the kitchen door flapped open and Fee breezed in.

"Sorry I'm late," she said, shedding her jacket and purse and tossing them onto the chair inside the door of Emma's office.

"You're not late. I'm early. How was Hildie's soccer match?"

"Oh, I didn't go. I just had to drop her off so she had time to get ready for it."

Emma nodded, completing the secure wrapping of the dough as she walked it to the refrigerator.

"What are you making?"

"Savannah tea cakes," she replied, and she carefully placed the dough on the top shelf. "It chills for an hour or two before I can do anything with it. I remembered the recipe this morning and thought it might be right for Ellen Caldwell's birthday tea."

"Yeah, okay. Sounds good." Fee shrugged into an apron and fastened the ties. "I covered the red velvet in fondant yesterday. It should be ready for decoration. Want me to start there?"

"Sure."

Emma approached the cake fridge alongside Fee, and they pulled open both doors. The gorgeous ivory cake appeared flawless, a perfect canvas for the delicate red scrolls that would soon cover every inch of it before the red chocolate roses, gracefully formed by the interns, surrounded the base of each of the three layers. It took both of them to lift the board and carry the cake to the stainless steel table.

"Listen," Fee said as she massaged the pastry bag of red icing, "I've wanted to tell you something for a while."

"If you say you're quitting, I'll come across this table and strangle you."

Fee chuckled. "Nah. Where would I go?"

"Wherever you went, I'd hunt you down and bring you back."

"Sean and I will be moving into the new house soon, and we . . . uh . . . Well, don't laugh."

"I won't."

"We've been talking about . . . kids."

Emma sat down on the closest stool. "Fiona. Are you . . . *pregnant?*"

"No!" she exclaimed, and she aimed the pastry bag at Emma for a few seconds. "No, we're in the process of . . . well , . ."

"Fee, just spit it out, will you? You're freaking me out here."

"We're gonna adopt Hildie."

Emma sat there for a moment. Despite the fact that Fee behaved as if this news would somehow come across as shocking, it didn't seem to Emma in the least bit surprising.

"I think that's great."

"You do?"

"Of course I do," she said, grinning. "The three of you are a perfect fit, Fiona. I'm so happy for you, and for Hildie."

"I know she's rough in places," Fee said, "but at the heart of her, there's a really great kid."

"Just like you," Emma said, and the validation brightened Fee's whole demeanor. "And you are going to be the best mom ever."

"Dude. You mean that?"

"Yes!"

"Good. Then . . ." Fee set down the pastry bag and glared at it. "Do you think you and Jackson could write us letters of reference?"

Emma laughed. "Of course! Just tell me what you need and when."

"Just, you know, saying we're like these stellar people with impeccable integrity, and how we'll make the best parents since June and Ward Cleaver. That kind of thing."

"Then . . . lie."

"Right."

"Sure. We can do that."

Aunt Sophie's Savannah Tea Cakes

4 cups all-purpose flour
(*plus another ½ cup for rolling*)
2 cups granulated sugar
2 teaspoons baking powder
1 teaspoon baking soda
¼ teaspoon ground cinnamon
¼ teaspoon ground nutmeg
2 eggs
½ cup buttermilk
2 sticks butter, softened
1 teaspoon vanilla

Sift flour into a large bowl, and mix in the dry ingredients.
Add the remaining ingredients and mix well.
Transfer the mixture to a floured board and
shape into a thick disk.
Cover the dough with plastic wrap and
refrigerate for 1-2 hours.

Preheat oven to 350 degrees.

Roll out the dough on a floured surface.
The dough should be about ¼ inch thick.
Cut the dough into desired shapes.
[Note: A round-rimmed glass works well;
also, thick cookie cutters or rippled biscuit cutters
create nice shapes.]

Bake on a lightly greased cookie sheet for 10 minutes.

21

"Just calm down, Emmy. Deep breaths."

Emma's father stroked her arm, and she marveled at the way the sound of his voice transported her back to childhood in only an instant.

"Just tell us what happened."

Her silent mother sat erect in the chair across from her, rubbing her hands as she waited, and Gavin remained perched on the edge of the plastic chair beside her.

"I stopped by like I always do," Emma told them, and a nurse behind the desk interrupted her to call out the name of Samuel Something, who hurried across the waiting room lobby toward her. "She didn't answer when I knocked, so I went inside. When she wasn't sitting in her chair, I called out to her, and she still didn't answer. So I went into the bedroom, and there she was, lying on the floor."

Emma's hands shook, and she pressed them against her trousers in the hope of making the trembling stop. "I tried to bring her around, and she stirred a little, but then she moaned and I was afraid she might have broken something. That's when I called 911."

The emergency room doors suddenly slid open, and Jackson rushed through them and headed straight for Emma. She jumped to her feet and hurried into his arms.

"Is Sophie all right?" he asked as he held her. "Is the doctor with her?"

"They herded us out of the examination room," she told him, her arms tight around his midsection. "They're doing some tests, and she should be back down in a few minutes."

The moment she released him, Jackson headed for Avery and sat down next to her. He took her hand and rubbed it affectionately. "Do you need anything?" he asked her.

"No, no, thank you, Jackson. I'm just eager to hear what the doctor has to say."

Jackson looked up and nodded at Gavin.

"Thanks for coming, my boy."

Emma heard Jackson's reply before he'd even spoken it. "Of course. Where else would I be?"

They settled into the hard waiting room chairs—except for Gavin, who paced in front of the glass window—and Jackson loosely held Emma's hand. The activity around them hummed, but the quietude of no answers about Aunt Sophie was mostly all that Emma could hear. When the nurse finally called out to them, she sensed a break in the silence that shattered like glass.

"Miss Sophie is in the third exam room to the right. Just one person can go on back and sit with her until the doctor comes in a few minutes."

Emma's mother didn't hesitate; she simply headed toward the door. "Third on the right?"

"Yes, ma'am."

Emma and Jackson returned to their chairs, and this time Gavin followed suit, occupying the chair his wife had vacated.

Emma realized that the distant thumping she heard was her own heartbeat pounding in her ears, and she inhaled sharply and closed her eyes. She couldn't shake the memory of Sophie's very pale face as she lay there on the floor, her eyes closed and her clothes uncharacteristically disheveled.

Nearly an hour ticked by before Avery reappeared, her porcelain face drained of color, nearly as pale as Sophie's had been when Emma found her. All three of them snapped to attention like family soldiers, waiting for the "At ease" command from Emma's mother.

"She has a mild concussion," she told them, and Emma gasped, covering her mouth with her hand. "She's going to be all right, and she's awake and talking. I had a little difficulty following her, but it seems she may have been trying to heat up some soup for dinner and got confused." Avery paused, sniffing back her emotions. When her husband placed an arm around her shoulder, Emma's mother broke down. "Gavin, she said she couldn't remember where she was. She didn't recognize her own apartment."

Emma's heart broke, both for her mother and for her aunt. How horrible to experience that kind of confusion, to become disoriented in what should have been the most familiar place.

"He says the Alzheimer's has obviously advanced to the place where very soon she won't be able to live on her own anymore, not even with assisted living. She's going to have to have care twenty-four hours a day."

"We'll figure it out, then," Gavin reassured her. "I promise, Countess. We'll figure it out."

Emma hadn't heard her father refer to her mother as "Countess" since her teen years. She'd forgotten all about the loving nickname he'd given Avery while their romance was still young, and it warmed her heart to witness their loving exchange now.

"They want to keep her overnight," Avery told them. she sniffed again and recovered her familiar stoic expression. "But you never know if it will extend to a couple of days or more. I'm going to stay with her until she's settled. Emma Rae, will you go to your aunt's apartment and pack her a bag, please?"

"Of course."

"I'll go with you," Jackson told her.

"She's going to need her bathrobe, and those embroidered slippers that she likes."

"Mother. I'll bring everything she needs."

Emma kissed Avery's cheek as she hugged her, and Gavin embraced her before she and Jackson headed out the door.

"Let's take my car," Jackson said, leading her by the hand. "You don't need to drive right now."

She slipped into the passenger seat and fastened her seatbelt. After a moment, she glanced over to find Jackson watching her.

"What?" she asked him.

Just one twitch, a minute little shift in his facial expression, and Emma caved into him, crying.

"I know you love her," he soothed. "We all love her."

"I don't even know if there's anything you can do. But I just have to do something to get more storage space in here."

J.R. tapped on the wall of Emma's office and listened to it like a doctor with a stethoscope.

"This wall is hollow. What's on the other side?" he asked her.

"I have no idea. Maybe Anton's back office?" She tried to visualize the layout on the other side of the wall. "Or it could be his pantry."

"All right, I'm going over to have a look. I'll be right back."

He ran a hand through his mane of shaggy hair and headed out of her office, leaving his leather jacket behind, draped over the corner of her desk. Half an hour later, he returned, grinning at her, his blue eyes sparkling.

"You are a very lucky baker," he told her. "There's a storage closet on this side," and he tapped on the far wall. "And over here is the storage shed on the back end of the courtyard. If we knock out the wall behind you and build into the storage shed, we can extend your office that way so that you'll have more space. Then we can push into the short wall and build some storage shelves and cabinets, whatever you need."

"Really?" She tried to imagine it, but felt turned around.

"All you really heard," he teased, "was 'blah-blah-blah storage shelves,' right?"

She chuckled. "Yeah, kinda. Maybe you'd better work something up and show it to Jackson?"

"Glad to."

"Will you be able to do the work?" she asked.

"Maybe. If we time it right. I've got a couple of obligations this month that I have to take care of out of town. I'll run upstairs and see if I can talk to Jackson now, and we'll go from there. Sound good?"

"Very. Thank you, J.R."

"Any time," he said, and his cell phone jingled an interruption. "Sorry. Just one sec." He checked the screen of his phone and raised his eyes to look at her. "Audrey wants you to call her."

"Okay."

"I'll see you later."

Once J.R. had gone, Emma called his wife.

"I can't find your cell number, Emma," Audrey said as she picked up the call. "Can you text me so I have it in my phone?"

"Sure. J.R. said you need to talk to me. What's up?"

"Don't panic, okay?"

Emma's stomach did a little somersault. "Oh, no. Something happened to my dress?"

"No!" she exclaimed. "No, not at all. The alterations are done, it's pressed and beautiful. Just tell me whether to deliver it to your place or to the hotel."

"The hotel, if you don't mind. I'll be getting ready here."

"You got it. I'll make sure it arrives the day before the wedding."

"Great, Audrey, thank you."

"Well, don't thank me just yet."

Emma swallowed around the lump in her throat. "Why not?"

"I have to fly to Chicago tomorrow, Emma. There's some sort of problem with the show we're preparing for, and Riley needs me back there."

"For how long?"

"Well, that's the thing. It could be a day or two, or it could be longer. I just won't know until I get there."

"You'll miss the wedding?"

"I don't know," she hedged. "But maybe."

Disappointment pressed down on Emma's ribs. "Oh, I hope not, Audrey."

"I know. I'll do everything I can to be there, but I just wanted to tell you up front . . . I just don't know."

"It's okay. I understand. We'll hope for the best."

Kat had dropped by just that morning to confirm the menu for the reception: a perfect duplicate of the one served at the gala hotel opening. She and Jackson had only just begun falling in love back then, and the exquisite menu seemed like a good representation—and reminder—of their romance. Emma still kept one of the menus tucked in her desk drawer as a memento, and she'd produced an engraved table card from that night's event that included the mouth-watering menu and showed it to Kat. She ran a finger over it before placing it back into the drawer.

Kat had also delivered a polite, watered-down reminder from a frantic Sherilyn about the design for the cake, and then they'd reviewed the guest list. It seemed a lot of their friends had sent sincere regrets; and now with her aunt in questionable health, Russell caught up in Brazil, and Audrey heading out of town . . .

After she texted her phone number to Audrey, Emma composed a second text for Jackson.

You don't have the measles, do you?

A few moments later: *Why? Do I look spotty?*

No, but they're dropping like flies as the wedding approaches. I just want to make sure you'll be there.

Who dropped today?

Audrey. Going to Chicago, doesn't know how long.

More cake for me.

Emma giggled. *And me.*

As long as u marry me, I'm good with no one showing. And after a few seconds he added, *Just u, me, a big cake and 2 forks.*

U assume I'll have a cake. Need to design it first.

Love u. How about dinner?

U can't, she typed, chuckling. *U have a meeting in a few.*

I do?

J.R. on his way up. Wants to knock out a wall or 2.

After a long pause, the reply arrived. *Here now. I'll get my hard hat and gear.*

Jackson followed J.R. out of his office and said good-bye to him in front of Susannah's desk.

"You know," Jackson said to Susannah after J.R. had gone, "I don't think we've exchanged ten words since you got back."

"You've been quite busy," she replied, smiling at him in that knowing way only Susannah could. "Did I overhear that you're going to expand Emma's office?"

"It's more like a closet," he said, perching on the outside corner of her desk. "I think we'll put that off until after we get back from Savannah. I don't think she can take any more upheaval at the moment."

"That's probably a very wise choice."

"You know," he said, reflecting on the parade of replacements who had occupied that desk while Susannah was gone, "I am really happy you're back. In fact, I can hardly express to you how much."

"A little birdie or two has told me you had quite a few undesirable temporaries while I was away."

"You have no idea. I can't even remember how many."

"Lauren sounded very competent when I spoke with her last week."

Jackson got up and headed for the door. Rather than sharing the sordid details, he leaned into the doorjamb and simply said, "Not a good fit."

"No? I'm sorry to hear that. But I'm sure I'll be able to find someone before I—"

"Don't say it! Can we please just not think about your retirement right now?" he interrupted, and he waved his hand at her over his shoulder as he walked away. Her laughter followed him down the hallway, and it seemed a little like music to him.

When he reached Emma's kitchen, he found it bustling with people and activity. Fee directed a line of three at the worktable in the center of the room, and two others faced the sinks and loaded the dishwashers on either side of them.

"Emma around?"

"Nope," Fee replied. "She's been naughty. Sherilyn has relegated her to the courtyard with a sketch pad and a pot of tea. She's not allowed to come home until she's chosen a wedding cake design."

Jackson chuckled and sang, "Thank you," and he left in pursuit of the site of her punishment. He crossed through the lobby and stopped at the courtyard, his hand poised over the brass doorknob as he peered through the glass at Emma.

With her hair piled into a messy bun at the back of her head and fastened with what looked like a pen, she leaned back into one wrought iron chair with her feet propped up on another. She nibbled her lower lip as she busily sketched on the pad that rested on her bent knees. An assortment of papers covered the tabletop.

No way was he going to disturb her now. Jackson simply turned and sauntered away.

༅༎༅༎༅༎༅༎༅༎༅༎༅༎༅༎༅༎༅༎༅༎

Welcome to the Gala Opening
of
The Tanglewood Inn

Your Menu
Award-Winning Chef
Anton Morelli
Celebrates Southern Cuisine

Starters

Proscuitto-wrapped Figs with gorgonzola and balsamic vinegar
Fried Green Tomatoes with buttermilk bleu cheese
Heirloom Tomato Salad with hearts of palm, candied pecans, and
citrus vinaigrette

Entrée Choices

Roasted prime rib of beef	Grilled salmon with pear vinegar
Shrimp & lobster cheddar grits	Petite ravioli with butternut squash
Shiitake mushrooms & caramelized shallots	Sautéed greens with shallots & Pancetta
White asparagus with pistachio vinaigrette	Candied cranberries with walnuts

Your Dessert
From this year's recipient of
The Passionate Palette Award
Emma Rae Travis's
Crème Brûlée Cake

Your Entertainment
Grammy Award-Winning Performer
Ben Colson

༅༎༅༎༅༎༅༎༅༎༅༎༅༎༅༎༅༎༅༎༅༎

22

*E*mma scribbled the title underneath the latest iteration of her wedding cake and tossed the pencil to the tabletop. She yanked the pen out of the twist at the back of her head and dropped it there as well, using both hands to tousle her hair.

She groaned as she arranged the various sketches she'd been carrying around for so long. First, the *Once Upon a Time* cake, beautiful in its romantic simplicity. She pushed the *Topsy Turvy* cake next to it; more and more, that aptly described their lives. Possibly her favorite of them all, she placed the *Classic and Simple* sketch next to the others.

She started a new row with the *Non-Traditional* cupcake-cake; she and Jackson were nothing if not unique. Next to that one, the scrunched-up-and-ironed-out sketch she'd made on the paper towel at her slumber-shower: *Pure and Uncomplicated.* And to complete the pattern, she tore the top page from her sketch pad and set the newest contestant into place with the others.

"My, how lovely!"

She nearly shouted in surprise and jerked her neck as she looked up to find a woman standing next to her, inspecting the cake design offerings before her.

"I'm sorry. Did I startle you?" she asked. "I wandered out here to wait for my husband, and I couldn't help noticing your project."

Emma sighed and leaned back against the cool iron chair to inspect the tabletop. "Tell me, do you have a favorite out of these?"

"Hmm," the woman said, adjusting her wire-rimmed glasses as she scrutinized the sketches, one at a time. "Are they all wedding cakes?"

"Yes. I'm a little decision-challenged, and my wedding is this weekend."

"Oh, dear! I hope you have a very understanding baker."

One corner of Emma's mouth tilted upward, and she groaned. "I'm not just the bride. I'm the baker, too."

The woman gasped, and she scraped the nearest chair close to the table and sat down. "Don't tell me you're Emma Rae Travis!"

Emma looked closely at her. "Do I know you?" she asked.

"No," she replied, pushing her light hair away from her round face, grinning sweetly at Emma. "My name is Bonnie Cordova. My husband and I are visiting the area to celebrate our thirtieth wedding anniversary."

"Then you're a good person to talk to about a wedding cake, aren't you?"

"I read about the award that you won for your crème brûlée cake. Will that be your wedding cake?"

"Yes. That's the one decision I *have* made about it."

"Ben and I know someone who visited the hotel when their daughter got married last year." Her brown eyes twinkled as she leaned forward. "You're the whole reason we're staying here at The Tanglewood. We're having tea right out here tomorrow afternoon, in fact. I can hardly wait to sample your baked goodies! . . . Probably no surprise, right? I wouldn't be this *fluffy* without enjoying baked goodies."

The twinkle in her eye charmed Emma, and she reached out and touched Bonnie's hand. "My grandmother used to have an embroidered sampler in her bedroom in Savannah," Emma told her. "It still hangs there to this day. A little round lamb, with cross-stitched words underneath that say, *Ewe's not fat . . . E.W.E. . . . Ewe's fluffy.*"

"I just think *fluffy* is a far friendlier word than any of the alternatives."

"I have to agree," Emma said on a chuckle. "So, thirty years, huh? How did you and your husband meet?"

"It's kind of a funny story, actually," Bonnie told her. "Ben worked with my mom, and he saw my picture on her desk. I was fifteen, and he was eighteen, and my mother set us up on a date. We went to the drive-in movies, and three years later . . . we got married! Would you like to see a couple of family photos?"

"I'd love to."

Bonnie produced a burgundy wallet from her large leather bag and opened it to reveal several photographs. "This is my Ben," she said sweetly. "And this is our son, Brandon, and his wife, Staci, our daughter, Brena . . . and here are Ceejay, Jayton, Kayla, and Leah."

"They're lovely. And they all resulted from a blind date to the movies," Emma remarked. "That might be one of the most romantic things I've ever heard."

"Our wedding wasn't elaborate or anything," she went on. "In fact, the pastor's wife made my bridal gown, and a woman in our church made the cake."

"And thirty years later," Emma surmised, "you wander into the courtyard at just the moment that I'm trying to figure out which of these cakes best represents Jackson and me. So tell me . . . which one?"

"Tell me a little about your intended," she prodded.

"His name is Jackson—"

"Not Jackson Drake," she cut her off. "The owner of the hotel?"

Emma nodded. "The very same."

"Talk about romantic."

She chuckled as she continued. "He's handsome and wonderful. Probably the most amazing man I've ever met. He's thoughtful in ways that you just don't expect. Do you know what I mean?"

Bonnie nodded. "I think so."

"He's so easy to be with, Bonnie. No demands or high expectations, just . . . easy. All of my past relationships have been so tangled, you know?"

As Bonnie grinned at her and nodded, Emma wondered for a moment why she felt so comfortable about sharing her personal emotions with a virtual stranger. Yet when Bonnie rolled her hand, inviting Emma to continue, she actually did!

"He really gets me, you know? He doesn't want to change me or control me or anything like that. He just . . ." She trailed off and smiled.

"Loves you," Bonnie finished for her.

"Yes."

"He sounds wonderful, and the spirit of each one of these cakes seems to fit your relationship with him."

"Welcome to my world. It's impossible to choose."

"Not really impossible, Emma," she said. "The emotion behind what you're telling me, well, it carries the message of one of these cakes, over and above the others."

"It does?"

Emma planted both feet on the ground and leaned forward on her elbows. "Tell me, Bonnie. Please."

Bonnie smiled at her and rubbed Emma's arm briskly before tapping her finger on the newest sketch. "This one. Absolutely."

Emma gazed at it for a long moment before she sighed so deeply that it felt as if she'd just taken her first breath in days. As a broad grin wound its way across her face, Emma began to laugh.

"Bonnie Cordova, you've saved my life!"

She jumped to her feet and frantically pushed the papers into a pile and held them against her ribs. "What time is your tearoom appointment tomorrow?"

"Two o'clock, why?"

"It's on me!"

"Oh, no, that's not—"

"Oh, yes, it is," she cried as she hurried toward the door. "I'm sorry. I have to go. It was so great meeting you, Bonnie. Thank you so much!"

"You, too, Emma. Best wishes on your wedding!"

And with that, Emma scrambled through the door and took off across the lobby at a full run.

∽≳≈

Emma could hardly wait to get to Sherilyn's. But when she steered around the corner of her street, a familiar sight sent her foot to the brake pedal, and her thoughts to revving. It looked like a repeat performance of her slumber-shower with familiar cars edging the driveway and curb in front of the house. Georgiann's BMW, Norma's Camry, Susannah Littlefield's Taurus, even Fee's PT Cruiser. The only car missing seemed to be her mother's.

When she reached the front door, Emma toyed with the idea of carefully turning the knob and tiptoeing inside to see what they had going on in there, but Andy's dog had a keen sense of killjoy, and he began barking before the thoughts could take flight into actual plans. She pushed the door open and let herself in.

"All right, Henry, all right," she said as she pushed her way past him. "They all know I'm here."

When she reached the end of the hall, Sherilyn looked up at her as if she'd just been caught reading her diary. "Emma, what are you *doing* here?"

"I have a better question. Why is everyone I know sitting in your dining room?"

They glanced around the room like thieves caught red-handed, but no one appeared to have an explanation to share.

"I'm not kidding. What's going on?"

"We're event planning, *sugah*," Madeline piped up from the kitchen. "One of Georgiann's charity functions."

Emma narrowed her eyes at Fee and asked, "You didn't think it was worth mentioning to me?"

"Well, you've been stressed. Norma thought I could pinch-hit."

"O-kay." Emma moved closer and scrutinized the scene before her. "So why do you all look like you're planning a bank robbery?"

"Don't be ridiculous," Sherilyn chimed in. "Why don't you tell me why you're here? Without calling. Just dropping in without any forewarning. It must be pretty important . . ."

Old Loose-Lips had resorted to an old mechanism: Anything could be avoided if enough fast words covered it.

". . . and I'd love to hear what that is. Although if you'd like some tea, I can put on the water for you and make you a nice cup. Would you like tea, Em? Hmm?"

"No." She hadn't realized she'd been holding her breath, and it felt pretty good when she let it out. "No, thanks."

"So what are you doing here, darling?" Georgiann asked her. "Is something wrong?"

She swallowed. Hard. Then she sighed. "I . . . uh . . ." And it hit her. "Oh! I wanted to dazzle Sherilyn!" She looked at her friend and grinned. "Brace yourself."

"No!"

"Yes!"

"You chose the cake."

"I have chosen the cake!"

Sherilyn gave a little shriek before lunging at her, grabbing the sketch from her hands, and peering at it.

"Oh, Em." She chuckled as she added, "It's perfect."

"Lemme see," Fee said, and she got up and snatched the paper from Sherilyn. After giving it a once-over, she smacked Emma's arm. "Dude. Way to go."

"Can we all see?" Susannah asked, and Sherilyn took the paper back and held it up for everyone to have a look.

"It's lovely."

"Just right."

"I think it says Emma and Jackson," Norma added.

Sherilyn glanced over her shoulder and asked, "So how did you finally manage it?"

"I met this really sweet woman at the hotel, and she helped me pick it. Speaking of which," she said, touching Fee's elbow. "Her name is Bonnie Cordova, and she and her husband, Ben, are having tea at two o'clock tomorrow. I'd like to comp them. And could you find out if they'll be around this weekend? If so, invite them to the wedding."

"God bless you, Bonnie Cordova!" Sherilyn sang, and she hugged Emma around the shoulders. "We have a cake!"

"We have a cake," Emma repeated with a sigh.

༄

Stretched out across the bed on his stomach and surrounded by half a dozen books of poetry and verse, Jackson landed on something that snagged a heartstring. He pushed himself up and sat cross-legged, a book open to one of his old favorites balanced his knee.

When his cell phone rang, he had to search for it to answer. "Guess what?"

Emma's voice tickled the back of his throat, and warmth washed over him.

"You're leaving me for a better-looking man."

"There is no better-looking man."

"Ah. Then what?"

"We have a cake."

"Don't toy with me."

"Nope. I'm not joking. It was a perfect storm of the right conversation at the right moment and the right sketch. We have cake liftoff. What are you doing?"

"I am writing my vows," he declared.

"We wrote the vows weeks ago, Jackson. We sat there and wrote them together."

"I know. But Sherilyn said we each need to choose a passage of Scripture or a poem or something to read to each other first. Something that sums up how we feel. Did you do that already?"

"Yes, I did."

"Oh."

Emma chuckled. "And you're just doing that now."

"Well, I'm just nailing it down now," he corrected, cringing as he scanned the many books scattered around him. "I'm narrowing down the choices."

"What have you been waiting for, Jackson?"

"Well, for most women," he explained with a teasing tone, "the wedding is apparently all about the dress. For you, my love, the cake is the thing. Now that you've landed on a cake, I have full confidence that this marriage is going to take place, so I need to kick it into gear."

"You doubted me? I'm wounded."

"And I am happy."

Emma giggled, and it sparked the flicker of a grin on him. A sweet silence followed, and Jackson's smile melted into an expression of pure tenderness.

His voice went raspy as he told her, "I wish you were here."

"I can come over," she offered.

"No. I mean . . . I wish you were here to stay."

"Ohhh," she breathed. "Me, too."

He pushed the book from his leg, closed his eyes, and sighed. "Do you have any idea how much I love you?"

"What a silly question," she replied softly, and he pressed the phone closer to better saver the earthy tone of her voice.

After another long silence, he remarked, "You sound tired."

"I am. But it's a good tired."

"Get some sleep," he said. "I'll see—"

"Hey," she interrupted. "I walked in on the strangest thing over at Sherilyn's tonight."

Jackson chuckled. "Do tell."

"Nearly every woman we know was there. All three of your sisters, Susannah, Fee. It was like I happened upon the meeting of some secret society of southern women that I hadn't been invited to join."

"Maybe your invitation got lost in the mail."

"Or they're up to something," she half-whispered, and Jackson laughed.

"And this would be surprising? Our wedding is in a couple of days, Emma. Of course they're planning something."

"Do you know what it is?"

"No."

"Aren't you curious?"

"No."

"Okay. If you're not going to play or be any fun at all, I'm going to sleep."

"Sweet dreams," he sang.

"Sweet vows," she returned. "And make it good, will you? I wouldn't want to have to trade you in for a sharper model."

Tips for Writing Your Own Wedding Vows

Make sure you work together to make a plan:

❖ Are you writing separate vows, or writing them together?

❖ Are you going to show them to one another prior to the ceremony?

❖ Have you agreed on the overall tone of the vows? For instance, will they display humor, or should they be serious and thoughtful?

❖ Will you write them TO one another, or will you choose an appropriate poem, Scripture verse, or passage from your favorite book?

23

"Did I wake you?"

Emma thought Sherilyn must be joking. "I've been up since four thirty."

"Why?"

"Uh, it's my wedding day?"

Sherilyn giggled. "I am aware. I just thought you might not feel well or something."

"Oh, no. I feel fine."

"Good."

"What's to be nervous about, anyway? It's not like anyone will be there to witness the wedding, aside from you and Andy, and possibly Jackson's sisters."

"It's not that dire, Em."

"Let's count the people who mean something to us who won't be able to make it, shall we?" she suggested. "Aunt Soph . . ."

"She's not doing any better?"

"Well, she's staying at Mother and Daddy's, and they have a nurse there to help. But she's still confused most of the time, and Mother doesn't think it's such a good idea to expose her to so much unfamiliar stimulation, so . . ."

"I'm so sorry, Em. But I think that's wise."

"I guess . . . And then there's Audrey."

"Audrey still might be back in time."

Emma groaned. "The wedding is in nine hours, Sher."

"So that's nine whole hours for her to get a flight."

"Why is it snowing in Chicago?" Emma exclaimed. "Seven inches. Didn't they get the memo that it's spring? Did you shirk your wedding planner duties and forget to send them the memo?"

Sherilyn chuckled.

"And Russell is still in Brazil."

"Yeah." Emma heard the pout in Sherilyn's voice as she acknowledged that fact.

"And Pearl e-mailed to say she woke up this morning with a tooth abscess, and she's trying to reach her dentist . . ."

"Well, it's better that she doesn't come, then."

"True."

"It's all going to come together, Em."

"It's only nine—"

"—hours away. I know, I know."

"Well, it is."

"Are you a little nervous?" Sherilyn asked her, and Emma dropped to the sofa and groaned as she gazed outside. The gloomy sky was painted dark gray, and the wind turned the leaves on the scarlet oak beyond the window.

"No. I'm just . . . I don't know what."

"I've been doing this a long time. And here's what I know about your wedding: It's going to be beautiful. Tomorrow at this time, you and Jackson will be married and blissfully happy, and none of these obstacles will even be remembered."

"Do you think it's going to rain?"

"I don't know," Sherilyn replied. "But Kat has got everyone on standby to move the ceremony to the Victoria Room if it does."

"So you think it's going to!"

"Em, stop it right now. It's just part of my DNA to anticipate every possible scenario."

"Including no guests?"

Emma knew Sherilyn well enough to understand her silence.

"I am heading to the hotel in about an hour," Sherilyn finally said. "I'll meet you in the bridal suite at two o'clock. Did you get my e-mail with the checklist?"

"Yes."

"Did you print it out?"

"Yes."

"See you at two."

"Yes."

Emma sighed as she disconnected the call. Something just didn't feel right. She'd waited for this day for such a long time, but something just felt . . .

Off.

The sour taste of dread stung the back of her throat. Had she really become one of those people who came to believe that, if they actually managed to get a firm grasp on the hem of their dream, the other shoe would surely drop out of the sky and *thunk!* them down with its big, disappointing heel?

No! she insisted. *I will not be that person. I will not give in to this.*

Especially when the most assured truth Emma knew in life involved Jackson, and Jackson alone. If every person they'd invited tripped over a prior engagement, a sick child, or full-on food poisoning . . . If an unprecedented spring snowstorm hit the greater Atlanta area two hours before the wedding . . . If

Ben Colson suddenly contracted laryngitis and couldn't sing the song for their first dance . . . . If every one of those disasters and more besides occurred simultaneously . . . the only thing that mattered would still be Emma and Jackson, facing one another, exchanging rings, and making vows.

One sudden thought sliced through her stab at positivity, spurring Emma to quickly dial the phone.

"Miguel? It's Emma."

"Emma, how are you? All ready to take the big plunge?"

"More ready than ever," she told him. "What about you?"

"Me?"

"Yes, I was just wondering how you're doing. Feeling okay? No unforeseen scheduling conflicts or car troubles?"

Miguel's laughter reassured her. "No, Emma, nothing of the kind."

"Oh, good. That's good. Okay. Because I was thinking that, no matter what else might happen, as long as you, me, and Jackson are there, we're pretty much golden, right?"

"Yes, Emma. No worries. I'll be there, and in just a few hours, you will be Jackson's wife."

"Right," she said on a sigh. "Okay."

"I'll see you at the altar, Emma."

"Okay, then." She chuckled nervously, wondering if she sounded as crazy to him as she did to herself. "You promise?"

❧

Emma had always known Sherilyn as a force of nature to her many brides, but experiencing this firsthand brought that knowledge alive for her. From the moment she entered the hotel through the glass doors in the front, she ceased to exist as the mere baker at The Tanglewood Inn. She had now morphed into one of Sherilyn Drummond's treasured brides.

Along with that distinction came a bevy of perks she hadn't anticipated:

1. Tomás, the handsome, uniformed bellman assigned to await her arrival;

2. Automatic check-in at the front desk where the clerk called her to the front of the line and handed her a key and a fragrant rose, the stem wrapped in a ribbon emblazoned with the word "Bride";

3. Tomás's personable escort to the bridal suite where the claw-footed table that greeted her brimmed with chocolates, sparkling cider chilled in a crystal ice bucket, a handwritten note on engraved stationery bearing the initials of her wedding planner, and an assortment of fruit, cheeses, and whole grain crackers; and

4. Fragrant arrangements of roses and hydrangea in low vases on every table.

The whole scene just smacked of Sherilyn's attention to the most minute detail, and Emma found sudden and profound common ground with all of those women who had preceded her—the ones who gushed about how the whole wedding experience at The Tanglewood had rocketed far above their hopeful expectations, mainly because of the recognizable fingerprints of their wedding planner.

"Will there be anything else?"

"No, Tomás," she told him as she poured cider into one of the crystal flutes on the table. "Thank you so much."

In sync with the click of the door as it closed behind him, Emma grabbed her glass, a strawberry, a wax-enclosed wedge of cheese, and Sherilyn's note, and she tossed herself deep into the corner of the overstuffed green chenille sofa.

Em, make yourself comfortable and relax.

Fee and I will be along in a bit with some bride-type surprises that will make the afternoon of your wedding a lovely treat with your two best girls.

xxoo Love you.

—Sherilyn

Halfway into the third wedge of cheese, a knock sounded at the door and Emma skipped toward it. Flinging it open, she expected to find Sherilyn on the other side; the face of her mother greeted her instead.

"Mother! I wasn't expecting you this early. Are you one of my *bride-type* surprises?"

"Can I come in?" Avery asked her.

"Of course." Emma closed the door behind her and asked, "Do you want some cheese? It's really phenomenal."

"No. Thank you." Just about the time that Emma began to realize the look on her mother's face did not exactly say, "Happy Wedding Day, Daughter!" Avery turned to her and sighed. "You'd better sit down, Emma."

"Oh . . ." She sat in the closest chair, which happened to be one of the ladder-back dining chairs at the round dining table.

"Is it Aunt Soph?"

"No, it's not. I don't want you to worry because everything is going to be just fine," her mother prefaced as she joined Emma at the table and took her hand.

"Mother, you're kind of freaking me out here."

"Sorry. It's just that I don't want you to overreact, Emma Rae."

"Well, tell me what I'm not overreacting to, would you?"

"Around two this morning, I had to take your father to the emergency room—"

"What! Why didn't you call me?" Emma popped to her feet and circled to the back of her mother's chair. "What happened?"

"He had a . . . mild . . . *episode* . . ."

"Mother, please."

Avery sighed and blurted, "It's his heart."

"His heart!" Emma sat down in a different dining chair, her hand clasped over her mouth. "Why didn't you call me?"

"Oh, honey, it's your wedding day. And your father didn't want you to—"

"That is so like him to make a harebrained decision like that."

"—worry. Or worse yet, postpone the ceremony."

"Well, of course we're going to postpone it! Is he crazy? What hospital is he in? Is he at Fulton?"

"Emma Rae—"

"I'll leave a note for Sherilyn," she said, jumping to her feet again. "Or I can tell them at the front desk to—"

"Emma Rae!"

She fell instantly silent. Emma wasn't sure she'd ever witnessed Avery resorting to . . . well . . . *shrill*. If she had, it had most certainly been directed at Gavin, never at Emma herself.

"Sit down."

She obediently sat in the chair across from her mother.

"Your father was very clear about this. He does not want you to rush over there, to postpone your wedding, or to do anything rash. He's going to be fine. The doctors have said it was just a mild episode of angina. They're going to monitor him closely and get him on some medication, and he'll probably be out of the hospital in a day or so."

Emma's heart pounded so hard that she wondered for a moment whether the bed next to him might be available. She could use a little heart medication herself at the moment.

"I want to head over to the hospital and see Daddy."

"Why don't you call him instead?" Avery suggested. "I think as soon as you hear his voice, you'll feel better."

Emma rifled through her bag until she found her cell phone. Avery handed her a card with the phone number printed on the front and a room number written in blue ink.

"Daddy?"

"Emmy! I hoped you'd call. How's my little girl on her wedding day?"

"I'd be a lot better if I knew you were well enough to be here."

Gavin released a bumpy little sigh. "No one wants to be there more than I do, princess. In fact, I've been working on this stubborn doctor of mine most of the morning, but he just doesn't want to give in."

"No, don't leave the hospital before you're ready, Daddy . . . It's just not going to feel right getting married without you."

Her mother got up when a soft knock sounded at the door, and she shushed Sherilyn and Fee as she ushered them inside, then whispered to them about Gavin's illness.

"I'm there in spirit, princess," Gavin vowed. "You know I am."

"You're sure you're all right?" Emma asked, tears welling in her eyes as Sherilyn tiptoed toward her, kissed her fingertip and touched it to the top of Emma's head. "I'm really worried about you."

"No need. I'm a tough old geezer, you know that. Look how long I've stuck with your mother."

Emma giggled, drying her tears at the same time. "You're impossible."

"This is what I'm telling you. I'm not going anywhere. But I'm sorry to say . . . it looks like I'm going to miss your special day. I'm very sorry about that, and I hope you'll forgive me."

Sherilyn handed her a tissue, and Emma dabbed at her nose with it. "Please don't apologize, Daddy. Just feel better, okay?"

"I have to go, Emmy. The doctor is here now, and he's going to talk to me about these fun little pills they want me to place under my tongue."

"Well, listen to him carefully," she instructed. "Don't make jokes. Really listen to what he tells you."

"Have a beautiful wedding, Emmy."

"I love you so much."

"I love you more."

She disconnected the call before bursting into tears and nearly choking on the sob she'd been holding back during her conversation with her father.

"Emma Rae," her mother said in a scolding tone. "He'll be fine."

"How do you know that?" she sniffed. "You don't know that, Mother."

"He's a tough old geezer," she soothed, tickling Emma's hair with her fingertips.

She laughed. "He said that, too."

"I'm going back to the hospital for a couple of hours," Avery told her. "Then I'll go home and change, and I'll see you at the end of the aisle. All right?"

Emma nodded, and she blew her nose.

"You two take care of her," she told Sherilyn and Fee before heading out the door.

Emma blew her nose again and wiped her eyes with tissues that Sherilyn handed her one at a time. "I had a bad feeling this morning," she told them with a sniff. "I just knew something wasn't right."

"Your mother seems certain he's going to be okay," Sherilyn reminded her.

"But how can I get married without my father there?" she whimpered, and the tears began again. "Who's going to . . . *give me away?*"

"Em, you don't need anyone to give you to Jackson. The two of you have belonged to each other for ages."

"And without my aunt Sophie . . . or Audrey . . . or Russell . . . or Pearl. . ."

"Emma Rae Travis," Sherilyn said as she grabbed several tissues from the box in Fee's hands and dabbed at Emma's eyes and nose. "You and Jackson don't need anyone there with you. We're all just spectators to what's happening between the two of you. We're lucky to be invited along, but it's not about who is there and who is not. It's about the lifetime of happiness you're about to begin."

Emma gazed at Sherilyn for a long moment before glancing at Fee and grinning through her tears. "She's good at this."

Fee peered down at her over the top of her glasses and nodded. "She really is."

"Now I want you to dry those tears," Sherilyn said, handing over a few extra tissues for good measure, "while I brew up a nice pot of tea. I've got Sheila coming over from The Ah Spa any minute, and she's giving us all facials and mani-pedis . . ."

"Some of us," Fee corrected. "I don't do group mani-pedis."

"Fiona, if the bride wants you to have a mani-pedi with her, you're having a mani-pedi."

Emma got up from the chair and headed toward the sofa. Fee grabbed her arm as she passed, her eyes ablaze with a "help me" fire, but before Emma could reply, Sherilyn continued.

"Then we've got Bruce from All Tressed Up coming at four to do your hair, and Millicent from Make Me Over for your makeup . . ."

Emma patted Fee's hand and whispered, "I release you from the mani-pedi ordinance."

"Bless you," Fee mouthed back to her.

". . . and I've ordered a very light snack for everyone that will be delivered around four thirty so that your blood sugar stays on track through the ceremony . . ."

Emma folded her legs underneath her and leaned back into the sofa cushions, watching her friend, the fierce wedding-planner tornado, with a grin.

"Oh! And Kat is taking care of things downstairs, but she'll stop by to have a bite with us before she receives the flowers at five o'clock . . ."

❧◆❧◆❧◆❧◆❧◆❧◆❧◆❧◆❧◆❧◆❧◆❧◆❧◆❧◆❧◆❧◆◆

Emma Rae Travis
and
Jackson Drake

cordially invite you
to join them
as they exchange the vows of marriage
on
Saturday, April 6th,
at
The Tanglewood Inn
Roswell, Georgia

The wedding ceremony will be held
in the hotel courtyard at 7 p.m.

Please join guests afterward
for an intimate celebration.
Dinner, wine, and dancing
to the music of Ben Colson
in
The Desiree Room
at 8 p.m.

"Set me as a seal upon your heart,
as a seal upon your arm;
for love is as strong as death."
Song of Solomon 8:6

❧◆❧◆❧◆❧◆❧◆❧◆❧◆❧◆❧◆❧◆❧◆❧◆❧◆❧◆❧◆❧◆◆

24

Emma peered at the reflection in the mirror, not entirely convinced that it was hers. Fee pinned the sheer lace veil into her wavy hair as Sherilyn expertly wielded a buttonhook, fastening the twenty-six rhinestone buttons down the back of her gown. When they were through, Sherilyn picked up the sparkly headband from its velvet case on the dressing table and gingerly set it into place on Emma's head, careful to cover each of the veil pins.

"You're more beautiful than I've ever seen you," Sherilyn told her, her turquoise eyes glistening with moist emotion.

"Really?"

Emma nibbled the corner of her bottom lip as she looked at them both in the mirror.

"Really," Sherilyn sniffed.

"Dude. You're an MGM movie," Fee added.

"Your mother's earrings are your something old, the dress is something new. But this is your something borrowed," Sherilyn told her as she clasped a two-strand diamond bracelet around her wrist. "It's the bracelet I wore at my wedding."

"Ahh, Sher. Thank you."

"Do you have something blue?" Fee asked.

"Her garter," Sherilyn said, wiggling her eyebrows until Emma laughed.

A knock at the door drew Fee away to the other room, and Emma sat down on the corner of the bed. "Just half an hour until I finally marry Jackson," she said on a sigh.

"And look!" Sherilyn exclaimed as she pointed out the window. "Clear skies. No rain, no wind."

"I'm so relieved that something's gone right," she replied with a smile. "I was starting to think—"

A gasp drew their attention to the doorway, where Audrey and Kat stood, and the expressions on their faces told Emma everything she needed to know about how she really looked in her gown.

"Audrey, you made it."

"My flight landed an hour ago," she told her. "I couldn't miss seeing you in that gown. You look exquisite, Emma."

"Thank you both." She crossed the room toward them and took Audrey and Kat into her arms. "For the dress, for the beautiful headband . . . for your friendship."

"You're welcome," Audrey cooed. "We adore you."

"Ooh, I saw Jackson," Kat chimed in. "He looks delicious!"

"I knew he would," Emma said with a giggle.

Sherilyn joined the circle and placed one arm around Emma and the other around Kat. "You see, Em? I told you it was going to be fine! Everything is rounding out beautifully."

"Did you have doubts?" Audrey asked.

"Oh!" Sherilyn exclaimed before Emma could answer. "I forgot to tell you. Pearl's here!"

Emma lit up a little. "Really? That's great. But Russell . . . you know. And my father is in the hospital . . ."

"No!" Kat exclaimed.

". . . and Aunt Sophie can't come . . ."

As if on cue, Emma's mother sang out a greeting from the other room. "Emma Rae? Are you in there?"

"Avery, wait until you see this daughter of yours in her wedding gown," Sherilyn called out as she headed through the doorway, but her words trailed off, replaced by a gasp.

"Emma Rae Travis," her mother declared when she saw her. "Look at you! You're a vision, darling."

Emma beamed. "Thank you, Mother."

"And she brought a surprise for you," Sherilyn sang as she danced past the etched-glass sliding door into the bedroom. "Look who's here!"

Emma's spirit soared for a moment, burgeoning with hope that her father had made it after all. But she wasn't as disappointed as she might have been when her aunt Sophie stepped into the doorway and smoothed the skirt of her beautiful pastel dress.

Emma gulped down a bubble of air as she rushed toward her. "Aunt Soph? You're here!"

"Of course I am, child. You know I love your weddings to Jackson."

Emma looked over her aunt's shoulder into the loving eyes of her mother. "She felt better today than she has in days, and her nurse thought it would be all right for her to come."

"Nothing could make me happier," Emma told her aunt as she kissed her cheek. To just her mother, she softly added, "Almost."

"I know."

"At the risk of reminding you that I told you so, just one more time," Sherilyn gloated with a broad smile, "I did tell you everything would work out, didn't I?"

"You did," Emma replied. "But don't make me say out loud that you were right, okay?"

"Consider it a wedding gift," she commented. "Now I'm going to call downstairs and ask them to bring the bouquets up here while I slip into my dress."

"You got one for Aunt Soph?" she whispered to Sherilyn.

She nodded, and then she leaned in toward Emma, looking her squarely in the eye. "Are you feeling good?"

"Perfect," she said on a sigh. "I feel like everything is right in the world again, and I can hardly wait to see Jackson waiting for me at the end of the aisle."

❧

"Help me with this, will you?"

Jackson set the ring box on the desktop and crossed his office to where Andy stood facing the full-length mirror Sherilyn had sent up. Once he'd clasped both cuff links, Jackson smacked Andy's shoulder and grinned at him before reaching for the black tuxedo jacket on the hanger in the corner and holding it for his friend.

"I don't know why I seem to be more nervous than you are," Andy said as he slid into it.

Jackson slipped into his own jacket and adjusted the satin lapels before tightening the solid black tie around the self-top collar of his starched white shirt. He tugged at the hem of the black vest before fastening the single button on his jacket and standing next to Andy in front of the mirror.

"We look pretty sharp," Andy remarked. "You ready to do this thing?"

"I was born ready." Jackson tucked the ring box into Andy's jacket pocket and tapped it. "Don't lose that."

Andy pinned a lavender rosebud to the lapel of Jackson's jacket. Once he'd reciprocated, Jackson opened the office door and waved Andy past. He took a few deep breaths as they waited for the elevator.

When the car doors opened, the two of them just stood there looking straight ahead at the unexpected sight before them.

"Come on in," said the man occupying the glass elevator car, and he tugged on the neon pink leash wrapped around his hand. A short, fat pig glanced up at them and snorted. "Justin won't bite."

Jackson didn't have a lot of fears or phobias in life, and he normally enjoyed the occasional dog or cat. But at that moment, he felt certain of two things: Pigs should not be walked on leashes; and if The Tanglewood hadn't already established a pig-free rule, one needed to be implemented as soon as possible.

"Go ahead," he said with a nod toward the pink pig. "We'll catch the next one."

Andy cackled at him as he stepped aboard. "He's kidding," he told the old man. "Come on, Jackson. It's go time."

Jackson puffed out a sigh and followed Andy. He tapped the button for the lobby several times before he turned and peered through the glass as the vibrant courtyard moved slowly closer. Guests had already begun gathering beneath the twinkling white lights, and candlelit chandeliers dotted the flowering tree branches above their heads. Rows of clear Lucite chairs shimmered with rhinestone-embellished ribbons and tufts of beautiful flowers.

Suddenly, the pig screeched as the elevator car thumped to a stop, and the force of it propelled Jackson backward into Andy.

"What was that?" Andy asked him.

"Looks like this old elevator has seen better days," the pig's owner offered. "Kinda like me." He clucked with laughter that sounded more like a free-range chicken than a man with a leashed pig.

The pig pulled on the leash and circled Jackson's legs before retreating behind his owner's. He attempted to step over the noose to no avail, and Andy finally helped free him.

"Excuse me," Jackson said, more to the pig than the old man, and he reached over and pressed the call button on the panel. Opening his cell phone, he quickly pushed #7 on his speed dial.

"Thank you for calling The Tanglewood Inn. This is Mason. How may I help you this evening?"

"Mason, it's Jackson Drake."

"Yes, Mr. Drake. Shouldn't you be getting married right about now?"

"Yes, Mason, that's the plan. However, I'm trapped in the elevator with my best man. Can you call for some help, please?"

"Oh, my. Yes. Yes, sir, I'll do that."

"And will you page Sherilyn Drummond and let her know immediately, please?"

"Yes, sir. Right away."

Jackson looked down at the pig staring up at him with one eye, the other eye hidden behind its owner's leg. The thing's glare was black and distrustful, and Jackson tried not to imagine the aggression level of a pig that didn't trust him.

"Morton Kuntz," the old man said, extending his hand with the leash still wrapped around it.

"Jackson Drake," he replied as he shook the proferred hand. "This is Andy Drummond."

"And you've met Justin."

"I have indeed," he said, glancing back at the one-eyed pig with the short, screwy tail.

"Is there a pet policy here at the hotel?" Andy asked softly, leaning toward Jackson.

Before he could answer, however, Morton Kuntz piped up. "They allow dogs," he said, pausing to suck something out of his yellowish teeth. "Don't know why Justin would be a problem."

Jackson shrugged at Andy. "There you have it."

"One of you fellas gettin' hitched?"

Jackson raised his hand slightly. "That would be me."

Morton sized up Andy for a moment before asking, "Best man?"

"Yep."

"My grandboy's followin' suit here in this hotel tomorrow night."

Andy and Jackson exchanged glances before they both nodded politely.

"Congrats," Andy added.

After a couple of silent moments—aside from the snorting, of course—Morton gazed at Jackson and said, "Hopin' the bride won't mind waiting around."

"Yeah," Jackson concurred. "I'm hoping that myself."

❧

"I knew better than to say everything was perfect! I did. I knew better. Why did I say that out loud?" Emma ranted as Audrey and Kat looked on in silence. "I just had to go and tempt fate that way, didn't I?"

"Sherilyn and Fee will know what to do," Audrey reassured her. "Don't worry about anything. Ten minutes from now, you'll be looking into Jackson's eyes as he slips a ring on your finger, and this will all be forgotten."

Emma hiked up the skirt of her gown and tossed herself back on the bed with a groan. "Everyone's already down there waiting," she exclaimed. "They're going to think we eloped! Or worse, that we're having second thoughts."

"Emma," Kat said. "Anyone who has met you will know neither of you has had second thoughts."

"You think?"

"We know," Audrey stated, and Emma decided to cling to her friend's confidence.

"You know what, I think I'm just going to take a stroll down the hall, see if I can find out what's going on with the ele—"

"No," Audrey sliced into her words. "You're going to stay right here so that no one sees the bride before she walks down the aisle."

"And . . . when will that be, again?"

"Like ten minutes," Audrey promised with a wave of her hand. "Fifteen, on the outside. Be patient."

Emma eyed the living room through the doorway. The sliding etched-glass door sat partially open on its track. For a moment, the thing appeared to shift, and she examined it more closely.

"You know, I think I need to take my glucose reading." Kat and Audrey exchanged panicky glances, and Emma raised her hand. "No, no, don't worry. Stress kind of makes things fluctuate a little, so I may need to nibble on some more cheese or something. It's fine. I'll be fine . . . Does anyone have any aspirin?"

❧

The elevator groaned, and the pig jerked toward the sound, its snout gyrating as it sniffed the air. The screech of metal on metal inspired a painful grimace, and Jackson watched as the car doors slowly opened a few inches.

One turquoise eye peered at them from the very top of the opening.

"Sherilyn?" Andy exclaimed.

"Hi, baby," she replied, blinking. "You okay?"

"I'm trapped in the elevator with a nervous groom and a pig," Andy answered. With a quick glance downward, he told the pig, "No offense."

"Andy, be nice!"

"No, honey, there's really a pig in here."

"A . . . pig? Really?"

"Yeah, he's on a leash. His owner is here for—"

"Sherilyn!" Jackson interrupted, gripping the partially open doors and staring up into her bright turquoise eye. "Is there any word on how long it's going to take to get us out of here?"

"Well, it could be an hour or two before they can get here," she told him, and Jackson felt his heart drop past his stomach.

"That's not—"

"Hang on, hang on," she cut him off. "We have a hotel guest in town from Kansas to attend another wedding this weekend, and he builds combines . . . those things they use to harvest wheat . . ."

"Clayton?" Morton called out, and he and the pig moved closer to the door as he attempted to peer through the small opening.

"Morton, that you?" someone returned.

"You gonna help get us outta here, or what?"

Jackson's sentiments as well, but he didn't say so.

"Clayton suggested we might be able to pry open the doors and see if you were stuck close to the floor," Sherilyn told them. "He thinks you're close enough that, if we can get the doors open a little more, you might be able to climb up."

"Let's do it!" Jackson exclaimed.

"Let's do it, Clayton!" Sherilyn concurred.

Just ten more minutes with what looked to be a crowbar inching in from the other side, and some real progress had been made. Andy and Jackson helped it along as each of them grabbed hold of one of the doors and pulled back. Just when it looked as if the opening they'd created might allow them to pass through it, Sherilyn stuck her head through and grinned at them.

"Oh!" she blurted suddenly. "You really do have a pig in here."

"Sherilyn," Jackson said with a clenched jaw. "How's Emma?"

"She's fine. She's with the girls, and all ready to join you once we get you out of there."

"Justin goes first," the old man piped up. When he picked up the pig and thrust him toward the open doors, Sherilyn shrieked and the pig oinked.

Once Justin disappeared through the opening, Jackson turned to Morton Kuntz. "You're next, sir. Let's go."

"Nah," he said with a yellowish grin. "Animals first, then wedding parties. You g'on and get hitched."

"You don't need to ask me twice," Jackson replied. "Thank you."

"No, wait!" Sherilyn cried. "Wait, wait. Take off your jackets first and hand them up here to me." Jackson shook his head as he slipped out of the tuxedo jacket, folded it neatly and raised it toward the top of the opening, where Sherilyn's manicured hands awaited. "I want yours too, baby."

Andy complied, and Jackson clasped his hands together and nodded to Andy. "Let's go."

"Okay. Be careful," Sherilyn cooed as Andy stepped into the leg-up Jackson offered and thrust himself over the edge of the second floor.

Once Andy's feet disappeared through the opening, Jackson looked back at Morton. "Are you going to be able to get yourself up there without a boost?"

Disappointment dawned in the old man's eyes. "Not sure, to tell you the truth."

"There's no shame in that," he reassured him. "Let me help you so I can go get married, okay?"

Morton fumbled a bit, and they made three tries before Andy could grab him from above. It took the efforts of the both of them, but he disappeared through the opening at last.

"Okay, Jackson. Your turn," Sherilyn called.

Jackson made one jump, grabbed the edge of the floor and pulled himself upward. He tried not to let on how difficult it really was, but with a picture of Emma in his mind's eye to spur him upward, he got a foothold against the side of the elevator door and shoved himself through the opening.

He lay there on his stomach just long enough to catch his breath as Sherilyn stood over him, cell phone in hand. "Fee, the groom is on the move," she said as she tugged at Jackson's arm. "Wait five minutes, and bring Em down." Helping Jackson into his jacket, she added, "Oh! And make sure you take the stairs."

⪻⪻⪻⪻⪻⪻⪻⪻⪻⪻⪻⪻⪻⪻⪻⪻⪻⪻⪻⪻⪻⪻

Welcome to the Wedding Ceremony
of
Emma Rae Travis & Jackson Drake

Prelude music

Processional:
Canon in D—Johann Pachelbel
The Travis Family
The Drake Family
Best Man, Andrew Drummond
Matron of Honor, Sherilyn Drummond

Bridal Entrance:
Mendelssohn's Wedding March

Introduction & Prayer:
Reverend Miguel Ramos

Uniting Family Honors:
From the Bride & Groom
to the members of their families

The candle at the altar burns in loving memory of Desiree Drake.

Bride & Groom Address:
Poetic readings between the Bride & Groom

Bride & Groom Exchange:
Exchange of the vows
Exchange of the rings

Pronouncement & Blessing of the Marriage

Presentation of the Married Couple

⪻⪻⪻⪻⪻⪻⪻⪻⪻⪻⪻⪻⪻⪻⪻⪻⪻⪻⪻⪻⪻⪻

25

$\mathcal{E}$mma ran across the lobby in bare feet, her Benjamin Adams four-inch pumps looped over two fingers, Kat and Audrey sprinting close behind her. At the courtyard door, she pushed her size six-and-a-half feet into the size-six shoes as Audrey pressed the bouquet into her hands. Four stems of perfect lavender-blue hydrangea, the stems wrapped in rhinestone ribbon that matched the Swarovski crystals adorning her designer shoes, the flowers just exactly like the picture she'd chosen with Sherilyn at the beach.

Kat adjusted Emma's veil while Audrey fluffed the front of her dress. The clomp of heels dashing across the lobby brought comfort to Emma's heart. She smiled and looked up at Sherilyn rushing toward her.

"You two get seated," she said. Audrey and Kat complied without another word. "Em, hold your bouquet right around here," she added, nudging her hands into place. "Anything you need?"

Her lips parted in reply, but it wasn't necessary. The only thing she needed at that very moment had sauntered through the door and stepped up beside her. Gavin smiled at her as he offered his arm.

"Daddy, what are you—"

"Do you think I would miss this moment?" he asked. "Come *wedding* bells or high water, I'm walking my little girl down the aisle."

"Gavin, you look good enough to eat," Sherilyn told him with a broad grin.

"Thank you, Sheri. Let's get this girl married, shall we?"

Andy jogged toward them and handed Sherilyn a rosebud boutonniere. "Ready?"

"Ready," she replied as she fastened it to Gavin's lapel. Turning toward Emma, she smiled warmly. "You look perfect. Like an angel."

Emma held back the wave of emotion as best she could. "Thank you for everything, Sher."

Sherilyn mouthed, "I love you," and slipped her arm into Andy's as they headed down the dark purple-carpeted aisle lined on both sides with trails of pastel flower petals.

"Me, too," Emma returned.

With a firm grasp on her bouquet, Emma pressed her hands against the swarming butterflies inside her stomach and looked up into the glistening eyes of her father.

"You're sure," he stated softly without the slightest trace of a question.

"So sure."

Gavin nodded, pressed his hand over Emma's in the fold of his arm, and the two of them stepped forward. The first couple of notes of Mendelssohn's "Wedding March" cued the guests to their feet, and they all turned to face Emma as she started her walk down the aisle.

The first face she recognized belonged to Bonnie Cordova, the lovely woman who had helped her decide on the final wedding cake design, and she tossed her a smile and a nod.

After that, every other face seemed to dissolve into stardust as she focused on the one and only face in the crowd.

There at the end of the aisle stood Jackson—serious and emotional. But the instant their eyes met, both of them broke into ridiculous, uncontrollable grins. Gavin placed a kiss on Emma's cheek that she almost didn't feel; all she could really think about was reaching Jackson's side. Sherilyn may have taken her bouquet . . . Emma couldn't be sure.

You look so handsome, she told Jackson without speaking. *I love you so much.*

"Please be seated," Miguel told the guests. "The story of Emma Rae Travis and Jackson Drake," he went on, "will make a nonbeliever truly believe in the concept of God-ordained soulmates. Jackson, a widower who bought this very hotel out of a sense of honor toward the memory of his late wife . . . and Emma, the baker brought in to contribute to furthering this crazy concept Desiree had of turning The Tanglewood Inn into a wedding destination hotel. How could that ever work, right? Especially without her."

Jackson glanced down for a moment, and Emma stopped breathing when the connection broke . . . but when his gaze met hers again, and he smiled that familiar, warm smile at her, the rhythm of her pulse restarted.

"Jackson and Emma wanted to honor Desiree today by lighting this candle at the back of what, for this moment in time, is our sanctuary." Miguel pointed out the purple pillar candle surrounded in flowers, front and center behind him. "Without Desiree's love for Jackson, and her dream for this hotel, none of us would be standing here today."

Jackson tilted his head slightly, and Emma couldn't help herself. She reached up and caressed the line of his jaw and smiled.

"Emma and Jackson found one another here. And they think it's only fitting that they make their lifelong commitment to one another here as well. So please join us in prayer."

Emma's racing heart settled inside her, and she bowed her head and closed her eyes as Miguel's words took root.

"Father God, everyone in this room loves Emma and Jackson, and we offer our sincere good wishes for their future happiness. But as much as we love them, we also know that it isn't a fraction of Your love for them. Your love transcends all we can think of or hope for, and we give You glory and honor for that love, Lord God. We ask for Your every blessing upon them as they commit themselves to one another and begin the journey of marriage. In Jesus' precious and holy name, we pray. Amen."

Emma joined the hum of agreement around her. "Amen."

When she opened her eyes again, Jackson's seemed glued to hers. She'd waited such a long, long time for this moment, and she'd pictured a thousand times what he would look like standing across from her, but the reality and depth of emotion in his deep brown eyes had escaped her. She never could have imagined such . . . *love.*

"Emma and Jackson know that they haven't arrived here, on this day and in this place, alone. They would like to take this time to honor the unification of their two families as one."

Emma stepped off the pedestal and approached the front row on Jackson's side of the aisle.

Looking into Georgiann's eyes, she tipped her head to one side and sniffed back her emotions. She then looked to Madeline, and to Norma, and smiled.

"I want to thank you all for welcoming me into the arms of your family the way you have," she said. "And according to the Book of Ruth, I ask you . . . 'Entreat me not to leave you, or to turn back from following after you; for wherever you go, I will go.'"

Georgiann lifted an embroidered lace handkerchief to wipe the tears from her eyes. Madeline and Norma grasped hands across their husbands' laps.

"Oh, *sugah*," Madeline crooned.

Avery burst into tears as Jackson approached her, Gavin, and Sophie. Emma grinned at her aunt, clutching the special bouquet she'd been given as *honorary* maid of honor.

Jackson took Sophie's hand as he said, "'And wherever you lodge, I will lodge; your people shall be my people, and your God, my God. Where you die, I will die, and there will I be buried. The LORD do so to me, and more also, if anything but death parts you and me.'"

Sophie fumbled to her feet and wrapped her arms around Jackson's neck until he nearly lifted her right off the ground. "And back to you, my boy," she said on a chuckle. Grinning at Emma, she added, "This is your best wedding yet."

A tear rambled down her face, and Emma laughed as she wiped it away. "I think so, too, Aunt Soph."

"Emma and Jackson, if you'll return to me?" Miguel invited them.

Jackson offered his arm to Emma as they climbed back on the pedestal in front of Miguel.

"The bride and groom asked if they could each choose a reading for one another at this point in the ceremony; something that summed up how they feel for one another. Neither of them knows until right at this moment, but I think it really says something profound about this young couple that they both chose different portions of the same poem."

Emma gasped, and she looked into Jackson's confused eyes. "E. E. Cummings?"

He nodded and laughed, then began to shake his head with understanding amazement.

"Jackson," Miguel directed, "since your segment comes first in the poem, why don't you go ahead and address Emma Rae first."

Jackson took Emma's hand in his. "You've always come to mind when I've come across this poem, Emma. I tried looking for others, but it was just . . . the only one. The way *you're* the only one."

Emma thought she might actually swoon, and the reaction of the guests told her she wasn't alone.

"I carry your heart with me," he began. "I am never without it."

And when he finished the passage, Emma sniffed as she took just a moment to compose herself.

"Here is the root of the root," she recited to him, "and the bud of the bud, I carry your heart . . ."

Emma couldn't take her eyes away from Jackson's. Without thinking, she leaned forward and pressed her lips to his.

"It's a little early for that, Emma," Miguel said with a snort, and the guests joined in with laughter. "But we're getting there."

When she realized what she'd done, a flush of heat rose over her and the top of her head tingled. "Sorry."

"Jackson, will you repeat after me?"

"Gladly."

"I, Jackson Drake . . ."

". . . take you, Emma Rae Travis . . ."

". . . to be my bride . . ."

". . . I pledge you all of my heart . . ."

". . . and all of my love . . ."

". . . to have and to hold . . ."

". . . to love and to cherish . . ."

". . . in sickness and in health . . ."

". . . in good times and bad . . ."

". . . in Paris or in Roswell, and anywhere in between . . ."

". . . for as long as we both shall live . . ."

". . . allowing only death to part us."

"And Emma, it's your turn. Repeat after me."

She repeated the same vows, with all her heart, and she grinned at Jackson like a schoolgirl as she did.

"And who has the rings?" Miguel asked.

"I have them," Andy said, and he stepped forward and offered the open ring box to Jackson.

Jackson took the diamond band from the box and placed it on the first knuckle of Emma's ring finger.

"Take this ring as a closed circle of my pledge. I give you my heart, my loyalty, and my respect, all the days of our lives."

Emma plucked Jackson's ring from the box and slipped it on his finger.

"Jackson, take this ring as a closed circle of my pledge. I give you my heart, my loyalty, and my respect, for all the days of our lives."

"The Scripture engraved on this couple's wedding rings is from the Song of Solomon," Miguel announced. "Chapter six, verse three. 'I am my beloved's, and my beloved is mine.' I think that's a good example of the mutual love and respect Emma and Jackson have for one another. So with that in our hearts, we all join in prayer for the Lord's mighty blessing upon them."

The corner of her mouth twitched as Emma looked up at Jackson. His eyes looked smoky and serious, smoldering with the thick haze of emotion.

"Emma, Jackson," Miguel stated. "By the power vested in me by the State of Georgia and God Almighty, in the name

of our Savior, I now pronounce you husband and wife . . .
Jackson, please feel free to kiss your bride."

He engulfed her in his arms and pulled her to him, kissing
her so deeply that she could hardly breathe. Emma's heart
raced as she returned his kiss . . . *The Marriage Kiss*. The one
she'd awaited for such a very long time.

～✥～

"Okay. You two wait here until I come back for you to make
your entrance," Sherilyn instructed. "It shouldn't be more than
five or ten minutes."

She disappeared inside The Desiree Room, and Jackson
turned to Emma. "After seeing her in action today, I don't
think I pay her enough."

Emma laughed out loud, and the music of her laughter
lulled something soft and warm inside him. He ran his fingers
through her hair where the bridal veil had been before Sherilyn
removed it. He touched the rhinestone band and grazed his
thumb over her temple.

"You look amazing."

"I feel amazing," she replied. "Except for my feet. My feet
are killing me."

He glanced down as she lifted the hem of her dress to reveal
crystal-covered shoes. Just a trace of pale pink toenails peeked
through the open front, and at least four inches of thin heel
tilted her poor feet at a steep angle.

"Take them off," he suggested.

"I can't. Sherilyn would kill me."

"Well, she can't expect you to walk around in those things
all night," he objected. "You're not used to wearing shoes that
high."

"Maybe I'll kick them off under the table later. When she's not looking."

The mischievous grin she shot him made Jackson laugh.

"Listen," he said, reaching into his jacket pocket. "I have something for you. Sort of a wedding present."

"Jackson. I thought we weren't doing that."

"I know. But I saw it, and I just knew. It had to be around your neck."

He opened the hinged lid of the velvet box to reveal the exquisite amethyst cross he'd purchased for her. She gasped when she saw it, confirming his belief that it was just Emma's style.

"Oh, Jackson. It's . . . ." Instead of completing the thought, she simply heaved a deep sigh. "I love it."

"I don't want to mess with the whole perfect ensemble you have going with your jewelry today," he said, "so I'll keep it in my pocket for you. But I just thought this seemed like the perfect moment to give it to you."

"You're joking, right?" she said, carefully unclasping her grandmother's diamond choker and dropping it into his pocket. "You hold on to this. I'm wearing that."

He helped her remove it from the box, and he secured the clasp around her neck. The marriage cross fell to just the right spot beneath the hollow of her porcelain throat.

"Yes?" she asked as he looked at it.

"It looks just how I thought it would," he answered.

Emma leaned in and kissed his lips softly, and she thanked him in a warm-honey whisper.

The distant thumping of running feet approached, and they both turned toward the sound just as Russell Walker raced around the corner of the corridor.

"I make it, mate?" he asked Jackson in that deep Australian accent. "Whoa," he interrupted himself as he got a look at Emma. "*Immah!* You're a sight for sore eyes, aren't you, love?"

"Russell, I can't believe you made it!" she exclaimed as they embraced. Turning to Jackson, she beamed. "That's everyone! Everyone we thought wouldn't be here, Jackson. We're all in one place after all!"

"I couldn't miss this now, could I?" Russell asked her. "It's a once-in-a-lifetime!"

When the ballroom door opened and Sherilyn laid eyes on Russell, she squealed and flung herself into his open arms. The two of them had always been oddly connected, and Jackson laughed as she continued to squeal from within his embrace.

"Bloody oath, Red!" he exclaimed. "You look bettah ev'ry time I feast my eyes on you."

"Russell, I'm so happy to see you," she cried. Then, with a gasp, she added, "Kat is going to flip her lid! Get in there so she can get it out of her system before I unleash the bride and groom!"

"Later, then," he said to Emma and Jackson before he disappeared inside. The wail of delight a moment later let them know that he'd found Kat, and they all shared a chuckle.

"Look what Jackson gave me," Emma said, tapping the chain around her neck.

Sherilyn leaned in for a closer look before tossing Jackson a crooked grin. "*Niiice!*"

At least she hadn't given him what-for over the missing wedding jewelry.

She pressed a button on her cell phone and spoke into it. "The bride and groom are about to enter. Are you ready, baby?

. . . What about Ben? . . . Good!" She closed the phone and gave them a nod. "You're on."

"Hey, Sher," Emma called over her shoulder as they walked into the ballroom. "Jackson says he's giving you a raise."

"What?" she gasped. Grinning at him, she asked, "Really?"

"Oh, yeah."

Jackson followed Emma inside. A lavender spotlight drew his attention to Andy on the stage at the front of the ballroom.

"Ladies and gentlemen," he said into a microphone. "It's my pleasure to present to you . . . Mr. and Mrs. Jackson Drake!"

Everyone applauded and they greeted flocks of well-wishers on their way to the dance floor, which featured a muted lavender paisley design in front of the stage.

"Jackson, this is Bonnie Cordova and her husband, Ben," Emma told him as she stopped to greet the couple. "Bonnie helped me pick the cake."

Jackson grabbed both of her hands and shook them between his. "Bonnie, I can't thank you enough." He leaned in closer and whispered, "At Emma's rate of confusion, I wasn't sure we'd even have a cake."

"I heard that," Emma declared. She laughed and pointed toward the beautiful cake on the pedestal next to the stage. "I call it *Free to Be Me*. That's how you make me feel. Completely free."

Bonnie turned to her husband. "Ahhh." With a second look toward the cake, she asked Emma, "Is it your crème brûlée specialty?"

"It is indeed."

"Any chance I can get the recipe?"

Jackson cackled. "Bonnie, I'm not sure even I could get that recipe from her."

"We'll talk," Emma mouthed back to her.

They moved forward toward the stage as Andy tapped the mic.

"I hope you'll all help me welcome the magnificent Ben Colson as he performs the bride and groom's special song for their first dance. 'The Way You Look Tonight.'"

Jackson and Emma waved to Ben and strolled to the center of the dance floor. Jackson took his new wife into his arms as Colson crooned the very song that he'd sung for them on the evening of the hotel opening. With Emma pressed against him, Jackson closed his eyes, holding her close, remembering that special night.

⋘⋙

Her eyes tightly shut, Emma recalled the first time Jackson had held her that way. She'd been so busy on the night of the hotel opening that she hadn't had the time to have dinner. He'd persuaded Pearl to bring them something after all of the guests had left, and he'd arranged for a private concert for two with Ben Colson . . .

"Emma, have you met Ben?"

"I haven't had the pleasure," she said, shaking his hand. "But I'm a big fan of your music."

"I appreciate that," he replied, and she couldn't help but notice what a picture-perfect man he was. The way he tilted his head and smiled, he looked like any one of his album covers. "Do you have a favorite song?"

"A favorite . . . Pardon?"

"Jackson tells me you didn't get to hear one song all the way through tonight. We thought you might like to, now."

Emma glanced at Jackson, then back to Ben. "Really?"

"What's your pleasure?"

"Oh, I just love the classics from your second album. Anything. Really, anything would be great."

Ben nodded, then he rounded the stage and climbed the stairs.

Jackson smiled at her sweetly, and she shook her head. "Thank you, Jackson. Really. What a nice thing to do."

On the first note from the piano, Jackson offered his hand. "Dance with me?"

Emma's heart thumped against her throat and she hesitated, but only for a moment before taking Jackson's hand and moving into his arms. As Ben Colson serenaded them with "The Way You Look Tonight," Emma leaned into Jackson and they swayed in perfect sync to the music.

It felt so good there in his arms, and she had the sensation of finally landing somewhere that she'd been struggling to reach for such a very long time. Emma nuzzled her face into his shoulder and closed her eyes, breathing in a deep whiff of the faint spicy wood and citrus scent that was becoming familiar to her now.

The music came to a gentle end, but the two of them remained in one another's arms, swaying softly to the silent song in the very large room.

"What are you thinking?" Jackson whispered to her now.

"Remembering," she replied.

"That first night? The night of the opening?"

"Mmm," she hummed, and Jackson sighed.

"Yeah. Me, too."

"Any regrets?" she asked him, lifting her face to his.

He thought about it for a moment before replying. "Regrets? Yes. But only one."

Her heart throbbed inside her chest. "Really?"

"Yeah. I went my whole life without appreciating hazelnut," he teased. "It took some irritating girl behind a bakery counter pushing it on me—"

"Many times before you gave in, as I recall."

"Yes! That's what I mean. I missed out on thirty-some years of hazelnut before that. I regret it. I really do."

"You're a jerk," she said with a giggle.

"I know. And you love me for it."

Emma smiled and nuzzled her head against his shoulder. "Yes, I do."

Free to be ME!

26

"Emma, can we see you for a moment?"

She looked up at Susannah's very serious face and wondered, *Oh no. Now what's happened?*

"It's nothing dire," she said, as if she could read Emma's thoughts. With a smile, she added, "In fact, it's a good thing."

Susannah offered her hand, and Emma excused herself from Carly and Devon's table to accept it and curiously follow Susannah's lead. When they reached the family cluster at the edge of the stage, the human sea parted for her, and Emma found herself at the center of the activity, standing next to Jackson. He slipped his arm around her shoulder.

"What's going on?" she asked him.

"No clue."

"Let's all sit down," Madeline suggested, and Emma followed them to the nearest table and sat in the chair between her father and Jackson.

Georgiann produced a small wrapped gift, about the size of a shoe box, and she slid it across the table toward them. Jackson nodded toward it with a smile, and Emma pulled the box the rest of the way.

"It's just a little something from your families," Norma explained. "Including Sherilyn, Susannah, and Fee, of course, because they're family now, too."

Emma's eyes caught Fee's, and her friend arched her eyebrows over the top of her small, rectangular glasses. "Have a peek."

Emma lifted the lid with some degree of caution, but she didn't quite know why. Inside, she found an array of folded cards in various pastel shades. She looked at her father and grinned, and he urged her on with a nod.

She picked up one of them, a mint green card that read, *Madeline & Georgiann—Shared Administrative.*

"What does this mean?" she asked Jackson in a hushed voice. He shrugged, and they looked around at the sea of eager faces. "I'm sorry," she told them. "I don't understand."

"Keep going," her mother urged her.

Emma pulled a lavender card from the mix.

Susannah—Delayed retirement.

Jackson, reading over Emma's shoulder, looked up at Susannah. "What's this all about?"

Emma unfolded a light blue card and recognized Fee's slanted penmanship immediately.

Fee—Bakery & tearoom admin.

Poking through the rest of the cards, Emma recognized a United Airlines logo, and she pulled the envelope from the bottom of the box. Her pulse began to race as she unfolded it, and she glanced at Jackson. He looked as confused as she felt.

"Two open-ended tickets," Georgiann explained. "Atlanta to Paris."

Jackson and Emma stared at one another for a long and frozen moment before they broke free and scanned the crowd of people around them.

"What is this?" Jackson asked.

"Each card bears one of our names," Madeline told them, "along with the role we will fill while the two of you go live out that dream you had of spending some time in Paris."

"What?" Emma cried. "Are you—?"

"No, no," Jackson interrupted. "You can't . . . Susannah, postponing your retirement?"

"Just for six months or a year, Jackson."

"And George," he objected, "you could hardly wait to get out of here once the hotel was up and running. You can't just—"

"I can, and I will." She sliced her hand through the air with that no-nonsense, this-is-the-way-it's-going-to-be expression Emma had come to know very well.

Gavin reached around Emma and placed his hand on Jackson's shoulder. "Don't fight it, my boy. This is bigger than you are."

"We've been planning it ever since the day you decided not to sell the hotel," Sherilyn told them.

"That's what I walked in on at your house!" Emma cried. Sherilyn nodded and grinned with sheer delight.

"We're all so happy that you didn't sell, Jackson," Sherilyn told him. "But it occurred to us that . . . well, why can't you have it all?"

"The Lord knows you deserve it," Avery chimed in. "Both of you."

Emma's voice remained stuck in her throat. Even though she didn't know in the least what she wanted to say, she struggled to push the random words up and out of her mouth.

"You need to take care of yourself, Emmy," her father said. "Nurse yourself back to health. I know a little bit about that myself."

"And Jackson has a book to write," Andy added.

"And there's pastry classes to take."

"And walks along the Seine."

"And a marriage to begin."

Wow. They've really been paying attention!

Jackson turned to Emma, searching her eyes for some sort of solid reaction, and she felt as if she'd let him down a bit when she finally shook her head and groaned in exasperation.

"You'll still go to Savannah tomorrow," Avery offered. "Spend a honeymoon week there, just the two of you. When you get back, you can take whatever time you need to set up your plans for the baking school, somewhere to live in Paris . . ."

"And make sure it has a guest room," Sherilyn chimed in. "Because if you think you're going to completely miss out on the first year of your goddaughter's life . . ." She paused, her turquoise eyes round as saucers. "Wait, we're going to have to speed up the christening, Andy. We have to have it before they leave!"

Andy chuckled and rubbed Sherilyn's arm. "Focus, honey."

"The thing is . . . you don't *have* to go for a whole year," she told them, and she looked around at the others. "I mean, there's nothing saying it has to be a whole year, right?"

"You can go for three months, six months, or even a year if you want to," Georgiann added. "But you *really must* go."

"This is . . . too much," Jackson stated.

"It's *nawt*," Madeline corrected in her low southern drawl. "It's our wedding gift, *sugah*. From all of us . . . to the two of you."

Norma rounded the table and stood behind them, touching their shoulders. "Build your 'Once Upon a Time.' Let us help you do that. We so want to be part of it."

Emma couldn't help herself. Propelled by pure emotion, she jumped up from her chair and hugged Norma, rocking her from side to side. When they parted, she turned toward the group of them, tearful and emotional.

"Who *does* this kind of thing?" she cried. "Every one of you . . . you're so precious to us. This is over-the-top ridiculous that you've put your heads together and done this for us."

"So you accept?" Susannah asked them.

Emma's gaze went straight to Jackson. As he looked up at her, she could almost hear the *click* of their eyes locking. It only took a moment for her to read his answer right there, swimming around in the warm, chocolate pools she knew so well.

"We accept," she said.

Hugs and kisses and good wishes flowed around the table in a sweet wave, engulfing the new couple. She could hardly believe what had swept her away, and she finally turned to Jackson and asked the question without speaking a word.

Is this really happening?

"I know," he replied, shaking his head. "We're . . . *going to Paris!*"

⊱❧⊰

Despite the wrinkles leading up to the day, Jackson had to admit that the wedding itself had bordered on flawless. All of the people they'd thought wouldn't make it had somehow managed to come, and every intimate detail of the ceremony and reception had added to the overall perfection.

And this new surprise!—the raised hands of an entire family of support, holding back the challenges, stopping time in order to send them on the adventure they'd been dreaming about for so long—it was almost too much to believe. He wondered if he might wake up tomorrow morning and realize he'd been reading some fairy tale novel or dreaming about such a well-coordinated send-off.

His beautiful bride had danced with her father, who looked fairly good considering he'd left the hospital just that afternoon

. . . The menu, if even possible, had turned out to exceed the original one on the night of the opening . . . Russell had sung to them from the stage, Ben Colson accompanying him . . . The exquisite cake had been cut and enjoyed . . . Most of the guests had said their good-byes, and just a remnant remained behind to toast the couple once more.

"It's been a perfect night," he whispered into Emma's ear as she clung to him.

"A week in Savannah, just the two of us," she murmured back at him, her face buried in the fold of his neck so that he felt the reverberation of her words against his skin. "And when we return, we'll start making our plans for *Paris*. It's like a dream."

Her shoes had been discarded somewhere around the time that she'd danced with Russell to a cranked-up version of The Animals' "We Gotta Get Out of This Place" from the variety of CDs Fee had brought along to play after Ben Colson packed up and left. And now, to the tune of "A Whiter Shade of Pale," they swayed from side to side, Emma's bare feet on top of his shoes while he took the steps for them both. He imagined it to be somewhere past midnight, but he had no idea how far past.

Emma moaned softly into his ear before humming along with the song. "I love you so much," she cooed as the music faded to a close.

Before he could reply, the first beats of the next musical selection elicited a wail from Sherilyn, and the next thing Jackson knew, they'd been mobbed to the tune of Bob Seger's "Rock and Roll Never Forgets." He recalled that Russell had sung it to Sherilyn at one of her wedding receptions, not long after they'd first met.

Every member of the group of stragglers hit the dance floor around them—Sherilyn and Andy . . . Devon and Carly . . . Audrey and J.R . . . Kat and Russell . . . Fee and Sean—

now dancing solo around them, just one large band of merry partygoers, most of the women barefoot, all of the men with their ties loosened and jackets strewn over random chairs.

The joy on Emma's face as she hopped from atop his feet thrilled Jackson to the core. He watched her as she danced with J.R., then Fee, then moved on to Sherilyn. The two women embraced, and their laughter rang like bells accompanying the melody of the music.

These people had somewhere along the line become their own inner circle. These were the people they had come to love, the people they trusted the most, would probably grow old alongside. Each one of them had wandered through the doors of The Tanglewood at some point, preordained, destined to become their . . . *family*. His heart surged into the depths of it.

Emma found her way back to him and wrapped her arms around Jackson's neck.

"Hey!" she exclaimed.

"Hey," he returned as she pressed against him.

"Remember when I told you . . . that I'd be . . . *worth the wait*?"

Jackson pulled back slightly and looked into Emma's brown eyes. "Yeaaah."

"Well, here's the thing. Your wait is over, my friend."

He stared at her blankly until she offered him her hand. And the instant that he grasped it, she took off running for the door. No need to think twice. Jackson joined her, stride for stride, as they flew from the ballroom and raced down the corridor, all the way to the elevators.

But as the elevator doors slipped open, they paused and looked at one another seriously.

The image of Morton and his pig, Justin, flashed before Jackson's eyes. But Emma said it first.

"Yeah. Umm, let's take *the stairs*."

Epilogue

*B*onnie Cordova flipped through the afternoon's mail while sitting at her kitchen table.

"Bill. Bill. Advertisement. Bill."

The final envelope in the pile bore a familiar crest. It had come from The Tanglewood Inn back in Roswell, Georgia.

She tore it open and removed an engraved notecard, one of those specialty cards people used to thank their wedding guests. But she hadn't given them a gift . . .

> Bonnie,
>
> Jackson and I were so happy you could attend our wedding and share in our joy. And I can't thank you enough for appearing at just the right moment to help me make the decision about our cake! The choice had been dogging me for weeks on end, and your input helped punctuate a perfect day for us.
>
> I've enclosed a little thank-you gift . . . but remember . . . it's a secret. You're only the third

person on the planet who knows this secret, and I'm trusting you to keep it.

All my love,

Emma Travis Drake

Bonnie unfolded the piece of paper tucked inside and immediately began to laugh. And the laughter morphed into a full-on shriek as she called, "Ben! Ben, she sent me the recipe! . . . Ben!!"

❧❧❧❧❧❧❧❧❧❧❧❧❧❧❧❧❧❧❧❧❧

Emma Rae's Award-Winning
Crème Brûlée Wedding Cake
A 6-Step Process

Step 1of 6: Crème Brûlée

Note: Prepare 24 hours ahead of time.

1 tablespoon vanilla bean paste (Lorann Gourmet)
2 cups heavy cream
8 egg yolks
¼ cup granulated sugar

Stir vanilla bean paste into the cream in a
heavy-bottomed saucepan.
Bring JUST to a boil and remove from heat immediately
to cool slightly.
Note: The cream must still be somewhat warm for the next step.

Whisk egg yolks and sugar together until mixed well.
Note: The fewer bubbles, the better.

Whisking constantly, VERY SLOWLY pour the hot cream
into the eggs.

Line two pans (the same size as your cake will be) with
non-stick aluminum foil (nonstick side OUT).
*Note: It is essential to get a smooth, bubble-free lining
on the bottom and to make sure the wrap stays up on the sides.*

❧❧❧❧❧❧❧❧❧❧❧❧❧❧❧❧❧❧❧❧❧

Divide and pour the custard mixture into the two
prepared cake pans.

Bake at 210 degrees for about 40 minutes,
until the custard is BARELY QUIVERY in the middle.
*Note: The mixture will be firmer than a regular crème brûlée
mixture, and it will not need a water bath.*

When the layers have cooled, stretch cling wrap across the
tops, and freeze in the pan.

❧❦❧❦❧❦❧❦❧❦❧❦❧❦❧❦❧❦❧❦❧❦❧❦❧❦❧❦❧❦

Step 2 of 6: Brown Sugar Crunch "Brulee" Layers

½ stick (¼ cup) unsalted butter
½ cup firmly packed brown sugar
2 tablespoons water

Cut two parchment paper rounds to line the
bottom of two pans,
the same-size pans that the cakes will bake in.
Leave the parchment liners in the pans.

Combine the butter, brown sugar, and water in a
heavy-bottomed saucepan.
Boil to a temperature of 260 degrees.

Immediately divide the molten sugar mixture onto the
prepared parchment,
and quickly spread to the edges.
Allow the sugar to cool and harden.
Once it is cool, use a heavy spoon to tap the sugar, cracking
it into small pieces.
*Note: Take care NOT to disassemble the circle. The smaller the
pieces, the better.*

❧❦❧❦❧❦❧❦❧❦❧❦❧❦❧❦❧❦❧❦❧❦❧❦❧❦❧❦❧❦

> ᜰᜲ᜕ᜲ᜕ᜲ᜕ᜲ᜕ᜲ᜕ᜲ᜕ᜲ᜕ᜲ᜕ᜲ᜕ᜲ᜕ᜲ᜕ᜲ᜕ᜲ᜕

Step 3 of 6: Sour Cream Cake

Preheat oven to 325 degrees.

2 sticks (1 cup) unsalted butter, softened
3 cups granulated sugar
7 eggs
3 cups all-purpose flour
¼ teaspoon baking soda
¼ teaspoon baking powder
1 teaspoon salt
1 cup sour cream
1 tablespoon pure vanilla extract

Prepare two 8- or 9-inch pans (NOT nonstick)
with the parchment paper liners coated with
cracked brown sugar.
Note: Do NOT butter or oil the sides of the pan!

In a large bowl, using a mixer, cream together the butter and
sugar until the mixture is light and fluffy (about 5 minutes).
Beat in the eggs, one at a time, mixing well after each.

Combine the flour, baking soda, baking powder,
and salt in a bowl.
Blend the sour cream and vanilla together in a separate bowl.
Add the flour mixture to the creamed mixture, alternating
with the sour cream mixture in 5 ADDITIONS.
Note: Flour, sour cream, flour, sour cream, flour.

> ᜰᜲ᜕ᜲ᜕ᜲ᜕ᜲ᜕ᜲ᜕ᜲ᜕ᜲ᜕ᜲ᜕ᜲ᜕ᜲ᜕ᜲ᜕ᜲ᜕ᜲ᜕

Mix until the flour is absorbed.
Turn mixer up to medium-high for 15 seconds,
and turn off mixer.
Carefully spoon the batter over the cracked brown sugar
in the prepared pan.

Bake in the preheated oven for 45-60 minutes,
or until a toothpick inserted in the center comes out clean.

Allow the cakes to cool in the pans.
When the cakes have cooled, carefully run a small icing
spatula around the pans.
Gently invert the cakes out of the pans.
Return the cakes to right-side-up,
and place the parchment-covered sugar bottoms on a
square of waxed paper.

❧❧❧❧❧❧❧❧❧❧❧❧❧❧❧❧❧

Step 4 of 6: Vanilla Filling

4 large egg whites
1 ¼ cups granulated sugar
3 sticks (1 ½ cups) unsalted butter, room temperature
1 teaspoon pure vanilla extract

Cut the sticks of butter into tablespoon-sized portions.
Set the heatproof bowl of an electric mixer over
a heavy-bottomed saucepan of simmering water.
Note: The water must not touch the bottom of the mixing bowl.

Combine the sugar and egg whites and cook, stirring
constantly until the sugar has dissolved and the mixture
is 160 degrees.

Attach the bowl to the mixer, fitted with the
whisk attachment.
Beat the egg white mixture on high speed until it holds
stiff peaks.
Continue beating until fluffy and cooled (about 6 minutes).

Switch to the paddle attachment.
With the mixer on medium low, add the butter,
1 tablespoon at a time, beating well after each addition.
Once all of the butter has been added, turn the mixer
to medium high.

Once the mixture comes together, turn the mixer speed
down to low.
Beat in the vanilla extract—about 2 more minutes to
eliminate air bubbles.

❧❧❧❧❧❧❧❧❧❧❧❧❧❧❧❧❧

Step 5 of 6: Whole Egg Buttercream Icing

4 large eggs
1 cup granulated sugar
½ teaspoon salt
2 teaspoons pure vanilla extract
4 sticks (2 cups) unsalted butter, room temperature

Cut the sticks of butter into tablespoon-sized portions.
Set the heatproof bowl of an electric mixer over
a heavy-bottomed saucepan of simmering water
Note: The water must not touch the bottom of the mixing bowl.

Combine the eggs, sugar, salt, and vanilla, and cook,
stirring constantly until the sugar has dissolved and the
mixture is 160 degrees.

Attach the bowl to the mixer fitted with the
paddle attachment.
Beat the egg mixture on medium high for 5 minutes,
or until it is light yellow and fluffy.
Continue beating on low speed until the mixture has cooled.

With the mixer on medium-low, add the butter, 1 tablespoon
at a time,
beating well after each addition.
Once all of the butter has been added, turn the mixer to
medium high until the mixture comes together.

Turn the mixer down to low.
Beat for about 2 more minutes to eliminate air bubbles.
Note: The icing should be silky smooth.

Step 6 of 6: Assembling the Crème Brûlée Cake

Level both of your cakes,
removing the dome top and ensuring that all sides are
the same uniform height.

Split the cake layers evenly in horizontal halves
so that you end up with 4 wheels of cake that are each
the same height.

Turn the sugar-coated bottom pieces over and remove the
parchment paper.
*Note: If the cracked sugar looks solid, give it a few gentle taps with
the back of a spoon.*

Place the first cake wheel (without the sugar) on a
flat cake plate.
Spread a thin layer of vanilla filling on the top of the cake.
Unwrap one of the Crème Brûlée custards, still frozen, and
lay it atop the filling.
Spread a thin layer of filling over the frozen custard.
Place a sugared cake wheel (sugar side down) on top
of the filling.
Press gently to seal the layers together.

Spread a generous layer of filling on top of the cake,
and repeat the steps.

*Note: From bottom to top, the layers should be as follows:
Cake, filling, custard, filling, cracked brown sugar/cake, filling,
cake, filling, custard, filling, cracked brown sugar/cake.*

Cover the entire cake with icing and decorate
for the occasion.

Discussion Questions

1. It's been a long road for Emma Rae and Jackson. As they approach the finish line to the altar, how do you assess the growth of their relationship?

2. Emma and Jackson are surrounded by many peripheral characters. Which ones do you think had the greatest impact on their relationship? On them personally?

3. How does the long-standing friendship between Emma and Sherilyn play into advancing the story?

4. How do you feel about the way faith and prayer were approached in the telling of this story?

5. Emma and Jackson have been together over the course of four books now. What do you think of their decision to wait until marriage for sex? Was it handled realistically?

6. How do you see Emma's relationship with her aunt Sophie affecting her and/or her marriage?

7. How did you feel about Jackson fielding an offer to sell The Tanglewood Inn?

8. How did the possible sale of the hotel affect Emma? How did it affect the others?

9. What did the arrival of Hildie represent in the book?

10. Emma really struggled to choose a wedding cake design. Of all the wedding details, why do you suppose that one was so difficult for her?

11. If you read the other books in the series, how did the major characters evolve and grow over the course of the series?

    a. Emma Rae

    b. Jackson

c. Sherilyn

d. Audrey

12. Did you have a favorite of the wedding cakes that Emma considered?

13. How did you feel about the stranger who helped Emma make her final choice?

14. Was Emma and Jackson's wedding a satisfying conclusion?

15. How did you feel when you closed the book after reading the final page? What stuck with you?

Want to learn more about author
Sandra D. Bricker and check out other great
fiction from Abingdon Press?

Sign up for our fiction newsletter at
www.AbingdonPress.com
to read interviews with your favorite authors, find tips
for starting a reading group, and stay posted on what
new titles are on the horizon. It's a place to connect
with other fiction readers or post a
comment about this book.

Be sure to visit Sandra online!

www.SandraDBricker.com

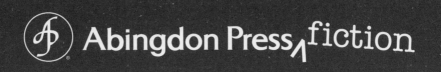

Discover Fiction from Abingdon Press

BOOKLIST 2010

Top 10 Inspirational Fiction award

ROMANTIC TIMES 2010

Reviewers Choice Awards
Book of the Year nominee

BLACK CHRISTIAN BOOK LIST

#1 for two consecutive months,
2010 Black Christian Book
national bestseller list;
ACFW Book of the Month, Nov/Dec 2010

CAROL AWARDS 2010

(ACFW) Contemporary
Fiction nominee

INSPY AWARD NOMINEES

Suspense   General Fiction   Contemporary Fiction

Abingdon Press fiction
a novel approach to faith
AbingdonPress.com | 800.251.3320

FBM112220001 PACP01002597-01

What They're Saying About...

The Glory of Green, by Judy Christie
"Once again, Christie draws her readers into the town, the life, the humor, and the drama in Green. *The Glory of Green* is a wonderful narrative of small-town America, pulling together in tragedy. A great read!"
—Ane Mulligan, editor of *Novel Journey*

Always the Baker, Never the Bride, by Sandra Bricker
"[It] had just the right touch of humor, and I loved the characters. Emma Rae is a character who will stay with me. Highly recommended!"
—Colleen Coble, author of *The Lightkeeper's Daughter* and the *Rock Harbor* series

Diagnosis Death, by Richard Mabry
"Realistic medical flavor graces a story rich with characters I loved and with enough twists and turns to keep the sleuth in me off-center. Keep 'em coming!"—Dr. Harry Krauss, author of *Salty Like Blood* and *The Six-Liter Club*

Sweet Baklava, by Debby Mayne
"A sweet romance, a feel-good ending, and a surprise cache of yummy Greek recipes at the book's end? I'm sold!"—Trish Perry, author of *Unforgettable* and *Tea for Two*

The Dead Saint, by Marilyn Brown Oden
"An intriguing story of international espionage with just the right amount of inspirational seasoning."—*Fresh Fiction*

Shrouded in Silence, by Robert L. Wise
"It's a story fraught with death, danger, and deception—of never knowing whom to trust, and with a twist of an ending I didn't see coming. Great read!"—Sharon Sala, author of *The Searcher's Trilogy: Blood Stains, Blood Ties,* and *Blood Trails.*

Delivered with Love, by Sherry Kyle
"Sherry Kyle has created an engaging story of forgiveness, sweet romance, and faith reawakened—and I looked forward to every page. A fun and charming debut!"—Julie Carobini, author of *A Shore Thing* and *Fade to Blue.*

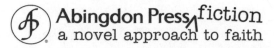

Abingdon Press fiction
a novel approach to faith

AbingdonPress.com | 800.251.3320

BKM112220003 PACP0103464642-01